THE GIFT OF A ROSE

A TWIN SOULS SAGA

Copyright © 2025 Lauren Gross All rights reserved

The characters and events portrayed in this book are fictitious. Any similarity to real persons, living or dead, is coincidental and not intended by the author.

No part of this book may be reproduced, or stored in a retrieval system, or transmitted in any form or by any means, electronic, mechanical, photocopying, recording, or otherwise, without express written permission of the publisher.

Dedicated to Carrie,
A local book club girlie who pushed me into reading at the age of thirty-five. The catalyst to finding my own destiny in creating my own stories.

And to all my girls that kept me reading.
From stellar books recs, to lending and gifting, and being in my inbox to theorize and review.

Also, to my Mum and sisters for our book club group chat.
Our meetups consist of; "yeah the book was good," then we fill our faces with snacks and prosecco. Very 'us' coded.

And to Bum,
for buying me my first kindle even though I have a habit of giving up on things if I'm not immediately enjoying it, and for actually showing interest, especially when it came to making my map

THANE

-1-

If you were told that today would be the day you would die, how would you feel? How would you want to spend that final day?

Would you spend it doing the most daring things you could think of because, 'Hey, I'm dying anyway'?' Perhaps you would surround yourself with loved ones and share one last meal together before you departed. Or would you frantically beg anyone and anything to save you, to grant you more time? Maybe you didn't get long enough to do all the things that you wanted to do.

I'd accept it.

I would hug Death like a familiar friend, and we would go hand in hand knowing that this life is one of many. This life is temporary. I would let him lead me to my mother and others that passed before me.

Anything you felt that you hadn't done or had missed out on could always be achieved on your next go at things.

I have loved and been loved for all my twenty-four years on this plane. Fed with kindness and caring until my belly's near to bursting. I spent the night with the man I loved while he kissed and caressed and satisfied me. My breath hitched at the flashes of memories and remnants of sensation fluttering between my legs. He spent the night holding me, and I was still surrounded by his warm muscled arms this morning.

What better way to be woken on your final day than by birdsong and luxurious golden light spilling through the cracks in the curtains, creating lacy patterns on the furnishings, dancing with the voile curtains that fluttered at my window.

I glanced around the room, an extension of me. The wooden beams decorated with dried flowers and macrame hangings. Glass sun-catchers cast flickering rainbows on the hand painted walls.

Father had encouraged my creativity. He told me this space was my own and that I could do with it whatever I pleased. He had even helped at times. A fond fuzziness washed over me as my gaze landed on the flower mural we had both painted together. Every flower he painted, I had painted over it. I chuckled to myself at the memory…

"You should probably just paint the leaves, Father."

My art was more realism and his, well, his was on par with an infant making marks with finger paints at the chapel nursery. A small giggle left my lips as I remembered what he did next.

He looked at me with mock offense and said, "But I want to paint a Rose."

Then he chased me around the room, paint brush poised to paint streaks of red on any part of me he could get hold of.

I had interrupted the slumber of the man next to me.

"Morning," I whispered to the handsome face beside me, whose eyes were lazily unshuttering. The epitome of relaxed.

I browsed his long lashes and the freckles that dusted his cheeks. I laid a kiss upon his nose and one on his lips that curved at the corners before his eyes, blue of the sky, had fully opened. He stretched out the tension that gathered in his muscles most nights from wrapping himself around me and keeping dead still to give me the most blissful slumber. Gods did I appreciate it, especially in the lead up to today. My pulse quickened at the thought.

Today.

His eyes danced over my expression and narrowed as he struggled to read it.

"How do you feel?" His voice still crackled from the leftover sleep.

"Excited." *Nervous.* "Happy." *Scared.*

I kept my tone light. I didn't know how to feel, but I knew I felt all those things at once. I showed him my biggest smile in hopes that I could reassure him. It seemed to work as he pressed my body into his in an embrace that filled me with warmth and his heady scent. I nestled close cherishing the gesture and his attempt to soothe me.

"It's a big day." He stroked my hair and placed a kiss on the top of my head.

"Indeed," I agreed, drawing a deep inhale through my nostrils grounding myself in his musk. "How do you feel?"

I'd been so wrapped up in my own mixed bag of feelings I hadn't given much thought to how he was feeling about today. I hadn't considered how different things would become for him too. Was he ready for it? Maybe he felt all the same things as me.

He slowly drew a breath filling his chest. "Like the proudest man in the world."

He said it with such fervour that it was hard not to believe.

"I think you'd have to fight my father for that title," I whispered.

Laughter erupted. "I think I could win," he whispered back.

We both laughed at the idea of Greer squabbling with my father over who was most proud of me. I knew they both were.

I was very much my father's daughter. I knew it was going to be hard for him to give me away today, but I knew he would do it with honour.

Emotion replaced the oxygen in my lungs, and my eyes glistened at the image of his face when he saw me try on Mother's dress.

The day they got married the weather was glorious. He told me the light from the sun was like a halo casting my mother in a golden aura as she walked down the aisle. I was there that day, the day they gave themselves to one another before the gods. They had yet to meet me, but I was there.

Father told me that Mother was sick that morning and he was unsure whether it was nerves or because I was growing inside her. Made of their love.

They had prayed so hard to conceive me. Conception wasn't something that came easily to our people. He told me he had felt so panicked all morning thinking she might not make the ceremony.

Enveloped in that golden glow she made her way toward him, her dress so long he could not see her feet. It looked as though she were floating like an angel. She took his breath away.

"I have something for you." Greer interrupted my daydream as he leapt from the bed and for a moment I mourned the loss of his warmth. Perhaps his embrace had grounded me more than I thought.

He turned to me with a smile and a box and took from within it a beautiful gold chain. Our eyes met and my smile twinned his.

"Hold back your hair," he instructed.

I did.

He unclasped the chain and the brush of his knuckles against the sides of my neck sent prickles all over my skin. The corners of his mouth quirked as he acknowledged the evidence.

He ran his fingers gently over the chain resting against my collar bones, to the pendant that hung between my breasts. I tracked his movements and watched as he appraised me.

"A rose for my Rose. A gift for my gift. Happy Birthday, Rose."

"I love you," I vowed.

"Me too," he replied. "I'll see you at the ceremony. Unless…"

Mischief coloured his features as he ran a thumb over the fullness of my breast causing my nipples to harden instantly. His hand smoothed over my skin to grip the back of my neck and he pulled my mouth to his with a possessive jerk. He hovered there temptingly.

"…unless you want to do some more of what we did last night?"

I slapped his bicep and chest while wriggling free of his grasp trying desperately to quash memories of him devouring my flesh in the small hours. The thoughts caused a flutter of excitement in my belly and as much as I would love for him to indulge in my body like the night before, I really was running out of time. He feigned hurt as I squealed and giggled and broke free from his grip and removed him from my bedroom.

"I have to get dressed!" I protested.

"Can I watch?" He cheekily responded while clearly undressing me with his eyes.

"Stop or I'll never make it to the ceremony!" I was playful but I did mean it. I had to bathe and dress and see my father. Priorities.

"Okay, okay." He held his palms to me in mock defeat. We studied each other in silence for a moment or two. I willed my eyes to absorb everything I loved about him. His shaggy blond hair that reminded me of my favourite season, summer. His lips that were mine to kiss that housed the most perfect white teeth. His skin was a contrast to my brown tones, but the bridge of his nose showed his exposure to the elements in the form of a smattering of freckles where the sun had kissed his face. Where I had kissed his face. His expression softened as he allowed me to take him in.

"See you there, Petal."

My eyes rolled at the nickname that he knew I despised, and I shut the door to the sounds of his laughter echoing the hallway.

"Right," I sighed with intention.

My wardrobe, although taller than me and about as wide as I could reach, only housed very few items. I wore the same mauve dress most days—it was practical and comfortable—it had pockets!

When I wasn't attending evening mass, I was shepherding the children to and from studies or tutoring the girls in domestic skills.

Greer, along with my father and Mr Anderson, taught the boys to rear animals, tend to crops, building and maintenance and collecting firewood from Cluster Wood—a small woodland our ancestors had planted some millennia ago. The wood was only about a two-hundred-and-fifty paces wide either way, and when the weather was nice, we would take the children there to study the flora and fauna and learn bush skills. It was also a favourite spot to rendezvous away from prying eyes.

Greer and I shared our first kiss in Cluster Wood. I had a gaggle of girls with me, and I was showing them the differences between male and female stinging nettles. The tiny geometric clusters of seeds that are produced by the female plant, we harvest and roast to make coffee. We make teas and soup with the highly nutritious leaves and treat aching painful joints with the stinging parts of the plant. This versatile weed had many uses in our community, and it was our job to pass this wisdom down to our younger generation.

Greer had a group of boys in the wood showing them how to use flint and steel to make fire. He had left the boys to practice before asking if he could 'have a word' in a most inconspicuous, 'responsible adult' way.

We had been flirting on and off for months and apparently, he couldn't resist any longer. He pushed me up against a tree out of sight of the children. He smelled of smoke and ash. There was a smudge of black on the tip of his nose and I swiped it off with my thumb and spittle. His face wrinkled at my attempt at mothering him before his gaze turned lazy.

"Be my girlfriend," he said. Not quite a question but more of a command and it caused my cheeks to blush and my heart to stutter. I'd never been someone's girlfriend.

"Yes," I replied with a nod and a grin.

I had been imagining this moment. I thought that if I played it out in my head over and over that I would somehow manifest it, and perhaps I had. He sealed our union with a kiss like a wax seal at the bottom of a contract. It was official. I smiled to myself for the way the memory was making me giddy.

I had a dress that I saved for best that I would wear to coupling ceremonies and celebrations like birthdays and death days. It wasn't much different in style from my everyday dress, but it was made from a lighter material in a sunflower yellow and I liked the way I felt when I wore it.

I had saved some of Mother's clothing, the ones that still had life left in them, but still I hadn't worn any yet. I'd told myself I was saving them until they would fit but I'm sure they would have fit me years ago.

I had only one pair of trousers, a tunic, a couple of pairs of stockings, a few under garments and one more dress.

My hand found the hanger instantly, but I paused for a moment and took a deep breath to steady my nerves. I knew exactly what was inside this garment bag so why did it feel like I was about to place my hand in a mystery box to find myself groping something grotesque inside it like those games we play at carnivals. I could still feel the moist bodies of the worms wiggling over my fingertips and the grit of the soil under my nails. Not being able to see them sent my mind running wild. I envisioned the hair-like nerves on the backs of eyeballs. I don't know why my mind had a tendency to think darker thoughts.

I had pulled my hand back and forth multiple times hesitating above the zip. Don't be ridiculous, Rose. It's just a dress. But it wasn't just a dress—it was *the dress*. This wasn't just me playing dress up like when I had tried it on for size a few years ago when Father insisted, after telling me how angelic mother had looked when she had worn it. He asked me to put it on for him just so he could try to envision her. "I'm beginning to forget what she looked like," he had told me solemnly.

My father had Mrs Cromer make alterations to accommodate my lower half. My breasts were just as small as hers but where my mother's hips were lean, mine were much fuller. Her legs were a little longer than mine too. Only by an inch or two, so Mrs Cromer had told my father she had added a panel to allow for my curves and taken up the hem, so I don't trip on my way to the dais. I was grateful for her consideration. With so many eyes on me, tripping was not on my to-do list.

I slowly lowered the zip of the dress bag hanging on the front of my pine wardrobe, a slither of ivory lace peeking through the opening. My fingertips ran over the bumps of the intricately woven floral detail of the fabric. I pulled the bag away from the shoulders and it dropped to the floor with a swooshing sound. I wished she could be here in person, but a part of her would be with me at least.

The tiny hidden zip stoppered between my shoulder blades. I smoothed the bodice and skirt with my hands. I hadn't dared look into the full-length mirror in front of me, I had kept my eyes to the ground. A few deep breaths and I was ready.

My gaze left my feet and made its way upwards taking in the skirt like an ivory waterfall draping to the floor. The under slip a sheer light fabric with the outer skirt made of delicate lace like the petals of cream-coloured roses. The bodice was fitted but not to the point of discomfort. The sleeves ended in the most beautiful fluid lace that hung loosely over my hands. I traced the low neckline—which didn't reveal too much, not that I had much to show, to find the pendant that Greer had fastened around my neck earlier and studied it properly for the first time. The golden chain of tiny hoops and the dainty rose—my namesake—no one had ever gifted me jewellery before. I smiled at my reflection before running my fingers through my hair and fastening a bow at my nape. My face was framed by my vibrant shoulder length crimson locks. Red—not like the leaves of autumn or copper faucets but red like blood, like cherry wine, like a deep red rose. I was an anomaly. Folks around here had shades of sand to mud, like the colours of nature but not me. I was the second of two redheads ever to have existed. Luckily for me they didn't make as much fuss as they'd seen it once before but still enough fuss to make me aware that I was odd.

I slipped on my white pumps that I wore most days. They showed evidence of the dirt paths that ran through the village. I'd had a go at cleaning them, but they were still more beige than white. My dress more or less covered them anyway and I doubted anyone would be looking at my shoes.

I studied myself for signs of her and found them there in the shape of my eyes, my full lips—we smiled the same—and the dimple in the centre of my chin. She was the reason why I didn't hate it. It took me a while to learn to love it. My skin was my own. A mixture of them both. A stark contrast to Fathers pale complexion and a warm beige in comparison to Mothers darker tone. My hair colour was hers; but the loose waves were his. I studied the finished product, the girl in front of me no longer a girl but a woman. When did that happen?

My focus found my mark, just peeking out from under the tiny scallops along the dress's neckline. A small brown freckle, sort of teardrop shape or half a love heart, branded onto my skin just left of the centre of my chest where my heart beats below my ribcage. It appeared just four days after I had turned twenty which was late compared to most who usually got it around eighteen.

My coming-of-age party was truly wonderful. Surrounded by friends and loved ones we shared food and drink in the square in the evening under the watch of the stars and the moon. Lantern flames flickered casting warm lighting all around us and of course I wore my sunflower dress and a crown of roses the florist had hand made for me.

Mother visited me that evening like she often did during the night. She told me I had been chosen and that she was proud of me. "You will do great things my love." Her voice carried a deep soothing tone. She had always told me I was destined for great things.

I was so excited—I'd been prepared for this possibility all my life. All the kids in the village were. The honour of being chosen and what that meant to the community. Father was over the moon and said that it was because I was made with so much love. 'Love is the force that keeps us all living. It flows through our blood and to our hearts. That's why we give our hearts to one another when we fall in love.'

Millicent, or Millie as Father called her, left this life when I was seven. When I closed my eyes and concentrated hard, I could still hear that rich velvety voice singing melodies that seemed to carry her wherever she went. She would share words of encouragement or sometimes just hold me when I needed her most. I had hoped to dream of her last night but alas, I did not.

Mother was a healer. She had a little annex on the side of our home filled with tonics and trinkets, potted plants and bunches of dried herbs hanging everywhere. The people of the village would come to her with all kinds of ailments. She could heal just about anything and was great with her hands. The whole community felt the loss. They had looked to me to follow in her footsteps but then the gods had another plan for me.

Greer and I had been friends for some time and were in the same study group growing up and had known each other for many years before we became a couple. He was the pastor's son, so I knew he was a good man—I felt it in the way he looked at me, the way he treated me. That's not to say I haven't had my doubts, and they've revisited me many times over the last few years. Just a little feeling deep in my gut. With my parents love story and the romances in books, I kept hoping for something a bit more but over the last four years I had grown to love Greer deeply. I wondered what thoughts would fill his mind when he saw me heading down the aisle.

The Crimson Moon is a sight to behold. No one knows why, but on the night when the moon is at its fullest it glows blood red. We witness a full moon every twenty-eight days or so but for some reason, unknown to us, she blesses us with her crimson beauty once every four years. A sacred day where we all make vows and promises and offerings to each other and the gods in return for prosperity, good luck and health.

Jennifer and Kane's celebration was on my twentieth birthday, just four days before my mark appeared, so I had to wait until the next Crimson Moon for my turn to make my offering—but tonight will be that night.

I took the steps one foot in front of the other. I'd learned every creak and crack of each tread on the wooden flight to the upper floor of our home. I'd become an expert at sneaking in Greer—incognito—after Father had gone to bed at night. It's not that he would have objected to us spending the night together; we were adults after all, and he loved Greer. Being 'chosen' meant he let me get away with things he might not have had I not been. I was just a little embarrassed. I didn't want him to think of his little girl that way.

Shuffling feet moved back to the kitchenette area as Father made himself look busy, like he wasn't just waiting at the bottom of the staircase with the same anticipation as a dog on the inside of a front door waiting for their owner to unlock it. If I hadn't seen him, his overcompensation for normalcy would have definitely given away the fact that he was so desperately impatient to see me. His shoulders slumped as if he had just emptied his lungs of a breath he'd been holding for the almost two hours it had taken me to get dressed. Tears spilled from his eyes. The reaction was almost immediate and exactly as I had expected.

"Excuse me for being a silly old sentimental man," he laughed as he dabbed his face with a red handkerchief with his initials embroidered in white stitching in the corner. He looked at me like I was breakable and precious.

"I don't know what you mean?" My sarcasm caused us both to chuckle.

"You look..."

"Like her?" He didn't have to say it, I knew what he was thinking.

"Does everything fit okay?" He twirled me around, surveying me.

"It's perfect Father, thank you." I smiled softly and I hoped that he knew what he meant to me.

"Dinner is almost ready," he said as he shuffled back to the kitchen.

"Father," I cut in. "Would you mind wrapping it in paper? I'd like to eat outside today. I'd like to go for a walk and... just take it all in really."

"Of course," he said chirpily. "We can do that."

"Would you be terribly upset if I went alone?" I asked in an almost 'tail between my legs' kind of way.

I saw the confusion and a slight flash of hurt on his face as he told me he didn't mind at all.

We were supposed to have a meal together just the two of us. We always connected over food. I definitely got my appetite from him as Mother was more of a grazer. She would joke that Father and I had two stomachs— one for mains, one for pudding. My father and I would always rub our full bellies laughing at one another as my mother shook her head in mock disgust.

As I'd gotten older, I had wished I'd had eating habits more like hers as the excess mouthfuls had seemed to store themselves around my hips, buttocks and thighs unlike my father's lean frame. He counteracted his larger appetite with laborious work around the village when we were not at the chapel tutoring the younglings.

I had taken over Mother's role at home. There wasn't much to do, being just us two. There was minimal cleaning as we were a tidy pair. Father wore the same flannel shirt and trousers to work every day. I hand washed our soiled rags on a Sunday. I cooked for us a few times a week, soups and stews and our favourite rabbit pie. It was a simple but fine life. I smiled to myself in gratitude as I scuffed the dirt path beneath my feet.

I came here often, whenever I needed to be close to her. This was the spot where they found her basket, with her secateurs, partly filled with nettles and yarrow. She had been foraging for supplies for her tonics and remedies.

The wood stretched as far as the eye could see. It surrounded us keeping us encased in a vast clearing of sorts. It would take most of daylight to walk the perimeter that lined our village. No matter where you stopped along the way one could only see past the first few rows of trees before all you could see was the dense darkness of the woods. The canopy so thick that it allowed little light to reach the ground. The edge of the world as we knew it.

The trees dwarfed me which was not at all difficult due to my short stature. These towering giants were like guards standing firm not allowing us to enter, or maybe they were guarding us and not letting something out.

We had been told tales of what lives within these woods, but nobody knew what was on the other side, if there was another side. As far as we knew the woods were all there was. We were told to stay put and our lives would be fruitful. The gods had never given us any reason to doubt them.

Just then, I heard a snap like a branch beneath a boot. My eyes whipped instinctively to the left where I was certain the sound had come from. I stepped closer to the trees squinting between the trunks, willing my eyes to see further.

I saw it then. A hooded figure moving swiftly through the shadows. My feet began to move in the same direction following the figure being sure to keep to the treeline and going no further in. I called out. The figure stopped, as did I, as though the boundary of the treeline was a mirror. I froze but held my ground staring purposefully into the abyss willing the stranger to react to me. I don't know where this fearlessness came from, but I didn't feel scared. It was like all fear and reasoning didn't exist and I was being led purely by instinct. Like the figure and I were attached by an invisible tether and as it moved, I was being dragged along too.

Maybe Death had come to claim me, just as it had Mother.

I called out again.

"Rose!"

"Father?" I turned to the familiar voice calling me.

"What are you doing?" He grabbed my arm with the force of his concern and abruptly turned me toward him and away from the wood, as though a horse and cart barrelled toward me, and he was pulling me out of its path.

"I...I...I thought I saw something," I stuttered. I definitely saw something.

"You know not to go into the wood. It's dangerous. What were you thinking? And today of all days!"

Today.

"I'm…I'm sorry." A tear escaped my eye. "I thought…" I glanced back to the blanket of darkness between the trees feeling an emptiness when I spotted nothing there.

"I know. It's okay." My father comforted me and swiped the tear from my cheek with his rough thumb.

"You know that the Wild of the Wood is a wicked temptress. She probably thought she could steal you from us today. Thank the gods that I found you in time."

"How did you find me?" I broke from his hold to look him in eye which I hadn't been able to do just a few moments ago. The shame had stopped me.

"Greer told me you were by the wood," he replied, eyebrows raised at my accusatory tone.

"But how did…never mind." The look on my father's face told me that it did not matter how Greer came to know my whereabouts, and I wondered was it Greer at all or had he in fact been following me himself?

The relief that he so plainly displayed made a pang of guilt run through me. I understood his worry, even if I didn't share it. I didn't feel the perilous energy that, according to others, emanated from the woods. The pull I felt toward this wood was like a yearning, like a rope tied around my waist attached to something deep in the wood and it was tugging the end, trying to coax me in. I dare not confess to him that I had had many meetings with the wood before this one. I had almost given myself to it when Mother died but found it was waiting there to give me comfort, offer sanctuary. The branches held out towards me like arms waiting to console me. I would tell them my secrets and they would keep them.

Words of wisdom came to me in the whispering of the winds and rustling of the leaves and when I felt I couldn't breathe they would fill my lungs with air.

Father had his reasons to worry. I had heard stories all my life of the Wild of the Wood. If not from the mouths of my parents, then from the mouth of the Pastor at daily mass. Most of the tales dated back as far as five hundred years but those stories had become entrenched in our traditions and history and had become somewhat lore.

Legend had it that the Wild of the Wood was a beast that feeds on our souls. She tempts us to commit sins and uses our greed, lust, violence and vanity to lure us to the mouth of the woods, then like siren song we are drawn into the forest by her melody where she devours our souls and leaves our bodies to be ravaged by the wilderness. Every now and then she would take one of our own to remind us, to keep us in tow. To keep us from our sins. To keep us subservient to the Gods. My mother was the last to be taken.

"I've been thinking of your mother quite often recently." My father broke the silence that had ensued on our walk back to the village.

We strolled leisurely hand in hand taking our time as if delaying the inevitable. We shared the meat, bread and potatoes he had packed for me. The sun was setting, and dusk was creeping in, and it was almost time.

"She would be so proud of you, you know?" I smiled in response to his claim. "You look just as beautiful as she did."

He paused before telling me the story of their union. I'd heard it so many times before but hearing him tell it and watching all of the emotion unfold was better than any romance novel in my collection.

"Everyone was gathered in the square and I stood out front of the chapel waiting for her to arrive. She was running late, and I was so nervous she had changed her mind. Pastor David kept reassuring me despite the murmurs from the restless crowd. The ground was quicksand, and I was sinking every minute she hadn't arrived. The sun had almost been swallowed by the horizon and the flames from the lanterns cast dancing shadows all around. I looked to the gods and prayed for them to bring her to me and as I lowered my eyes, there she was. She was so beautiful. She had this aura around her of yellows and pinks and her dress, that dress, was so long that it looked like she was floating. She had a few red roses in one hand and the other rested on her stomach." His eyes always welled up at this part, every time. "She nodded at my acknowledgment of her hand placement and we both smiled the biggest smiles in the world. You were with us that day. Our Rose."

We had made it to the chapel by the end of his story. I had been so captivated by him that I hadn't even noticed.

They were waiting for me. There must have been around three-hundred inhabitants in the village of Sandy, and it looked like most of them were here. The elderly and less abled were seated toward the front but the majority stood.

My father told me he loved me and gave me the strongest, heartfelt embrace before walking me slowly toward the dais.

Mrs Cromer handed me a red rose as did Mr Sykes, Mr Tunwell, Mrs Ellison and some of the smaller children I recognised from tutoring, and just like my parents' wedding day the light from the lanterns cast dancing shadows in the dusk.

I was carried down the aisle by Father's reassuring hand and the smiles of the locals. I saw flashes of relief on faces, I imagined their anticipation like a groom waiting for his bride who suffered with poor timekeeping, much like my father in his story.

Some folks hid sadness behind their smiles. Today was bittersweet in many ways. I saw others had no problem hiding their greed. They weren't here to support me but here to see the fruits of my labour, the gifts we were to receive.

Pastor David waited for me at the end of the aisle dressed in his ceremonial garb of rich purple embellished with golden patterns. He looked almost regal, like the kings of fairy tales I read as a child. I suppose he was kind of royalty here. He was the leader of our community. He was advisor, chieftain, representative to the gods. Yes, he was our king, and I was the lover of the prince.

My focus landed on Greer to the side of his father. His eyes lit up when mine found his and my heart skipped a beat.

"I love you," I mouthed to him.

"Me too," he mouthed back.

Me too? I thought today he might say more than just *'me too.'* Oh, how it bothered me, but I had always let it go. It was like a tiny splinter of wood lodged in a woollen sock. You could feel a sharp sting pricking the arch of your sole but could not locate the little bastard. It was one of those itches that seem to be embedded deeper beneath the top layers of skin, and you scratch, and you scratch, and you just can't get it.

It had become our way. I would always be the one professing my love and he would reciprocate with those same two words every time. Me—fucking—too.

Oh, this was new.

A stinging feeling I had no idea how to describe. I felt my cheeks redden with the sensation of it. It was like anger, jealousy and irritation all rolled in to one and causing a prickly heat to rise in my cheeks. Greer's brow furrowed and I realised my face must've portrayed what my brain was thinking. I quickly corrected it with a false smile and hoped that he would see my blushing as embarrassment, as the symptom of all of the eyes that were scrutinising me in the same way he was. Now was not the time to nit-pick and point out tiny flaws in an otherwise lovely life. I assumed that this was the 'cold feet' that people spoke of. When making such a massive commitment, doubt starts to chisel away at certainty like a stonemason etching letters into gravestones, chipping away tiny pieces like little niggling hesitations chipping away at confidence.

My father shook hands with Pastor David and bowed his head to Greer before leaving me for his seat on the front row. I looked out to all the happy expectant faces. This was it. The day we had been preparing for was finally here.

I drew the air through my nostrils greedily, savouring how it felt and tasted, the intake filling my lungs and spreading a surge of energy through my veins.

"Thank you all for coming," Pastor David began. "Thank the gods and the Crimson Moon…"

We all raised arms to the heavens and let the energy of the Crimson Moon wash over us and, just like that, she erased the irrationality that skewed my vision for a moment.

"…and thank you, Rose. May I say you look incredible this evening." His shoulders lifted and fists bunch with an expression that exuded excitement. His salt and pepper hair sometimes looked like a wig, especially when freshly washed, giving it that extra bit of bounce. He had tucked the mid length locks behind his ears and smiled benevolently at me.

"We will start by remembering the ceremony of Jennifer and Kane on this very evening four years ago."

We all bowed our heads and closed our eyes.

"We've had such a fruitful four years since. Our crops were plentiful, rain came, our well was fixed. We received food, tools, books, even new tiles so we were able to repair the chapel roof. These vows bring with them good fortune and we thank the gods." His voice seemed to project and fill every nook of the clearing in the centre of our village.

"Thank the gods," we all chanted in unison.

"Rose, please repeat after me."

His smile was kind, and I felt at ease, and the words I repeated after him flowed freely from my mouth.

"I, Rose Elodie Harlow, surrender myself to the gods in return for your stewardship over our land and our people. Please continue to bless us with health, happiness and prosperity. I thank you for selecting me as tribute and promise to honour you in this life and the next."

Pastor David gestured to Greer. He uncorked a bottle of deep cherry wine with a pop and poured the liquid into a silver chalice. Pastor David held it in the air.

"Rose, you shall drink the blood of the gods and as they give to you, you shall give to them and know that you will be received into their kingdom."

The vibrant pink hues of dusk had given way to dark blues and there above the chapel roof, right on cue, was our Crimson Moon.

I took in my surroundings one last time. This town square held many a happy memory—market days, carnivals, weddings and celebrations of life. I could spot the roofs of the Pipes bakery—A Slice of Life—a clever play on words but their baked goods really were one of the great joys of life. The Whistle Inn—the largest public house in Sandy—cooked a fantastic steak with wild garlic butter, a flicker of regret at the fact that Father and I didn't have one more meal there; the band stand where we had held hands and danced with merriment after every tribute under the Crimson Moon. I glanced upon the faces, many familiar, many not and I wondered if maybe I should have made an effort to get to know some of them more.

I looked up to the big, beautiful full moon, a glowing globe of deep red like the cherry wine in the chalice I was clutching. I noticed my hands tremble and for a split second I felt a pull in my gut like my body might just refuse to swallow the contents. 'It's just like falling asleep,' we had been told over and over, 'completely painless and nothing to be scared of.' I had believed it too, right until this moment.

What if it did hurt? What if the poison felt like spikes and knives and other sharp things? What if, when I took my final breath, the toxins burned like fire in my lungs?

I was terrified. I had been terrified from the moment my mark had appeared. I had gotten good at storing those fears away in a box. Every time someone told me they were proud or told me I should be honoured, every time Mr Pipe offered me free buns to take home for me and Father as I strolled by at closing, or every time Brock told me 'It's on the house.' With every kind gesture I channelled more fear into my locked box. But now the box had cracked under the strain, and what was a trickle was now pouring like the tears that welled in my eyes as panic struck my body. I didn't want to die.

The crowd started to grow restless and those smiles that had carried me down the aisle had now turned to scowls and faces of confusion. Some looked to be leaving as the mass started to scatter. Then I heard the screams.

My eyes darted around looking for the cause of the commotion while my feet stayed rooted to the spot. Then I saw him, Death. It was him from the forest earlier and he had come to claim me. He didn't trust me to go willingly so he had come to take me himself. Clever Death. He knew what I would do before I even did.

He was huge. So tall I had to crane my neck to look at him. His hood covered most of his face, but I could still see the very bottom. A strong jaw jutted out from beneath the hood. I could see stubble there on his bronzed skin. Funny, I always assumed Death would be pale, like colour was too alive. The fact that his facial hair was cropped so closely to his skin told me he was groomed and that surprised me too. How could death even grow facial hair—he was well, dead?

"Sorry to break up the party but I will be taking Ms Harlow now." His deep tone sounded almost humorous in command. It had a 'try and stop me' tone to it. He reached a strong arm around my middle.

"I wouldn't do that if I were you," Pastor David practically spat at him. "You will damn us all!" He bellowed.

The figure, covered in a heavy black woollen cloak embroidered with small red roses that trailed the opening and framed the hem of his hood, grinned cunningly.

"Oh, but I am going to do it, David, and you can't stop me."

There was something arrogant about the way he said it. My senses came rushing back, and I was present, no longer watching some kind of play unfold.

"Father?" I shrieked.

My head spun as I scanned the row where he had been seated. Everyone once there had left their chairs—all except him. He was gawking in shock with a look on his face that probably matched my own a few moments ago. I tried to get to him, but Death's grip was too tight.

"You're hurting me," I shouted.

They'd said it wasn't supposed to hurt. Surprisingly he loosened his grip ever so slightly giving me enough leeway to wriggle free.

"Wait," he ordered. I felt the words stop me physically. Like he had uttered a spell. I was at a crossroads. One path led to my demise tonight and the other lead to who knows what. It could very well lead to death that way too but call it curiosity, a small voice in the back of my mind was telling me which way to choose.

"Please. Come with me," he begged, and like the pied piper's song I followed.

"Rose, where are you going?" Greer ran forward and grasped both my arms. My mouth tried to form words, but I didn't know my answer. Where was I going? I looked to the cloaked man trying to steal me away from destiny.

Full lips parted. "The gods have decided to let you live. I'm saving your life. You were made for greater things."

-5-

Mother. She's the reason I went with him. She's the reason I ignored all rational thought and followed my gut, and my gut said I should go. Or was it false hope? His words reverberated in every corner of my mind. Had those recycled words been but coincidence?

Greer begged me, and the caped crusader had laughed at him. He didn't try to come after me. He adhered to my captor's orders. I would challenge anyone to stop me from going after Greer if someone had taken him from me.

Me too.

There was that feeling again.

I was a tight knot of reluctance with stubborn feet. There was a war raging within me and as it was coming to a head, regardless of which side I was on, I would still lose. Stay and die, go and die...probably. I had taken root watching him ransack food and clothing from a house on the verge of the woods.

Better the devil you know, I decided.

"Listen, I don't know what's going on here, but we were kind of in the middle of something really important that can only be done on this very day, and if we don't, then the people of this village, my people, will have nothing. Our crops will die, our wells will dry, and the gods will not deliver the things we so desperately need." I thought, if he heard what was at stake, he might return me. Perhaps he didn't know, which would be impossible; everyone here relies on the tributes to the gods... Unless he wasn't from here?

"Thank you," he replied. I raised my brow at him in question. "It's what you say when someone saves your life." He unsheathed a knife from the knife block before studying the blade and swapping it for another.

"Saving someone implies they were in danger. I was not in danger. I was chosen. Chosen by the gods as tribute. It's a tradition from the beginning of time, and it's how we ensure our community thrives. It keeps our bellies full, our bodies healthy, and warm. Not only that, but it also keeps us safe from the Wild of the Wood and monsters, like you, I suppose."

I didn't know why I was telling him this. He should already know the details, but just in case he was a time traveller, or from another dimension, or perhaps not of this world entirely. I scoffed at myself for the implausibility of any of those reasons.

"Grab that blanket," he said, completely brushing over everything I'd just stated.

"Are you listening to me?" I snapped. My patience was wearing thin.

No reply.

"Who the hell are you, and what gives you the right to save me?" I stabbed my finger at his chest and my finger bent the wrong way under the firmness. He stood there like a brick wall, unreactive.

I reached for his hood, whether to get a better look at him or to force his hand, I just wanted a reaction. I managed to move it slightly before he grabbed my wrists. The motion swift, but the grip light. My heart thundered in my chest, and I forgot to breathe for a moment, like I'd been caught doing something I shouldn't. Like the time Father caught me sneaking out past curfew. I had frozen then, just the same.

A deep inhale, and I could feel him engulfing me—his scent like campfires and forest floors, like he'd slept under the night sky and hadn't bathed in a month. Not dirty, just undiluted man. A shuddering breath escaped my lips and my reaction surprised me. My traitorous body. As if I was allowing myself to fall under whatever spell he was casting.

"You said I was needed for greater things?" I didn't intend to sound so vulnerable and small, but I was having a hard time accepting that the things that I'd been conditioned for—the thing that I had been building up to for four years—might not actually happen and my brain couldn't comprehend the what ifs.

And with a voice tender and empathetic he said, "You will know everything soon, but for now I need you to trust me, please."

In the cover of darkness, we trailed around the outer edge of the village. We paused several times for him to scout and listen out for people coming to my aide. No one did.

We eventually made it to a large cave, an imposing shadow against a navy sky. My attention caught on a mound of items just in front of the cave. The Crimson Moon, like a muted flame, cast just enough light for me to make them out.

"It's all here?" A puzzled expression adorned my features. "But I'm still here?"

There were barrels and crates of all the things that were promised upon my sacrifice. Books, herbs, medicines—new tools, building materials, and fabric for garments. I'd been told about this place. That this place, the Giving Cave, was where our rewards were left. The Collins family were the ones responsible for retrieval and had been for as long as anyone had known. Only they were permitted to come here. The gods had said so.

"It's not possible," I whispered, dumbfounded.

"This way is the safest and easiest route. Keep close," he commanded, ignoring my obvious turmoil.

Jet black swallowed him at the mouth of the cave like a huge creature. By the time I had joined him, he had lit a lantern, the light of which was guiding him through the tunnel. It smelled of dirt and wet stone. The cold damp sent a shiver through me, pebbling my skin. I wasn't prepared for this, nor wearing the correct attire for such a place.

The tunnels seemed to be a way to distribute the gifts, and it very much looked man-made, not gods made. There were unlit lanterns hanging at intervals along the walls. Tracks at my feet, rails on which wheeled crates would run. We walked past a small table and two stools, an abandoned stack of cards on the tabletop. It was evident that it was used recently.

"What the hell is this place?" My demand echoed up the passage.

He froze and turned back slowly and placed a single digit against his lips, highlighted with the lantern he held to his face. Before an argument could escape my open mouth, I noticed light in the distance up ahead.

"Who goes there?" A gruff voice shouted from further up the tunnel.

"Shit, Plan B it is," he sighed.

Whatever Plan B was, it didn't sound as though I should have much faith in it judging by the girth of his sigh. It felt like he had relied on the success of Plan A, and Plan B was last resort.

Feet thundered and metal clanked.

"Time to go," he urged.

Argument would have to wait as he pushed me to get moving. I ran alongside him as fast as I could, I was sure he had to slow himself so as not to lose me. My breaths were rapid. I hadn't really run from a potential threat before. I didn't need to.

I braved a look behind me even though I knew I shouldn't. It confirmed they were closing in on us fast, whoever they were.

Shit.

Fear was a force behind me, pushing me forward, and as I sped up, my body lurched ahead of my feet, hurtling me towards the ground. Two strong hands grasped my ribcage and righted me.

After some frantic minutes that felt like more, we exited the cave and continued to run the outskirts along the treeline.

"Who was that?" I gasped for a breath that was not enough to satisfy my need for oxygen.

"Kingsmen," he answered matter-of-factly.

"What does that mean, Kingsmen?"

We didn't have a king. Pastor David was probably the highest authority. We had no need for enforcers in our peaceful village. Had a problem, we fixed it as a community and usually at the chapel with the pastor as mediator.

Struggling to fathom this new information, I hadn't realised that we had run much further into the trees than I would ever dare to go. More than I would ever be allowed to go. I felt the colour drain from my face as unawareness cleared the way for panic.

"I can't be in here. We must go back!"

"Why?" He scoffed at my fretting as if I was being absurd, and I didn't appreciate it.

"The Wild of the Wood!" I exclaimed. I would have thought that was obvious.

"And what might that be?" He probed with an air of ridicule.

I told him about the temptress in the trees that stole many a member of my village, but not that she had taken my own mother. That felt too personal, and I wasn't about to show further vulnerability to a man that scoffed at my fear.

"Well, there's some truth in that at least. There are many dangerous beings in this wood, and out of it. But if we go back, you face certain death. They may even kill your whole village. At least in here, with me, you have a chance of living," he replied with a haughty tone. I think that was the most he'd said to me so far.

"What do you mean, the whole village will be in danger?"

"Right now, your village leader will be covering your rescue with another lie. They won't want everyone to start asking questions, start to think for themselves. They will be told that you have betrayed your village and that you hired someone to rescue you to evade your duty, or something along those lines. They may say that we have escaped into the woods and will be sure to speak of our guaranteed demise. They will blame the possible forthcoming of bad luck on you."

Bullshit.

"Where are you from? At least tell me who you are!"

I didn't realise I'd raised my voice until he whipped himself around to face me and charged at me like I was waving a red cloth, grunting with each heavy step. For a second, I thought he was going to seize me or accost me or show me something other than the minimal that he was giving. But whatever he was going to do, he changed his mind, turned away and proceeded to walk deeper into the wood.

No! I deserved some answers. You can't just abduct someone and say nothing and expect them to follow you—no question.

"I'm talking to you!" I made a grab for him. I would have answers, and I would not go any further until he told me. I'd glue myself to the spot, and he would have to throw me over his shoulder if he wanted me to go with him. I would not move until I heard some truths.

Suddenly, my feet left the leaf-littered forest floor, and I was slammed into the thick trunk of an oak tree. My head hit the bark, and my vision dazed as he held a firm hand across my mouth. Panic-stricken tears immediately poured from my eyes. The collision hurt and my nostrils were not adequate enough to give me back the air that the impact had forced from me.

I had made a grave mistake. In his attempt to save my life, I had somehow assumed I was safe with him. I'd never been so scared. The tears that fell made tracks across the back of his hand. My knees buckled, and he pressed himself close, keeping me from dropping to the ground. He leaned to my ear until his rough jaw brushed against my cheek, his warm breath coated my neck.

"Nathaniel," he breathed. "My name is Nathaniel Blackmore."

He pushed off the trunk with the hand he had kept braced above my head. A rush of air whooshed between us as he pulled a sword from under his cloak. My eyes popped from their sockets as I took in the lethal weapon and the attacking stance he'd cast.

I was so consumed by my thirst for information that I hadn't noticed it. Not until it had sauntered into my peripheral. Antlers as thick as my arms protruded from a massive head covered with a bony plate and tapered into sharp points. A sleek feline body as tall as my shoulder. A growl rumbled in its throat as it halted, scenting the air next to me. Nathaniel whistled for its attention, and he got it. The beast's yellow glare landed on him as the predator immediately lunged. He held his position, sword up high over his head, refusing to back away, either part of his plan or he was scared stiff, as was I. The beast lowered his antlers on his approach as the blade of Nathaniel's sword came hurtling down. An almighty crack of steel on bone as the force threw them both backwards. The beast growled ferociously, unphased by the attack, protected by his exo-skeletal helmet.

It charged again.

Nathaniel rolled to the side with mere seconds to spare. The beast crashed into a tree. The impact shook the forest. The attack was so swift I hadn't even spotted that Nathaniel had managed to nick its side until I saw the blood oozing from a slash near its rear.

Nathaniel crouched low. He moved with the stealth of a predator, sizing up his prey. The beast rounded to face him once more, shaking his head side to side. It mimicked Nathaniels low stance and stealthy movements. Its belly brushed the forest floor leaving streaks in the debris. It huffed air from its nostrils and crept toward Nathaniel. Nathaniel stayed put and did not move an inch. He let the animal get ever closer. I felt my bones liquidise and any minute now I'd be nothing but a gelatinous pile on the floor. It was not that I particularly cared for my captor, but I'm not sure I could cope with having front-row seats to a death match.

The beast's movements quickened from a creep to a gallop, and still Nathaniel did not move. My heart thundered in my chest, rattling my ribs like a caged animal. I pushed back into the solid trunk behind me, wishing it would swallow me up.

The beast had reached its target. Its body coiled like a spring and launched from the ground with powerful hind legs. A fraught squeal escaped my mouth. Time slowed as Nathaniel took a knee and lowered his head seemingly surrendering. I slapped a hand to my mouth and bent at the knee, sliding down the trunk of the tree. I didn't want to see it anymore, but I couldn't look away.

As quick as lightning, as the predator arced over Nathaniel, he launched his sword skyward to the soft underbelly of the beast. A howl pierced the forest as the beast collapsed with a thud on top of him. Concern lifted me from the ground and moved my legs. I got to him just as he'd managed to roll the carcass from on top of him.

He stood quickly with his back to me and righted himself, securing the hood to its usual position, obscuring his face. I wondered why he was keeping his identity so secret. Did I know him? Had I seen him before? Was he horrifically ugly? Or maybe his face had been maimed by a beast in a battle not unlike the one I had just witnessed, and maybe he was too self-conscious, so he hid himself away.

I waited in anticipation for him to turn around.

"Nathaniel?" I whispered, my throat still clenching from the tension that had coiled in my body moments ago.

"I'm okay," he replied, picking up on my tone. He sheathed his sword back under his cloak. "We better move. We have a lot of ground to cover."

"Thank you."

He froze at my offering. I was grateful. Grateful that he came out of the attack unscathed and for not leaving me alone in this unknown territory. Grateful that I did not end up in the belly of the beast.

He turned slowly and closed the gap between us. "Are you okay? Are you hurt?"

If I hadn't known any better, I'd say he sounded worried. I know I hadn't exactly been friendly so far, but my thanking him really wasn't an indication that we were now friends.

"I'm okay." Maybe physically yes, but emotionally, no. I felt like I was teetering on the edge of a precipice with a pack of wolves behind me and rushing rapids ahead of me.

I am not a brave person. I've never had to be. The most difficult dilemma I had faced was my mother being taken by the Wild. We searched for hours when she hadn't returned, and when her belongings were found and the pastor addressed the village to reveal what had happened, I was devastated. I was her shadow. I could no longer exist if she didn't. My father worked so hard to build me back together. Our people came together and helped me to become my very own person, no longer a shadow of a person. That was seventeen years ago.

I no longer hid in her shadow, and I didn't want him to hide from me either.

We stood face to face; his hands braced my arms. I could feel an energy pulsing in the small gap between our bodies. His aura like the steam of a warm cup of tea after a crisis. I accepted it and drank him in and instantly calmed my quivering. I reached a hand to his jaw but stopped myself from touching him. I wanted to, but my want confused me. He took my hand and lowered it back to my side. No touching then. Got it.

We stayed there silently, comforting one another with the soft strokes of energy rippling in the minute space between our bodies. His breaths were lazy, and I could tell I wasn't the only one feeling a sort of ease. I could feel my bones regenerating and a little bit more of something, like extra reinforcements, were infused into the marrow and bone. The heat from his body so rich it practically caressed me.

My eyes roved over the floral border edging his hood. Tiny blood-red rose heads encompassed with tiny green leaves and fine gold swirls dancing around them. It was such a pretty detail in contrast to the stark black wool and the dark and dangerous way in which he carried himself. My gaze left the floral arc and danced along his stubbled jaw, and I wondered how it would feel under my fingertips. Then I found his lips. The bottom full and velvety, the top all sharp edges and I wanted to feel them on my own.

What was happening?!

Nathaniel lifted his hands between us and rested them on the edge of his hood. He obviously thought I'd seen too much.

But just when I thought he'd conceal himself further, he began to lower it.

He didn't miss the way my throat bobbed when I took him in. The corners of his mouth upturned briefly when he spotted it. My heart stammered. He was beautiful. Black hair framed his face. It was cropped short around the sides, but the top was thick with glossy coils. Some strands had fallen to just above his eyebrows. His eyes were so dark that they swallowed all colour, like deep inky pools that I could fall into and drown. They were severe and cryptic and framed by feathery black lashes. I could tell that his nose had been broken by the bump on his bridge, but it added character, like that small imperfection made him more real. His high cheekbones were as defined as his jawline, and I wanted to see what they would do with a real smile. He chewed on his bottom lip, seemingly nervous, but his eyes willed me to speak.

"You're…" I didn't know what to say. I was astonished. Why had he been hiding this?

"Yes?" He urged eagerly.

"…very handsome?"

Good one, Rose.

My face flushed with the embarrassment of my admission. He seemed…disappointed.

"Oh, I'm sorry, was that not enough for you?" I scoffed. "You're devastatingly gorgeous." My voice, steeped in sarcasm. Maybe he had been used to more enthusiasm when it came to the big reveal. A bit pretentious if you asked me. Did he really think he was such a gift that he had to conceal himself so that he could open himself like a present on winter solstice?

He rolled his eyes and shook his head. His tone reverted to that familiar reticence—his default. "We have to go. It's not safe out here at night."

-6-

Before long we had ventured deeper into a dense thicket. The undergrowth grabbed at my ankles and dress with sharp claws and talons, leaving angry lines on my bare flesh. I trudged through the spiked vegetation and huffed and complained to myself as I kept close behind him—if he heard me, he didn't let on.

Looking around, visibility was poor. Natural light was kept out by the looming treetops, and trunks were rooted so close to one another that everywhere you looked felt like a dead end.

"Where are we going?" I called as a root snagged my foot. I stumbled forward but managed to keep myself from toppling. For every one of his strides, mine were doubled. "Will you slow down? You're going too fast!" I pleaded.

Nathaniel's cloak was so dark that he almost merged with our surroundings. I kept as close as I could in fear of losing him as he weaved in and out of the trunks. I had no idea how he knew where to go. I looked around for signs or markers but found nothing.

Eerie hoots and trills sounded around us, some very close by. I wondered, were they calls from creatures or the ghosts of victims of the Wild of the Wood? I hated to admit it, but I was scared and cold, and the groaning in my stomach was right at home with all the other beastly calls around us.

Suddenly Nathaniel stopped, and I collided with his back. He paused while I righted myself, then stepped to the side, leafy branches held high, and he gestured for me to go ahead.

"After you," he said, doing his best gentleman impression. I rolled my eyes and stepped under his arm to find more darkness, even blacker than before.

I felt a breeze as he passed by me, and the darkness devoured him. My heart started a quickstep until click, click, click, a spark hopped from his hands to the ground. Embers quickly grew to flame as Nathaniel fed it bits of dry grass and kindling.

A warm orange glow lit up a pocket clearing in which a large canvas draped over sticks, just behind the arrangement of rocks that encircled the flickering flames. Nathaniel made himself at home and hung his heavy cloak on a broken branch protruding from a tree trunk. His black collared shirt was loose-fitting on the body, but the sleeves were tight like they were struggling to contain all of his burliness—the top buttons unfastened revealing some of his broad chest. His fitted trousers—tucked into black military-style boots—were also black and hugged his strong thighs equally as tight.

Nathaniel cleared his throat. Had I just been caught ogling this man again? What was wrong with me? You would think I'd never seen an attractive person before. Greer was arguably the best-looking guy in the village, although I'm sure when his father was younger, he'd have given him a run for his money. Taking both of them into consideration, I quickly concluded that yes, I had witnessed attractiveness but nothing on this scale. This man took my breath away without even trying to impress me.

Nathaniel crouched and grabbed a blanket out of his pack. I recognised it from the house he had ransacked in the village. I felt an ache in my chest as I thought of my father, Greer, home. I wished I could go home. He passed me the heavy blanket. I knew that someone had spent valuable time hand-stitching each little square to the sides of others—it was lined too. It would have taken weeks to make, maybe even years, with what little materials we could get our hands on. That's why it was patchwork—most of our blankets were, and many of our garments were repaired with scraps that did not match, and in a few seconds, he had bundled it in his bag, claiming it for his own without a second thought for whom it belonged to. I felt the ire warm my skin, or was that the heat from the flames? Either way, I knew the emotions I felt for this blanket were just symbolic. I knew that the welling in my eyes was caused by a collection of events, and that this blanket was just the final crack to burst the dam.

I opened my mouth to demand he take me home immediately, but before I could say anything, he simply commanded, "Eat."

He held a lump of dry bread and a water-skin out towards me.

"You can sleep in there tonight, and I'll keep watch." He pointed at the make-shift shelter. I was so weary I could sleep anywhere right now. I would save my demands for return for tomorrow.

"And what about you?" I snapped. The shelter was small. I would not be sleeping in there if he intended to share it with me. He ignored my question.

"Would you like to change into something more comfortable? I have a tunic and..."

"No." I cut him off and moved to sit in front of the fire.

He placed his pack on the ground and sat on the log next to me, passing me a small block of cheese. I didn't want to accept it, but my stomach all but lurched from my mouth to take it itself. I snatched the cheese from his hand and immediately felt rueful. I had been raised to be respectful and polite, even when faced with someone as rude as Nathaniel Blackmore.

"I'm sorry," he offered, his voice gentle. My brow creased. I hadn't expected him to be able to feel remorse, let alone express it.

"What for?"

"For everything," he said. "Back at the village, the beast, this..." He gestured around us with his hand that held the lump of dry bread.

He looked at me softly, and I realised that his eyes were not black at all. They were rich mahogany and chestnut. They were whisky and honey. The light of the fire illuminated golden flecks and rivets, like the bark of an oak, all encompassed in a charcoal ring. They were mesmerising and warm and kind and sincere. I had to change the subject.

"My dress was my mother's." I surprised myself with that announcement as much as I seemed to surprise him. I startled him as if he had broken free from a trance.

He nervously ran his hand through his ebony curls.

"She died when I was seven."

He looked at me as if he felt her loss personally and those kind eyes told me he would listen, and something compelled me to continue.

I told him all about her. The way my tiny hand would fit in hers when we would walk to evening mass together, Father on the other side, me in the middle. The way she stroked my hair every night until I fell asleep. The way she made me feel so completely safe. I followed her everywhere and copied everything she did. She would call me her little helper—they would call me her little shadow. I told him about her ebony skin that smelled of vanilla and her hair the same colour as mine. I told him about my father and about their love and about my dress—her dress. I spoke of how I would hold her basket while we walked around Cluster Wood foraging for supplies for her tonics and potions, noticing his confused expression at the name 'Cluster Wood.' I went off on a tangent about the origins of it while he held my stare with fascination. I told him about the day they found that basket… a tear escaped my eye, and before I could swipe away the evidence, Nathaniel stopped me from raising my arm.

"You can cry."

His permission seemed to be the only thing I was waiting for. I had always been a bit of a cry-baby but when I did, I cried alone. It was personal and private moments where I allowed myself to be vulnerable, but right now I felt exposed. My attention focused on his calloused thumb rubbing soothing strokes up and down the exposed skin of my forearm. The tender gesture matched with eyes that were warm and compassionate. Why was I sharing my deepest thoughts and memories with this stranger like we had been lifelong friends? Even my oldest acquaintances, even Greer, would never have seen this side to me.

"I can't quite process what's happened today…I really need to know what's going on," I pleaded.

"I promise you that you'll know everything soon. I just don't have all the answers right now."

Disappointment nipped at my senses, and he didn't miss it. He inhaled deeply.

"I'm from Oakenvale," he began. I heard the hesitation as he said it, and he spotted my puzzled expression. "There is so much more to this world than your village, Rose, and I want to show it all to you. I have some friends—well, a lot of friends, actually. We found out about your village and what the king had you doing in the name of the gods, and we decided to put a stop to it, to show you the truth."

He told me about the tyrant king and his oppressive reign. He told me about the things we found at the Giving Cave and their true origin. He told me about the mark of the Twin Souls and the magic a pair can create and how the king started the tradition of sacrifice to eliminate potential threats and sustain his position as the most powerful in the realm.

"But the Crimson Moon ceremonies have been going on for centuries?" His king couldn't have started them—they predate him. Nathaniel nodded with a sympathetic smile.

"You should get some sleep."

"Don't you sleep?" I asked.

"Tonight, I'll watch," he insisted.

"Oh, to make sure I don't get out," I quipped.

"No." His voice deepened. "To make sure nothing gets in."

-7-

Two thousand years earlier

"Let's get out of here." Bellinus took Lisandra by the wrist and pulled her away.

A stream of boiling, angry lava was roiling through the village, devouring buildings and shrubs like a hungry beast devours flesh. Timber dwellings with thatched roofs began to smoke, and picket fences smouldered.

"I need to find Leonora first." Lisandra turned and headed back toward the chaos. Vibrant orange molten rock spewed from the peak of the Sacred Volcano.

"It's too late," Bellinus insisted. "We must go now."

Lisandra's face crinkled with his betrayal. "But you said we would bring her."

"I did and I meant it, but now it's too late." Bellinus was firm with her. He would take her by force if he had to.

"But she's my sister." Lisandra pulled her wrist from his grasp. She couldn't believe that he would do this to her. He knew what Leonora meant to her.

"Not really. She isn't exactly blood." The words hung in the air between them and hurt her more than any molten rock could. She knew he could be a cruel bastard. She had even loved him for it, most of the time, but he'd never been this cruel to her. She glared at him with glistening eyes and panting breaths, daring him to stop her.

Mama and Papa had died when Lisandra was only young. At fifteen years old she was left with a five-year-old Leonora. Papa had been crushed in a terrible accident whilst repairing the town hall after damage from fire. He had stayed behind after everyone had gone home to finish some woodwork when he fell from a ladder, knocking down a support beam for the floor above, burying him under rubble. By the time anyone had noticed, and the geomancers were able to lift the rubble from on top of his body, he had gone cold. After a few days, Mama had begun to fade, and before long, she died of a broken heart.

Lisandra became Leonora's everything, and she hers. They were inseparable, and she would not be separated from her now. That was one of her conditions in helping him to raise this world to the ground.

His face softened as he took her in.

"Be quick." He would burn the world for her. He could at least give her this.

Lisandra wiped her eyes roughly and sniffed her watery nose. He watched her like a hawk as she shot through the streets, leaping onto debris like stepping stones.

They had waited for night to fall before they began. The last light went out at almost midnight. Everyone was tucked up in their beds, resting before another day in the ghostly shell that was once paradise. Despite the stories of the creation of the motherland and the first men, when the gods breathed life into this place, thousands of years ago, the harmonious existence between man and beast, all detailed in the sacred book, The Book of Man, Lisandra and Bellinus grew up in a world much different from that which was told.

Mama and Papa had so much love to give. They were desperate to bear life, to give all the love they harboured to a baby. They tried for decades, but like most couples, conception was a difficult task, even when the environment was so perfect, even when the home they'd created was desperate to hear the cries and coos and joy that new life brings.

One day, when Mama had finished her fertility tea: a blend of green tea leaves, raspberry leaf, nettle leaf, and chaste berry, she went to the east-facing front door, as she did every morning to absorb the light of dawn—this was common practice in Nova and was encouraged at dawn and dusk to aid in maintaining a healthy circadian rhythm.

With her face pointed skyward and her eyes closed she drew a deep breath and muttered her daily affirmations—I am loved, I am happy, I am grateful, and what is for me will not pass by me.

Just then, she heard a faint cooing noise amongst the twittering of rising birds and buzzing of honeybees collecting pollen from the flowers in the hanging baskets on either side of her door. She shook her head. This wasn't the first time she had heard phantom infant noises. She almost expected it now with how desperate she was to be a mother. But then, piercing through the peaceful sounds of nature at dawn, an abrupt, shrill cry rang out from below her, on the ground, at her feet. She yelped and stumbled backwards, knocking the coffee from the hands of her husband.

"What is it, Maeve?" Peter asked his wife. His concern was not for the boiling hot beverage that he was now wearing down his front, but for his wife's sudden turmoil and the crying sound that he could not see the source of.

"It can't be," she breathed. She pulled her hands away from her mouth, which she had slapped with shock, and reached down for the bundle laying on her doorstep.

Swaddled in the softest lambswool shawl was a tiny, perfect human baby. There was a note tucked into the folds of the blanket.

Dearest Peter and Maeve,

Please take this baby and show her the love that I know you have both been so desperate to give. She is a gift from the gods. They know how hard you have worked to bear a child; this is their way of honouring you.

I must go now.

Please don't let his death be in vain.

Love conquers all.
Jacobi.

That afternoon, with their baby held close, her belly full of milk from the nanny goat they kept in their yard, Peter and Maeve decided to visit the chapel. By now, word had spread across the land that something was amiss. No one had heard from the founding fathers, and news had travelled fast about a baby being left on a doorstep. Peter and Maeve found this odd, since they hadn't shared the news with anyone.

Despite the worrying letter, Maeve had pleaded with Peter to spend some hours together as three, in case for some cruel reason, the baby was taken away. She had cried at the idea that this was all a mistake, or someone was playing a mean trick on them. Peter had assured her that they would get to the bottom of it and accepted her request.

After Peter had milked Dotty the goat, he put some of the warm liquid into a small milk jug from their tea set. He joined Maeve, who was cradling the baby on the sheepskin rug. He sat behind her, enveloping them both, and while Maeve cuddled the baby in the crook of her arm, Peter poured tiny sips of the golden goat milk into the babe's mouth. They both smiled and laughed at the way she slurped hungrily, making little satisfied humming noises. This was everything they had ever wanted, and so they decided to address their neighbours with honesty and express their desire to keep this gift, their baby.

The chapel was triple the size it was when originally built. Peter, a skilled carpenter and builder, had taken part in crafting the newest extension to the building. The building was now made up of three arched roofs, side by side with enough floor space and pews to accommodate up to five hundred people. It was rarely ever full, but most did try to make at least one mass a week. There were other places of worship throughout Nova, but this chapel was the hub.

Since the beginning of this world, Jacobi and Adama, with the assistance of the gods, had created a paradise for the people. The land was fertile, lush and green. The people were happy, healthy and modest.

Over the last four-thousand years, the community had grown to around two-thousand inhabitants. Their abodes were quaint and charming, and each home was surrounded by great gardens, each with the purpose to sustain Nova. The community was peaceful and kind. People would help other people, trade with each other, socialise, and celebrate one another.

When Twin Souls found each other, everyone would come together to sing their prayers, and the founding fathers would look on with pride at what they had created, pride at the sanctuary and haven they'd developed in the name of the gods and the love they had found in one another.

There was a hum of unrest in the chapel as Peter and Maeve made their way towards the chancel. Maeve glanced around at the crowd. She'd never seen so many people in the chapel at once. She trembled at the thought that this might not go as planned. Sensing her hesitance, Peter placed a reassuring hand on Maeve's lower back. She smiled at him as he looked into her arms at the baby. Their baby. She was the reason. Maeve's confidence grew, and they walked further along the nave. Upon the chancel, Peter recognised Trevor Hobbes, a close associate of the founding fathers. His wife Ann hid behind him, her face blotchy, and her eyes red. She clutched a piece of paper in her hands.

As soon as Trevor spotted Peter and Maeve, he stopped in his tracks.

"You have the other one?" He called.

Peter's gaze fell upon the identical bundle in Trevor's arms.

Someone from the crowd stood up. "What is happening?"

Someone else shouted. "Where are the fathers?"

The room was abuzz, like someone had just kicked a wasp's nest. Peter took Maeve's hand, and they made their way toward the far end of the chapel.

"This morning, my wife opened our front door to find this baby girl and this note." He held up the handwritten article and read it aloud for all to hear.

"What does it mean?"

"Why is it only signed off by Jacobi?"

By now they had joined Trevor and Ann on the platform, in front of the audience of panic-stricken Novans. Wide eyes, tarnished with fear and unknowing glared at the four of them on the stage.

"We too discovered a baby and a note," Trevor responded. "But our story is different."

He addressed the whole room now. "As you know, Ann and I have a very close relationship with our founding fathers, and some of you already knew of the prophecies that she and Adama bore witness to." Faces looked to either side, heads shook, brows creased. "Adama had a dream, more a nightmare actually. In this dream, he foresaw that on this latest Crimson Moon, the final babes were to be delivered from the mouth of our Sacred Volcano and would grow up to wreak havoc on the land. They would grow to be more powerful than any one of us."

"Nonsense," someone called. "No one is more powerful than the founding fathers."

"Maybe so," Trevor continued. "But Adama has not been wrong before."

"So, what happened?"

"Where are they?"

Trevor carried on with the best explanation he could offer. "The counsel could not come to an agreement. Some of us thought it best to return the children from whence they came, whereas some of us," he looked sternly towards his wife, "some of us, including Adama, believed that if we showered these babes with love, and lead by our wonderful example, we could save them from their fate."

More murmurs. Some couldn't believe what they were hearing. Kill innocent infants? Others agreed that returning them would have been for the best.

"So, what do we do now?"

"Where are our leaders?"

Ann began to cry hysterically. Trevor patted her shoulder to console her.

"In the middle of the night last night, Ann had a premonition. She saw Jacobi and Adama fighting over the fates of the babes on the top of the Sacred Volcano. Wind thrashed, and voices bellowed. They both clutched a babe each. When they had left that evening, the counsel had agreed to spare the infants, but somewhere on the journey, Jacobi had changed his mind. Adama was upset. He was furious that Jacobi could have such evil intentions. They were men of peace, not violence. There was a tussle as Jacobi insisted he was doing this for the good of Nova and its people. He snatched the baby from Adama's arms, and as he did so, Adama stumbled and..." Trevor's voice cracked as he realised that his wife's premonition had seemingly come to fruition. "Adama fell...into the pit."

Horrified yelps and yowls rang out from the crowd. Some simply left the chapel without looking back, as if running away from the truth would make it not so.

"Please settle...please. We can't begin to lose our heads now. We must stay calm." Peter tried to soothe the crowd to no avail.

"What do we do?" Peter asked Trevor.

"You can do whatever you want, Peter." Trevor seemed defeated as the mayhem from the crowd burst outside the chapel doors. "I fear that what is written is already upon us."

"What does your note say?" Maeve asked Ann, meekly. Ann sniffed and wiped her tears with a navy handkerchief.

Dearest Trevor and Ann,

I fear the worst has happened. Adama has gone and now I will fade. He believed with his whole being that we could save the babes. I doubted him, and now, I will die knowing that he left this world feeling my betrayal. Please don't let his death be wasted.
Ann, go day by day. Whatever you see, make sure to share it with the counsel, and Trevor, please make sure they listen.
Good-bye, my friends. Nova is now in your hands.
Love conquers all.
Jacobi

-8-

Lisandra and Leonora knew nothing but complete adoration. Lisandra never realised anything was missing until Leonora came along. 'A beautiful surprise,' was what they'd say when folks asked if she was planned. She hadn't been planned. Peter and Maeve had gotten everything they'd ever dreamed of the day they'd discovered Lisandra on their doorstep. The world they had known was gradually coming undone at the seams, but behind closed doors, their seams were bursting with blissful happiness.

They spent her early years sheltering her from the chaos until it finally started to settle. It never returned to how it was before, but Maeve still started her mornings with her affirmations. When Lisandra was able to talk, she joined her mother in her morning mantra, even adding one of her own. "I'm the luckiest girl in the world," she would say gleefully.

Mama and Papa were always honest with Lisandra about her origins. Although it was unfair, she would have to work extra hard to convince the people of Nova to accept her. She would be on her best behaviour, always smiling, always polite. She would try her best to be helpful, and even volunteered at the chapel to help collect donations or hand out pamphlets. She would help the elderly with tending to their gardens and would always pick up any litter she saw to help keep the streets clean. None of these things were hard for Lisandra; her parents were wonderful people, and if she didn't do it for herself, she did it for them.

When she was nine, Mama and Papa shared the news that the three of them would be expecting a gift in the next few months, making them a family of four. They had fed Lisandra with so much love, she was overflowing, and she was ready to share that love with her new brother or sister.

Leonora was born at home on a summer day. It was hot outside and even hotter indoors, so Lisandra did her best to keep Mama cool with cold flannels and a fan she had made herself by pleating a sheet of paper. Mama was in a lot of pain, and Papa was trying his best to help her to control her breathing and rub her aching back. When Lisandra got worried, Mama would smile at her and tell her it was all normal, between ragged breaths.

After hours, and just as Lisandra had dozed off on the daybed that Mama was leaning against, with her folded arms creating a shelf for her head to rest upon, she was woken by the noise she had waited so patiently to hear.

A raspy 'wahhh' jolted Lisandra from her dozy state. The baby filled her lungs and screamed as she adjusted herself from the confinements of Mama's warm tummy to the wide-open air of their sitting room. Mama instinctively brought the baby to suckle at her breast as Papa cleaned up the area in a state of euphoria, smiling the whole time.

"Is that how I used to eat?" Lisandra asked Mama curiously.

"No," Mama replied. "You didn't grow inside Mama's tummy, Lisandra," she reminded her. "You grew from our prayers. The gods heard our pleas and delivered you to us." She smiled at her eldest daughter. "Mothers only produce milk if the baby has grown in their womb."

Lisandra felt a little jealous that her mama and her little sister shared something that she did not get to experience.

"You are still my firstborn daughter. You made me a mama," she told Lisandra. "That is something that Leonora cannot say."

"Leonora?" Lisandra questioned.

"Mm. What do you think?" Mama asked smiling widely at the gift she had just given to Lisandra.

What did she think? She was elated. Leonora was her suggestion. They'd had many discussions of names, and no one ever agreed.

"Leonora." Papa joined their bubble.

"Your arms will have to grow now, Papa," Lisandra joked. "I've grown up quite a bit lately, and now there are three of us to fit around."

"Indeed," Papa chuckled.

"You little scoundrel. Get back here!" Old man Tompkins bellowed as his apples cascaded from his toppled cart.

Bellinus giggled mischievously as he sprinted past stall after stall on market day, holding a wooden peg that had held the cartwheel of Mr. Tomkins cart in place. He pocketed the peg for later, he knew he could make use of it—perhaps to throw it at a windowpane or an unsuspecting victim on a peaceful evening stroll.

Trevor and Ann had tried. It only took a few days before they were smitten with the baby. Bellinus was only ever happy if he was in Ann's arms. He would cry every time she put him down. She constructed a type of sling out of an old pair of curtains so she could hold him to her body, freeing her hands for other tasks.

They decided to be known to Bellinus by their forenames instead of Mother and Father. This saddened hopeful Ann, but Trevor was sceptical. There were several occasions when he felt himself warmed to the idea of being Bellinus' father; in fact, he found himself falling for the child several times. However, the events that led to Bellinus being in their custody were a constant reminder of what could come, and to protect himself and his wife from the inevitable, he'd erected a wall to prevent him bonding too closely with his adopted son.

Over time, Trevor began to feel resentment towards Bellinus for his attachment to his wife, and when they reached the terrible twos and the troublesome threes, when Bellinus' tantrums were explosive and he started to lash out and bite, the love that began to burn when he was a babe was now just nothing but slightly warmed coals.

Bellinus would put his ear to the floorboards and listen in on the frequent bickering between his parents, of which he was always the topic. He grew to be obnoxious and rude, and everyone that tried to befriend him soon regretted going anywhere near him. He was consistently sent home from classes, which saw him permanently excluded at the age of eleven. He would vandalise and steal and get a kick out of being a nuisance to the other Novans.

One day, he heard Trevor and Ann talking with members of the counsel in the town hall. Ann sniffled and blew her nose and dabbed at her eyes.

She constantly had red patches around them or a lump in her throat these days. Bellinus scoffed at her craven character.

"We need to come to an agreement. We can't allow this to continue," one council member said.

"He is one person, and a poor excuse for one at that," another stated.

"Can't we just imprison him? Lock him up somewhere?" another said.

"Sure, let's just get to building a prison especially for one person."

"We need to be realistic here," a large man spoke from the head of the table. The leader, Bellinus guessed. He had lived amongst these people for around fifteen years now and still hadn't bothered to get to know anyone. He couldn't tell you which name belonged to which face. He had no interest. Soon it wouldn't matter anyway. Bellinus dreamed of a world where none of these people existed. None of them had treated him with respect or kindness. Ann had, but then her loyalties lay with her husband. He knew nothing but hostility from the people of Nova, and they'd be mad if they thought that he'd beg for their acceptance. No way.

The large man continued. "Bellinus is one person. We are many. We need to rid Nova of him for the good of the majority."

Bellinus felt the rage curl and coil inside of him. He will show them what one person can do. He spotted a flickering torch mounted on the door frame of the tavern, and with the alcohol he had stolen from Trevor's personal stash, he doused the wooden structure with the potent liquid and lit it with the torch flame.

The discussion had become heated as the members argued back and forth about ethics and morals. They were so consumed with the debate that the flames had managed to engulf a good portion of the building before they noticed. Bellinus watched on with sinister pleasure as they all began to cough and splutter on the smoke that had swept through the hall and stolen the air. He smirked as he watched the large counsel leader try to open the front door. Bellinus had already braced it shut. There was no escape.

'How do they like being imprisoned?' he thought.

The heat of the flames caused the glass windows to shatter. Some of the smaller people were able to squeeze through the frames, but not the larger ones. The air from the broken windows fed the flames, causing them to rise higher, sparking a hunger in the arsonist. He would burn the whole of Nova to the ground, but first he might just try to see if he could be a leader. Yes, he quite fancied this newfound power that he felt. He would be the new leader, not of a counsel; he didn't need a counsel, but of a kingdom. This would be his kingdom, and he would be the king.

-9-

Although Peter and Maeve had always been honest with Lisandra, there was one vital piece of information they'd withheld. They never told Lisandra about her Twin Soul. At first it wasn't a conscious decision; their home was on one side of Nova, and Trevor and Ann lived on the other side—around four miles away—and for the first couple of years they kept themselves in their little blissful bubble away from the prying eyes and interfering opinions of others. They didn't go out often, but you could bet that when they did, someone always liked to give their two cents about what the town should do with the pair.

As stories of Bellinus the bad, Bellinus the bully, Bellinus the bastard, started to spread around the town, Peter and Maeve felt that they had made the right decision to keep the kids apart. They had assumed, and maybe immorally so, that Bellinus would meet a grizzly end sooner or later, and if they could prevent their daughter from imminent heartbreak, they would. They knew that the pair may come together one day, but they were confident that the effort they'd made to ensure Lisandra would be the best version of herself as she could be, when the time came, Lisandra simply would find Bellinus incompatible.

Lisandra had thrived, and their neighbours had grown to love her, and although she heard comments sometimes about the local scoundrel, she felt it was best to stay out of it.

One day, she was taking Leonora for a stroll. The youngster's tiny hand grasped Lisandra's fingertips and warmed her heart. It had rained in the night, and Leonora's new favourite pastime was to see how big a splash she could make in the puddles the rain left behind. She squealed with glee as her tiny boots pitter-pattered in the muddy water. Lisandra watched on as her little sister got such enjoyment from something so simple, when suddenly someone barged into her shoulder and knocked her onto the wet dirt path. Brushing the soggy grit from her damp knees, she glanced up to see a boy smirking over his shoulder at her. His hair was black as raven feathers, wisps of it caressing his jaw. His nose was sharp, and his cheekbones too, but his eyes, his eyes were like ice, and they sent a chill of pimples over Lisandra's flesh.

Lisandra was haunted by the strange boy's face. It was all she could do to erase him from her mind, but she couldn't. The way his mouth crooked at the corner in a smug grin. She hadn't even called out to him to apologise or to do the right thing and help a young lady to her feet. She had just stared. Stared at those wolf-like eyes and the primal energy that came from them.

She never saw the boy again, not for lack of looking; she thought she must have imagined him, dreamt him up from the darkest parts of her mind. Lisandra's mind was light, and her thoughts were sweet, but everyone had dark parts. She had just gotten so good at perfecting her persona that she had pushed anything that she thought could jeopardise her place in Nova, or make things difficult for her parents, in a tiny compartment right at the back of her mind—like a dusty old cabinet of classified documents that no one was allowed to access unless authorised.

She had to admit, though, that since she had become a teenager, her desires for intimacy had peaked, and no boy had ever intrigued her as much as this one. She wanted to tell Mama, but she was frightened it would displease her. Lisandra knew about Twin Souls. Her parents were bonded, as were most couples in their world, but whenever Lisandra had asked her Mama whether she had a Twin Soul, Mama would wring her hands and struggle with words before changing the subject. Lisandra did not mean to upset her parents, and after a while, she gave up questioning it.

The locals stepped up when the girls lost their parents. The two lived alone in the house they had grown up in, despite some well-meaning locals offering to take Leonora as one of their own. Lisandra refused. She was more than capable of looking after a sister, and her parents would have wanted the girls to stay together.

Lisandra did a fantastic job taking care of Leonora. She put the child's needs before her own, cooked nutritious meals, which they ate at the table, and slept together every night in Mama and Papa's bed. She would tell Leonora stories at bedtime about their parents to make sure that Leonora never forgot them. She took the little girl to school and made sure to teach her important life skills like laundry, sewing and mending, tending to the animals and produce that grew in their garden, hygiene, and cooking.

One day on the way to market, after dropping Leonora at school, the sun's rays lighting her path and kissing her pale skin, her sandy blonde hair flowing in the summer breeze, she suddenly became aware of the shadows. She wasn't afraid of the dark like Leonora was. She knew that light followed darkness, and one could not exist without the other. They defined one another. But today, the shadows felt like a living thing. They felt like they had arms and legs and were following her on her way. A gloomy rain cloud that was about to unleash a great downpour. Breathing down her neck and watching her every step. She could run, she thought, but then that would mean she feared the shadows, and she did not.

She came to a halt. The shadows stopped a moment too late. Her excellent hearing had noticed the scuffle that continued mere seconds after she had stopped. Excitement tickled her ribs, and a smile drew wide on her face. A cat chasing a mouse. She carried on, pretending that she hadn't noticed the poor act of stealth. This time she would try something else.

She felt the presence just behind the stone wall surrounding the resting place. She stopped and spun her head to glance at the wall. She saw no one, but she knew there was someone there, and the flutter in her stomach told her exactly who it was.

She crouched and ran to the wall and ducked low. After a few moments she heard the mutterings and huffs of someone behind the wall. She heard their feet scuffle one way then the other, clearly searching for her.

She braved a peep over the wall and saw the raven-haired boy, just as she had suspected, his back turned to her, rubbing his hands through his hair. He seemed frustrated that he had lost sight of her. He was much taller now. His back was broader, his legs longer.

She crept over the low wall displaying much more efficient stealth than he, landing with light feet and creeping towards the boy who was scanning an area of the square. She straightened herself and brought her hands up to reach around him and cover his eyes when suddenly, she was snatched from the air and tackled to the ground.

Frosty blue eyes peered into hers only inches away from her face. His smoky breath panted into her mouth. He felt dangerous, and exciting, and electric. His body lay flat on top of hers as she felt a pull in her lower abdomen, she was unsure what it meant. He braced himself on one arm to the side of her head, and the other began to unfasten the wooden buttons of her dress. Lisandra's heart raced, and she wondered whether she should tell him to stop, but she didn't want him to.

He placed his cold palm against the warm flesh between her breasts.

"Your heart beats for me," he declared with an intense stare that pierced her soul.

He lifted his palm and trailed a fingertip around the teardrop freckle on her sternum. Her nipples pebbled beneath the thin white fabric of her smock. His eyes flicked to the visible bumps before recapturing her gaze.

The pulsing in her ears was so loud, it drowned out the sounds of the shoppers in the market on the other side of the wall. It matched the thrumming between her thighs. She wondered if he could feel it beneath his body, where he lay atop her.

He tilted his head to one side as if assessing her, she intrigued him, she could see it in the way his eyes bore into hers and the way his lips were parted with his trembling breath. 'Kiss me,' is what she wanted to say, had she been able to form words.

As if he could see her thoughts, his eyes widened a fraction before he gave in to their yearning. His lips clashed with hers as they parted for him. He swept his tongue of spirits and ash over hers, drew her bottom lip into his mouth, and sucked before sinking his teeth into it. She yelped at the sharpness, but the buzzing in her core told her not to protest.

"You taste sweet, like pear drops," he said. "I want pears every day."

His tone was demanding, and she knew he was it. She knew that he was her Twin Soul. She could feel it in every fibre of her being. He wanted her, and she would give herself to him no matter the cost—and she could sense that the price would be incredibly high.

-10-

Present day

My vision was awash with blood red, like I was basking in the ruby glow of the Crimson Moon. Everything was hazy, as though my eyes were full of the residue of a deep sleep that I hadn't yet rubbed away.

Suddenly, I realised I was unable to move. I was held still in a vice-like grip. Layered sounds were a blur of echoes that my ears struggled to recognise. Bewildered and overwhelmed by yet another entrapment, I did what I should have done when my conscience had clawed at the back of my brain—when I gave myself up to die, or when some outlander stole me away from that set of circumstances. I harnessed all the fight I could find within my usually imperturbable default and let it burst outward like a force pushing anything perilous away from me. I gasped for air to recover from the surge of power that stole my breath.

"Rose, what's wrong?"

Eyes like mine stared back at me beneath a glower, and her face betrayed the upset she felt at my sudden outburst. It disarmed me in a way I hadn't expected. A moment ago, I'd been dynamite, and she had just pulled my fuse.

"Rose?" Her hands cupped my shoulders and firmly squeezed. Worry crinkled her features.

My eyes locked on her familiarities, her perfect round face, and that dimpled chin, and it brought me back to her. Brought me home. My mouth moved as it tried to convey my feelings, but I couldn't find the right words. Why was I here? Why was she here?

"Mother?" I managed to whisper her name.

"There she is. You had me worried there." That sunshine smile, that I'd always tried so hard to be the cause of, curved her lips.

My eyes roamed over her once more. Her hair, that was the red that had taken over my sight. When she was working, she always kept it tightly braided, but at home we got to see her in her natural state, and that was my favourite. It was thick and fluffy like a cloud lingering in front of the Crimson Moon and tinted by its hue, and when she embraced me, it was all I could see and feel.

"I miss you," I told her.

She smiled. "I'm always with you, my love."

Her expression darkened and her voice became serious.

"Rose, the journey will be tough, and you will have to do things that many would struggle to do, but it's imperative that you do it. Do you hear me? You have to save them, Rose. You must save the kingdom. You must save your father."

"What do you mean, save Father?"

"It's up to you, Rose. The gods have chosen you."

I jolted awake, lying on stiff woollen blankets on the forest floor, aware of all the rubble digging into my back that I couldn't feel last night due to the exhaustion of almost dying…twice, running for my life and walking for hours. I rubbed the residual dream from my vision and glanced through the opening of the makeshift canvas shelter to see Nathaniel leaning over the fire, stirring it to life with a stick. I crawled through the gap and stood up, acclimatising myself to reality once more.

Nathaniel gulped down the contents of a metal mug, refilling it before handing it to me.

"Pine needle tea," he said.

I smiled as I accepted it. Mother's favourite, full of vitamin C and great for ridding the body of mucous, I remembered her teachings.

"Hungry?" he asked, as I inhaled the fragrant steam, the foresty scent relaxing me.

"Not really a breakfast person," I told him.

"Me neither," he smiled. "Although we have quite a way to go, we'll have to skip lunch if we are going to get there in time."

"I'll take a biscuit then," I replied just to ease his paternal style fretting.

I wondered did he have children? I couldn't figure out his age. He seemed like he could be my age or maybe slightly older.

He handed me two, and I put them in the pocket of the cardigan I now wore. I woke up with it covering me. He must have added it as an extra layer during the night. I smiled to myself at the thought.

"What is this place?" I asked him, surveying the rather snug camp where we had spent the night. The morning light was trying its hardest to pierce through the dense shrubbery acting as a wall. It was still dull inside, but it was bright enough to see that someone had spent significant time clearing the place, weaving a wall from leafy branches, and setting up camp.

"My friends that I mentioned," he began. "We've set up a few checkpoints like this throughout the woods. The walls are woven thickly so the firelight can't be spotted easily, and it gives us some safety from the creatures that live here."

Satisfied with his answer, I braved asking another question. I bobbed on my toes with my hands behind my back.

"Where are we going?"

"To get you some answers," he replied.

Another satisfying answer. I hoped my luck would continue for the rest of our time together, however long that should be.

We continued our trek without a word. In such a vast forest, how could it also feel so small? Maybe it was because of how dense it was. All these different tree trunks so close together. It was so overcrowded, yet the trees made space for each other, and they flourished. I glanced above my head at all the branches and leaves blotting out most of the light from the sky. Small cracks between them showed me the blue I knew, and it gave me comfort. I may be far from home, but we are still under the same sky.

I wondered what Father ate for breakfast this morning. I wondered if he missed me as much as I missed him. I wondered if Greer was there for him, like he said he would be. I looked over my shoulder and wondered, if I ran straight, would I reach him? What if Mother's message in my dream last night was just my subconscious trying to tell me something? I ignored my gut before, and I'd promised myself I wouldn't ignore it again. Nathaniel could be feeding me lies to keep me compliant. What if Father, the village, were in danger? Heat rose to my cheeks, and my temples started to throb.

"Everything okay?" Nathaniel asked me.

It was the first time either of us had spoken over the last few hours. My mind was racing with possibilities and what ifs. My heart was heavy, and I really wanted to go back.

I responded with a slight nod and turned my eyes back to the front. Nathaniel had walked behind me, watching our backs. He said he wanted me upfront so he could see me—I didn't like that, but I obeyed.

For the first few hours, I could feel him like the cold chill across your shoulders when you feel you're not alone—like when you read a spooky story and need a glass of water in the night, and the dark feels weighty and thick. My senses were on edge until we had walked so far that the only thing I could think about was how tired and hungry I was. My legs were lead weights, and my stomach had a sharp stabbing pain in the middle just behind my navel. I could eat the biscuits, but I was so thirsty that I knew they'd be like sand in my mouth, and I was still too shy to ask for a drink. He had offered some a while ago and I'd refused. I don't know why.

Suddenly, Nathaniel strode ahead of me, eyes and ears alert. He held a hand out to instruct me to stop moving and then held a finger to his lips and listened intently. I watched his eyes squint as he turned his head side to side to better hear. Whatever he thought he had caught on to, I hadn't heard a thing.

He brought both hands to his lips and warbled a peculiar sound, somewhere between a bird call and a terrible impression of a turkey. My eyes widened and my lips tightened into a line as I struggled to conceal laughter. Never did I think that someone so serious would be doing a half twitter, half gobble in the middle of this, well, wherever we were. Had he gone mad with the hours upon hours of walking and feeling like getting nowhere? The backdrop never changed. We could've been walking in circles the whole time.

It was darker now, and the gaps above showed no light. Nathaniel made the call again. A few seconds later, the call came back from the distance.

"Let's go," he said as he grabbed my wrist with a firm grip and led me onwards.

Before long, I could smell fire and spotted a dull glow. Nathaniel led us towards it. Just like last night, he pulled back a collection of branches and shrubbery to reveal another camp. Only this time, this one wasn't dark and empty.

"Hey, you made it!"

A large man tended a fire with a spit of meat roasting above it. Dressed in the same garb Nathaniel wore, without the cloak. Yes, I was interested in this new face, but my mouth was watering, and my attention was definitely on the deliciously fragrant flesh roasting on the spit. A small lump of bread last night was the last thing I had eaten.

"Brother!" Nathaniel barged by me and embraced the blond male with a grunt and a back slap in the most masculine show of affection I'd ever seen, that's for sure.

Either these men just happened to be on the larger side, or men from my village were much smaller than men from wherever these guys were from. They did not look alike. Both seemed to carry muscle, though Nathaniel was slightly bigger. Where Nathaniel seemed dark, this man seemed light. Nathaniel seemed to harbour pain as though he had endured torment or hardship, whereas this man seemed so jovial and carefree. His attention turned to me.

"Ah, the chosen one." There was a playful tone to his voice, and his face was alight with a huge smile. "Nice to meet you. I hope this one hasn't been too hard on you." He gestured to Nathaniel with his thumb, and I spotted the corners of Nathaniel's mouth curve for a moment before he looked down almost bashfully reminding me of the kids back home when they received praise for their achievements.

Our host's voice had a beat to it and was full of enthusiasm. It was really endearing. I couldn't help but smile. Stranded in an ocean full of sharks and mortdags, he was a life raft.

He strode to me and drew me in for a bear hug, just as big a squeeze with a lot less back slapping. A bit too familiar, considering we had just met. He pulled away and braced my arms with his hands as he took me in. His eyes and mouth crinkled at the corners, giving away that this man had experienced a lot of laughter. His eyes sparkled, although I couldn't quite make out the colour in the dim light.

"You must meet my wife," he said with pride. Oh fantastic, now I wouldn't feel so outnumbered.

White-blonde, silky hair fluttered around the head that emerged from the tent, her face beaming with delight.

"You're here!" She dampened her excitement when she realised that I hadn't greeted her with the same amount of enthusiasm. In fact, I was finding it hard to feel anything but utterly perplexed. It was like I'd been told everything I'd ever known was a lie, and I'd just been provided with concrete evidence that even I couldn't argue with. Although maybe I could. The woman in front of me was familiar, yes, but not. She was like an impersonation of someone, a doppelgänger or a theatre costume.

She looked me dead in the eye, and with a smaller smile now, an almost straight-lipped smile that exuded cautiousness. She nodded her head at me as if to say, 'Yes, Rose, I'm exactly who you think I am.'

My feet worked in reverse as she approached me. I can't do this—I've seen a ghost. I turned to run and slammed into a brick wall. I didn't even try to focus; I just threw my arms and kicked my legs and tried so desperately to exit the haunted house. Strong arms restrained me, and I stopped when I realised, they weren't going to let me go.

"Breathe."

A deep whisper like a charm, instantly doused my raging flames until I was a steady flickering glow. My heavy arms dropped to my sides, and I submitted to the command. I pressed my cheek into his chest, and I let his scent fill my nose. A gentle touch hovered over the skin of my back like he was unsure if he had my consent to touch me.

"I know this must be hard for you, Rose. I really do," Nathaniel's voice rumbled below my ear.

I turned to see flawless porcelain skin and crystalline blue eyes and pink-blushed cheeks. She was ethereal and definitely could not be who I thought she was.

"This isn't real," I croaked, my voice hoarse from all the wailing I had subjected my throat to mere moments ago.

"I can explain if you'll let me." She offered gently.

I shook my head vigorously. "But I saw you die?! I saw it! You drank the blood of the gods and lay on that dais. I saw it with my own eyes, Sylvie." I widened my glare as if to prove that they were in fact open and had been when she'd given herself to the gods.

"Boys, can you make some tea and bring us some food?" She asked. Our host shuffled nervously for a moment, but Nathaniel's eyes were on me, his whole body positioned towards me—feet planted hard, and his expression looked as though he was fighting the urge to approach. My brows creased as I cast suspicious eyes over him.

Sylvie led us to the tent. "So, you've met Colm." Her face lit up in the same way his did when he mentioned her name, although her joyous tone did not appeal to the sternness I felt right now. She noticed and dropped her head.

She took a deep breath and sighed. "Ooh, okay."

She was preparing herself to talk, but I could see she was having trouble getting started, and I'm sure my glare wasn't helping matters.

"So, did Nathaniel tell you anything?" she asked.

"No," I replied. "I suppose he thought you would do a better job, but I'm thinking maybe he was wrong."

Harsh, but I was so done with this.

"Right." She accepted my insult graciously. "A few weeks after turning eighteen, I found my mark, and well, you know how that story goes."

I looked at her with a raised brow as if to say, 'Do I?', she noticed and moved swiftly on.

"The wine I was given that day was just that, wine. My death was fake."

My stomach flipped at her admission.

"A few days earlier, I felt it. It was like a magnet. I was the south pole, and he was the north. I followed the pull, and it led me to the Giving Cave, and that's when I met Colm for the first time." I noticed her eyes well. "He too had the mark, Rose, but it was the mirror of mine. He's my Twin Soul."

I remained silent. I didn't have anything to offer. Everything that I had learnt was just not feasible. It felt like an ambush. A set-up.

"You know how, back in the village, they use the word 'soulmate' for people who are in love? Well, for some of us, the marked ones like you and me, when we were born, our souls were split in two. On the same day I was born, so was Colm, and he is the other half of me."

A scoff of disbelief escaped my mouth. It was accidental, and I'd tried to catch it with my hand. I wasn't a rude person usually, but everything about what was happening was making me question who I really was. She continued despite my interruption.

"Eight years ago, Colm had been dropping supplies at the Giving Cave in preparation for my sacrifice. He too felt the pull while in the tunnels. When we came together, everything happened so fast it was a blur. There was a man with a crown, a king, and he told me everything, and I believed him because Colm verified it, and he was the other half of me, so if he said it was true, then I must believe it."

She looked at me with eyes pleading with me to believe her story. I wanted to, but it was so ridiculous. It was all nonsensical ramblings, and she was different. Sure, the last time I saw her, it was through the eyes of a sixteen-year-old me, and back then she was eighteen, barely a woman, now she must be twenty-six, but she was like something out of a painting.

She noticed I was studying her features. "I look too different, don't I?" she asked.

Yes, she did. The Sylvie I remember had fair, wispy hair, not luxuriously silky, platinum hair. She always did have nice skin and beautiful eyes, but the eyes and skin I saw before me were unblemished and flawless. She seemed so much bigger too.

"Colm and I had our ceremony not long after we met, and it changed me. They're not like us, Rose. When you find your Twin Soul and complete the ceremony, things change. I'm larger, stronger, and faster. I have powers."

My head whipped up to meet her gaze. Powers? Come on.

Once she was in Oakenvale, Sylvie was told the history of how our village came to be. The Queen told her that to keep the kingdom pure, you are only permitted to have romantic relations with your Twin Soul. If you collude with someone before you come of age who is not your Twin Soul, then your mark never forms; it results in normal humans—magic-less people, impure blood, short mortal lives. The bonding ceremony unlocks your full potential and makes you somewhat immortal. They can be hurt, they can die, but they're superior in every way. I couldn't believe what I was hearing. It was like a work of fiction.

Hundreds of years ago, the queen's sister fell in love before coming of age and got pregnant. The king ordered the execution of her and her lover. The queen begged and pleaded with him. The king's love for his queen convinced him not to execute her sister but to banish her instead. They continued to banish the unmarked until the problem started to get out of hand. More and more youths were breaking the rules, and engaging in coitus before coming of age, thus their marks would not develop resulting in inferior weak humans. Their counterparts would form marks but would never be matched, forcing upon them a lifetime of service to the king.

The king then ordered public executions for anyone that broke the law of colluding with anyone but their Twin Soul. No more banishing people. He placed trusted people in the ever-growing village to oversee them, and over time the history of the origins of the village were lost to its people. The king and his plants fabricated the story of the marked ones in order for the village to willingly execute their people, keeping the inhabitant's human and the rest of the kingdom pure.

The village community continued to thrive and live harmoniously for hundreds of years, long after the death of the queen's sister, and the king grew fond of his little pet villagers, the inhabitants of Sandy (named after his wife, Queen Lisandra Thane). Those within the kingdom who were marked but were unable to find their Twin Soul joined the Kings Army, took a vow of celibacy, and dedicated themselves to the service of the kingdom.

"I couldn't let it go, though. It was eating away at me and Colm could see how unhappy it made me."

I could see that her sorrow was real.

She continued. "I told him I had to put a stop to it. I was scared he might give me up to his father, but I didn't care. I was prepared to die for Sandy and my people before, I would do it again. But Colm's love for me far exceeded his love for his father. He is me, and I am him.

"He offered to help me. We started to dig through hidden archives and found books full of history. Texts of the old gods and truths the king had kept well-hidden to assure his successive reign. We found prophecies that spoke of his certain demise, and the queen that would unite us all. We decided to take our knowledge and carefully recruit help. We found families of victims that the king had executed due to colluding before coming of age. They were just kids. There were soldiers forced to give up their lives to join the King's Army due to their lack of a mate. They were beaten and broken into submission and forced to enforce the king's unjust laws and deliver punishments to those who broke them. They were willing to join the fight for freedom, to find the queen that will put an end to all of this."

It was so much to absorb. Sandy had once been my whole world, and now it felt so small. We were so simple, so naive. We lived our tiny little lives with our heads in the clouds. We had been so conditioned that we never questioned anything. We stayed in our clearing with our invisible boundaries, got on with our ordinary lives, and sacrificed our chosen ones willingly, even happily. The oldest person ever recorded in our village was one hundred and two, and now, I'm told people in the kingdom live into their thousands, but only if they've managed to find the other half of them, because alone, they are not only half a person, but they're half as intelligent, half as strong, half as attractive, and half as worthy of freedom. The sacrifices we made back home were in order to make sure that no one from the village was drawn to the kingdom and vice versa. No one was to know about the king's secret village apart from his lackeys and confidants.

"Can I have some time alone?" I asked her. That was all I could say to her after what she had just revealed to me. She looked disappointed but did as I asked and left the tent.

No sooner had she left than Nathaniel entered.

"I just want to say that I'm really sorry," he offered, but again I didn't have anything to say. "I wanted to tell you, but I just didn't know how. I've never been very good with words."

Did he just tell me something personal? I offered him a small smile. Not a real one. I couldn't smile when my loved ones were back in that village. I had no idea if they were in danger because of my fleeing. I had to know if they were safe. What if they hurt my father? What if they believed he was behind it, and they imprisoned him, or, worse, killed him? A tear slipped from my eye at the thought, and I brushed it away roughly with my sleeve.

Nathaniel edged closer and took my hands in his. They were so big they dwarfed mine. They were rough and calloused but gentle and warm at the same time.

"When I got my mark, I was beyond excited," he began. "I couldn't wait to meet my Twin Soul. I had been surrounded by those who had found their mates. My parents, grandparents, and cousins, they had all found their other halves. I had no doubt I'd find mine. But months passed, then a year, and when I still hadn't felt the pull of the bond, my time was up. The King's Army came knocking to take me away." He swallowed a lump in his throat, and I looked up at him from our joined hands. His misty eyes looked distantly over my shoulder, pain etched into his features, as if he could see that memory playing out on the canvas behind me. "I spent the next year being broken and tortured to toughen me up, to prove my loyalty to the king."

I was floored by his truth. I hadn't considered what he had had to go through. I hadn't really considered that he had his own story to tell, and whatever his reason for sharing this with me, I was glad he felt comfortable. It seemed like it was his first time saying it out loud, and I was honoured to listen. Although, I felt somewhat like a hypocrite for being so dismissive of Sylvie.

"Colm was part of his father's army before finding his Twin Soul. He hadn't expected to find her since so much time had passed, so like all the other untwinned, he was enlisted. Of course, he was given a lieutenant position rather than just a regular soldier. He commanded my troop. We became friends, and he told me how he found Sylvie."

I had totally skipped over the part where Colm was a prince. Did that make Sylvie a princess? I was in a makeshift camp, as a fugitive, in the middle of the forest with kingdom royalty. This was madness.

Nathaniel continued to talk, bringing my attention back to his beautifully tortured face. Like Sylvie, he told me about their discoveries and how they knew they could not let this go on. He told me they had around two hundred and fifty rebels from different settlements, and it was growing by the day. He told me he felt confident that they could bring down the king, and he felt it was his purpose, his duty to do so.

"I'm sorry that happened to you," I told him.

"It's okay. It made me the man I am. I'm a good man, Rose. I've done some terrible things, but I will make it right."

Is that what this was? Nathaniel thought that saving everyone would redeem him for all the evil he'd dished out in the name of the king. A chance at redemption so that he could make good with the gods.

"Would you be opposed to me sleeping in here tonight?" he asked. "I'll stick to my side and won't bother you. I swear it."

A small laugh escaped my lips. I don't even know why. Maybe it was the awkward boyish way in which he asked. I was used to him making, shall we say, requests not asking politely.

"What?" he asked.

"Nothing. Of course you can sleep here."

He deserved to. He kept watch last night while I slept, and quite frankly, he looked completely spent.

Three deep breaths in and out, in and out, in and out. Two heavy eyelids tightly shut, drifting further to sleep. One fingertip trailing softly along my brow, tucking a strand of hair behind my ear.

-11-

Despite sleeping soundly, I woke up exhausted. The weight of all that happened, and all that I'd come to know, was bearing heavily on my shoulders. I was grateful that Nathaniel had saved my life, and as much as the fact that my actual existence was inexplicable, the reality was even more dire.

I didn't want to die, but I did it gladly for my people, as those before me had done for centuries. If he hadn't saved me, I would have been none the wiser and the village would have continued in its crazy little bubble. Ignorance was bliss, and I didn't mean to sound so selfish and dismissive of the wider issues.

Only a few days ago, I thought the world was a clearing a couple of miles wide surrounded by vast woodland. I hadn't given much thought to anything beyond that. We were taught to follow, not wonder.

Even though I knew what I now knew, I couldn't just leave it like that. I couldn't leave my father. I couldn't let him live without knowing what had happened to me. When mother died, I gave him reason to go on. He told me so. He told me he could live, knowing that she lived on in me. He said that if I hadn't existed, he would've succumbed to a broken heart. I had to go back. I had no choice.

Nathaniel slept so peacefully next to me. He'd really earned the rest. I felt guilty for what I was about to do, but I knew he would understand, and I hoped that he would forgive me.

I let my eyes trace the curl of the dark strands that hung at his forehead. They wandered along his brow and danced along his incredible lashes that many women would envy. He looked so peaceful as he breathed deeply. I wondered if he dreamt at all. A twitch drew my attention to his lips and along the stubble that lined his jaw. My hand started to wander of its own accord, and I caught myself before my fingertips reached their target.

"Morning." I kept my voice low when I greeted Colm and Sylvie outside the tent, so as not to wake Nathaniel.

Colm was perched on the same log on which he sat when I'd entered the camp. He was sharpening sticks with a penknife. Sylvie was making tea. She offered me a cup.

"Yes, please." I accepted, a little too cheerfully, considering how we had left things last night. I made a note that if I ever got the chance again, I should apologise. It wasn't right for me to be angry at her. Although Nathaniel was the one to physically save me from the clutches of death, it was her insistence to act that placed him there.

"Is there anywhere I can relieve myself? In private?" The pair shared a glance as if conversing without words.

"I'll come with you," Sylvie replied. "It's quite dangerous out here. You don't want to get spotted by a briar wolf looking for breakfast."

I laughed nervously, unsure whether her concern was genuine or if they were suspicious. She said their people had powers. Could they read my mind? I was still struggling to believe that part.

She had told me that the most common powers were what they called 'Elementals.' These powers consisted of having the ability to control earth, wind, fire, and water. I know, ridiculous.

Not every twinned pair possessed special abilities, and sometimes only one of each pair was gifted with these magical powers, and usually they could not possess more than one power. The dishing out of gifts seemed to be rather sporadic.

There also existed 'Rare Powers.' Some of the Twin Souls were able to read or control minds, some were able to rejuvenate themselves and heal others. She said that some had the power of foresight in the form of visions or prophecies, and some were able to throw shields around themselves or others to protect them from harm. Those powers were rarer, but they did exist. Apparently.

"I'll be okay," I insisted. "I'm not comfortable with going in front of someone else."

I might have dramatized my embarrassment, but I wasn't lying. If I really did need to go to the toilet, in the way I was trying to imply, then I was absolutely not going to do that in front of anyone, especially not people I'd known or reacquainted with only a few hours ago.

They finally agreed and pointed through the trees in front of us. It may have been dark last night, but this was definitely the way we came. I could feel it, my internal compass pointing me home. If I just kept straight, I would eventually find my way back to Father, to Greer. Once everyone saw me, they would know that we had been lied to. I'd be the evidence just like Sylvie was to me. When I tell them how I met Sylvie and everything she told me.

I felt the wind of determination under my wings. I could do this. I could make it back to the last camp we had stayed in by nightfall. I would spend the night there and then make the last stretch in the morning.

I patted the pocket of the chunky knitted cardigan I'd worn since waking up with it over me yesterday. The two biscuits Nathaniel had given me that morning were still in my pocket. They were probably rather stale, but by the time I would eat them, I'd be too hungry to care. I grabbed a canteen and was relieved to find it full of water. I took a sip and calmly told them I'd be back in a moment despite the tremors of adrenalin starting to infuse my body.

I started the walk slowly, pretending to find somewhere to squat, until I was certain I was out of sight. I picked up the pace to a light jog for several moments until I accelerated to a panicked sprint. My heart was racing, adrenaline pumping to my legs, moving them so fast I was almost flying. I was covering a lot of ground, and in five minutes I reckoned I'd covered what would've taken us twenty minutes to walk. This was going to be easier than I thought

I was so impressed by my speed and determination to get home that I hadn't even thought about the Wild of the Woods, or the Briar Wolves, or the horned feline beast Nathaniel had saved me from. Maybe I'd be too fast for them to catch anyway. That's it, Rose, think like lightning as it breaks through the sound barrier. My internal monologue giggled at the idea.

I dashed between tree trunks and leapt over fallen branches. Leaves whipped my face, but I didn't care. I felt so free, like I'd been trapped in a cage all my life and I'd finally been released.

When my energy started to deplete, I set myself in a steady jog, drawing air in and out my lungs like the rhythm of a beating drum. I must have been running for fifteen minutes now. I wondered if they'd called for me yet.

I started to feel guilty. I realised that fifteen minutes of running was probably equivalent to thirty minutes of walking, and then I remembered that we had walked from dawn till late into the night yesterday. And then I realised that there was absolutely no way I was making it to my checkpoint any time soon. Shit. I had made a major miscalculation. My desperation to get home had outweighed any logic I had.

My jog slowed to a walk of defeat as I hunched over, placed my hands above both knees, and tried to catch my breath. I tried and I tried, but I couldn't. My realisation had taken away my ability to breathe. My chest tightened and my eyes welled. Dizzy little dots floated in my vision. A few more gulps of air, and I exhaled a growl of frustration from deep within my gut. It was hopeless. I was hopeless. I couldn't do this on my own.

I accepted defeat. I'd acted rashly, and now I would go back to camp with my tail between my legs. I turned to walk back and rolled my ankle on a rock. Another guttural wail left my mouth. My knees and palms slammed the ground. Tears of frustration splashed the debris beneath me.

One minute, I was a sobbing mess of painful hands and knees on the forest floor with wounded pride. The next, I was clawing for anything I could grab onto as I was ripped through the undergrowth.

-12-

The last thing I remember before waking up, was cracking the side of my skull against a tree trunk as I was dragged over the floor of the woods, and up towards the canopy above me. The thud rang in my ears, echoing endlessly. I was still here, suspended high above the forest floor, bound by white ropes covered in a sticky, gluey substance.

I hollered for help and tried to wriggle free. It just made things worse, and I became more stuck. Making things worse seemed to have become a habit of mine. I tried to calm myself down. My thoughts were racing and I had to find a solution to get me down from here. Where even was here?

I looked around to assess my situation. From this height, the view was pretty much the same as when I was on the ground—endless tree trunks and leaves. My view was restricted to a few paces ahead of me.

I seemed to be ensnared in the centre of a snowflake-like structure but on a much larger scale. It resembled a winter solstice dartboard, and I was the bullseye. Sticky sinews trapped my arms and legs to my body like bandages around a mummified corpse, limiting my ability to move. I followed their lines. I noticed that some were thicker than others, and they seemed to be supporting the finer threads spiralling from me in the centre. Where the last loop of the circles ended, the thicker ropes singled out and attached themselves to various trees surrounding me.

Only a fool would fail to work out exactly where I'd found myself ensnared. I had known from the minute I saw those sticky threads, but I continued to analyse, hoping, wishing that there could be another explanation. But all evidence confirmed my biggest fear. I was prey and I had just spotted my predator in the shadowy cover of the crown of an oak.

I wriggled again, trying to free any part of me I could. I dared not take my sight off the beast for fear it would initiate a surprise attack if I looked away, but then again, did I want to see it whenever it did decide to come for me. I could see its eyes—eight of them, and underneath, were two shiny black fangs as long as me with glistening points. Pure terror rose from the tips of my toes, like water-level rising, threatening to drown me. That death would be a kindness in comparison to what was surely inevitable. All hope abandoned me.

I had learned that spiders have poor eyesight. People often think that the number of eyes must mean they have perfect vision, but they do not, they sense vibrations.

Shit, shit, shit.

I couldn't move. I had to stay statue-still and hope that it was an opportunist, and I had been caught on a whim and was being stored for later, hope that the arachnid had eaten only recently. If it could wait to eat me,

I could possibly come up with a way to detach myself or maybe someone might discover me.

I tried to scream for help again, but in my fear of movement, it seemed my vocal cords had frozen too. My call was just a whisper on my lips.

Tears streamed in despair for the fact I was about to become spider food, but mostly, for how angry I felt towards myself. I had promised myself to listen to my gut and this is where it landed me, in the middle of a fucking, mammoth web belonging to a creature fresh out of my nightmares. My life had become a tangled mess of lies and deceit, kind of poetic really, that I should be literally stuck in the middle of a web.

I had cried so much more than I ever had, I was surprised there was anything left. My whole body shuddered with fear no matter how much I willed it to stop. It seemed the more I tried to suppress it the greater I trembled.

The gigantic arachnid noticed. It edged forward ever so slightly. I was overwrought with despair. My desire to live wanted me to chew through the sticky ropes, and thrash my appendages to try to break free, but hopelessness told me I should resign to the predator above me.

Maybe this was a sign from the gods. I'd escaped death by poisoned cherry wine, death by vicious feline beast and now I was caught in a glorified pantry as the ingredients of someone's next meal.

Back home, we always said that what is meant for us would not pass us by, maybe I've cheated the game. You can't run away from what's already been told. I should already be dead. Fate is just doing some housekeeping to restore order.

I closed my eyes, and sampled the forest air, appreciating the cool freshness entering my lungs. I thought of Father, and the meal that I wished we had shared that night. My stomach rumbled to taunt me. I thought of my failure to get home to him. I hated myself for the fact that he would never know what happened to his daughter. I wondered if any scraps of me would be left. If Nathaniel or Sylvie found my remains, would they take me home? Would they continue their mission without me? Of course they would. I'd just be a blip, a minor inconvenience in the grand scheme.

I imagined I wasn't constricted by webs but tucked into a cocoon-style sleeping bag, camping under the stars. I thought of the boundary of the woods. The place where I would sit when I would need to feel close to Mother. I imagined I was there, and I let that feeling wash over me. The peace it would bring me, watching the leaves dancing in the breeze, listening to birds and insects chirp, the rustling of the trees and creaking of branches. The throb of terror in my ears was replaced by natures melodies.

My eyes closed, I allowed myself to be lulled by the symphony while I awaited my fate, like an orchestra playing out my last scenes. An animal call sounded somewhere in the distance. I focused on it, familiar but I couldn't quite envision its bearer. A roar sounded in the mix of rustling and chirrups. There it was again louder this time. Not a roar, a shout, a desperate bellow.

"Rose!"

I knew that voice. The way that he uttered my name had etched itself in a part of my brain.

"ROSE!"

"Here, I'm here." My voice was shaky with relief. "Guys, I'm here." I sobbed.

Out of the dense shrubbery they strode marching forward with purpose, eyes wide and frantically scanning.

"Up here." I directed their eyes.

"Hold tight, Red. We're coming," Colm promised me.

He and Sylvie dashed for the trees acting as posts for the spider's web, Sylvie on one side, Colm on the other. They climbed with so much strength and pace.

"Rose, look at me." Nathaniel stood below me with worry in his eyes. "They're going to cut you down and I will catch you. I promise."

I nodded my head in understanding, but the truth was I was cracking under the pressure. I was so high up, what if he missed me or what if my impact brought us both to the ground and we both got hurt?

As they began to cut, I felt the vibrations on the strands constricting me and so did…it. It unfurled giant, gnarled legs. The sheer size of it was a hand wrapped around my throat. It touched the strands with the spiked tips of its legs like it was testing the different strings to determine its next move, as if tracing lines on a map. It found its path and edged forward from its hiding place.

Spine-like hairs covered its skeletal legs. Its bulbous, black body burned amber where the light hit it. With its front legs splayed, it scuttled forward in a way that made my skin crawl. Beads of sweat formed across my forehead, and I gasped the air greedily to force it down my constricted throat.

"Please hurry," I begged Sylvie.

Both of them were sawing as fast as they could at the tough ropes. What was this stuff made of? I saw Colm's gritted teeth and heard curses escape his mouth. Their swords weren't sharp enough, were they? He glanced quickly at the spiders' movements, and leaving his knife part way through the rope, grabbed one of his spiked sticks from his belt, and threw it with force at the spider. The spider shrieked as the spike lodged in its side between two of its legs. It changed direction and retreated to the cover of the trees above.

A few more saws of their blades and I was falling. I wanted so desperately to grab hold of something, but my arms were still constricted by the webs wrapped around me.

The ground rushed up to meet me, fast, but he was there. Nathaniel with his arms outstretched snatched me from the clutches of Death…again.

He took a knife from his belt and began to cut and rip at my bindings impatiently. He righted my skirt and brushed my hair from my face, removing the sticky remnants of my rope prison. He greedily grabbed my body, and pressed me to him, letting out a relieved sigh. I felt his lips brush lightly on the top of my head. I wasn't sure if he intended for me to feel it, but it was definitely there.

I glanced up at him from where I was pressed against his chest. This man had a habit of being my saviour. He lowered his eyes to meet mine and his icy glare thawed. He stroked my hair and with it all the anxiety, the despair disintegrated. Whatever was happening behind us didn't matter in this moment.

"Er guys, can we catch up later?" Sylvie screamed.

I instantly turned to see Colm in a battle with an eight-legged monster. Nathaniel moved me behind him protectively and drew his sword from its scabbard.

Sylvie grabbed a boulder that seemed far too heavy for one person to pick up and hurled it at the gigantic creature. It shrieked as the rock connected with one of its legs. There was a loud snapping sound, and the creature stumbled.

Following Sylvie's lead, Colm grabbed a boulder from his side and hurled it. It connected with another of the spider's legs and brought it down.

Nathaniel dashed forward, leapt from the ground, and as if in slow motion, ran through the air before landing on the beast's bulbous back. He drove his sword through its head, and ripped it right open, before tumbling off the giant, and landing in a squat in front of me.

Brain-matter exploded, coating us in a rancid fluid. I grunted as I swiped the putrid, yellow ichor from my face.

If scowls could kill, Nathaniel would be dead.

"What the hell was that?" I squealed. I had to stop myself retching at the smell. It was in my hair and in the shell of my ear and no matter how much I tried to get rid of it, it stuck.

"An aranimmanis," Colm gasped, crouched over with his hands braced on his knees, catching his breath.

"Did you have to cover me in this, this, shit?" I squawked at Nathaniel.

"Better to be covered in him than inside him, wouldn't you say?" Colm laughed.

Nathaniel's face had returned to that hardened expression. He took my wrist in his hand and pulled me along.

"Let's go," he sighed.

-13-

I heard the babbling of water just beyond the trees ahead of us, and I looked heavenward, thanking the gods for their gift. I could not convey how desperate I was to wash my hands. To feel plentiful water washing away the pent-up tension and days of dirt that had burrowed under my fingernails and crusted in the tiny fissures of my palms.

Colm had tried to make light of the situation, saying I looked as though I'd been dragged through a hedge backwards—which was funny, because it was true. He licked his sleeve and attempted to wipe the muck from my face like a nurturing father. I had, of course, squirmed away, just as a child might, to which he told me I'd need more than a damp sleeve to fix it. He circled a finger in the air outlining my face with it. But since then, we had walked in silence.

We stopped at a shallow bank. The water ran clear over the pebbles. It looked so refreshing I had to stop from throwing myself headfirst into it. I was so dehydrated I was sure I would suck the entire water reserve up like a sponge.

I lingered at the river's edge, watching it ripple over the silt—much like the guilt rippling through me. Like the river, I had hoped the ominous atmosphere caused by my selfish actions would flow upstream. Maybe an apology might help it along.

Nathaniel, Colm, and Sylvie began to remove their outerwear. After scanning around us, they laid their weapons on their cloaks. I guessed we were safe. I noticed each of them kept their smaller daggers still attached around their thighs. They reached for the laces of their boots. They all looked fed up and quite frankly exhausted. I felt responsible for adding to their already hefty load.

"Everyone, I owe you all an apology."

Three sets of eyes looked at me for the first time since my latest escapade. We had walked together, but we'd felt so far apart, like we were unsure what to say to each other, or they were holding back from what they really wanted to say. Colm tried once or twice to make remarks unrelated to the events. Sylvie had offered him small smiles but no words, and Nathaniel had trailed behind me. I felt like they had purposefully boxed me in, front and back, so that I wouldn't try to run again. They needn't have worried. I'd learnt my lesson now. I wasn't going anywhere, especially not alone.

"I truly am sorry," I tried again. "I acted rashly. I put myself, and you all, in danger. I just…I just wanted to see my father." I burst out. "I need to know he's okay. We lost my mother a long time ago, and we never knew what happened to her. I was all he had left, and I'd hate for him to put himself in danger trying to find me. Please, I will do whatever you need me to do if you just let me see him. I'll keep my distance. I won't even let him see me if I just see that he's okay."

Colm and Sylvie glanced at me sympathetically before they continued downriver, leaving Nathaniel and I alone.

He took my wrist—more gently this time—and led me to a large rock, and pulled down on my arm until I sat. I had planned to just express my regret for being so stupid, but I continued to blabber on, giving him excuses for my leaving without telling anyone. I apologised for my error in judgment, but mostly, I tried to build a case for why we must go back before we move forward. He answered in 'hm's' here and there and continuously pottered around me, and it wasn't until I finished nattering that I realised he had been picking twigs and leaves from my curls, and was now wiping smut from my forehead with a piece of his shirt that he had ripped off and dampened with the river water. He studied my face for more smudges, his plump bottom lip pinched between perfect teeth, and my chest tightened. His eyes, like coffee and honey, warmed me. When he finished wiping my face, he wrung the water out of the scrap of shirt. He smoothed my wild hair with his palms and gathered it at my nape and secured it with the fabric scrap. I had frozen, taking in the way he was silently caring for me.

I didn't take my eyes off him as he crouched to my feet, the fabric of his trousers almost tore with the pressure of his bulging thighs. He slipped my pumps off and emptied the grit that had built up inside them. It was so enraging at first, having to stop every few minutes to empty the contents of the entire forest from them every few metres. In the end I got fed up and just learnt to live with it. I placed my hand on his shoulder and noticed a slight pause at the contact before he dipped my feet in the river.

The water flowed over my aching soles and through my toes. I hadn't realised just how much I'd put them through the past few days. They were sore and tired, and the water was so cool and soothing. He rubbed thumbs into the arches with the perfect pressure, and I almost let out a groan of satisfaction. He dried my feet on the bottom of his shirt before he tucked it back into his trousers. He then fished around in his bag and unrolled a balled-up pair of socks that he placed attentively on my freshly washed feet before replacing my shoes and lifting me off the rock. I was completely taken aback.

My mouth opened and closed not different to a creature you may find in this river.

"Okay," he said. His neutral expression gave nothing away.

"Okay, what?" I quizzed.

"Okay, we can go back."

"You really mean that?" I grabbed his forearms, clutching on to them like the very words themselves.

"I do," he smiled. "If it means that much to you, we will go. We will do it together."

Elation surged through me and lifted my spirit. I jumped to wrap my arms around his neck in an excitable hug. His hands held my waist at the smallest part, just where my hips began to curve. His fingers squeezed lightly, and I blushed at the contact and dropped my arms bashfully.

I took his hands from my waist and placed my palms in his, his rough, calloused skin telling stories of battle, survival, and labour. I wondered if he would let me in on them one day. My fingers swept the soft warmth of his wrist, finding his pulse, which matched the beat of my own. I slid my hand along his muscled forearm, firm from wielding heavy weapons and engaging in brutal brawls. I placed my other hand on his chest, and he flinched beneath it. He bowed his head, watching my every move.

"Should I stop?" I whispered.

His dark eyes dilated and captured mine. "Never."

His hand splayed on the small of my back, tugging our bodies close together. The abruptness stole my breath. Nathaniel pinched my chin between his thumb and forefinger and tilted my head back, forcing my gaze. His beautiful, full lips lingered in my eyeline, and I so badly wanted them on mine. The pause between us was full of tension and longing. He leaned closer, so slowly. My heartbeat hammered in my chest. I was certain he had to have heard it.

The kiss was so delicate like the brushing of fingertips against a silky rose petal. A light brush like velvet on my skin. My hands found the back of his neck and delved in his thick hair and brought him back to kiss me again. Once was not enough. I parted my lips, and he swept his tongue across mine in one sensual movement. I tilted my head to the side and returned the favour, earning me a deep groan. Our tongues met again and again, like we were desperate to taste one another.

Nathaniel pressed his forehead to mine and looked at me through the lashes of his lust-glazed eyes, lids shuttering heavily. Had time slowed? We basked in the euphoric haze of synchronised breaths and heartbeats.

"Home," he whispered.

"Home," I repeated.

His dimples dipped with a smile so wide it reached his eyes that sparkled like a kaleidoscope of excitement and pleasure. I saw his face in a way I never had before. It was like hope and new beginnings. He looked at me with awe, like he was pleased with me.

"What?" I chuckled.

He shook his head, but there was something he wasn't sharing. Words were dancing on the edge of his tongue. Not something sinister. Something nice.

He lifted his cloak from the ground, shook off the dust, and draped it across my shoulders, fastening it around my neck.

He held out his hand.

"Lead the way."

-14-

The sound of his voice buckled my knees. It took everything in my power not to step out of the shadows that concealed us and run to him.

"I just need to see her, David. That's our way. I was supposed to spend time with her before she was buried," Father agonised. He was still holding onto the hope that I was still out there, and he was as desperate to see me as I was him. I completely underestimated how palpable the temptation would be.

"I understand that, Joseph, but it didn't exactly go to plan now, did it?" There was spite in his tone.

"I know," he replied. "She must have been so scared." His voice cracked as he relived the traumatic events of a few days prior, and I felt a pang of grievance at the man that had stolen me away from him. The man that I had allowed myself to be become enamoured by.

"You have my utmost sympathy, you do, but Rose made things incredibly difficult for us. She caused so much unrest. Her accomplices are still out there. What she did may have a significant impact on future ceremonies. What if others decide to deny their destinies as the god's tributes? What if they decide to put their own lives ahead of the lives of the community?" His volume rose with each question as did my ire. Nathaniel was right. He had told me this would happen but witnessing it was like a knife in my back.

"I'm sorry, David, I truly am. If it helps, I will address the village myself."

My father, apologising, sounding utterly crestfallen and it was all I could do to stop myself from going out there and throwing my arms around him. Who would comfort him in his time of grief? The thought of him crying alone was almost unbearable. I thought he would have Pastor David to turn to, but it seems I was mistaken.

Pastor David cut him off. "I think the Harlow's have done enough already. What with Millicent consistently bending rules and her venture into the forbidden woods leaving us without our healer. Seems your daughter inherited her defiant streak," he scoffed. "Quite the mess your family has caused."

Anger bubbled through my veins, threatening to boil over.

"I…I…" Father struggled for words. "I just need to know what happened."

Pastor David had calmed down now and resumed his usual ruse of kind, caring, village leader. A role he had fine-tuned to perfection.

"Of course, I'm sorry, Joseph. I am under a lot of stress. You've been a great contributor in this community, and I hope we can continue to work together for the good of our people."

"Of course." My father's voice quivered.

"Rose returned later in the evening and begged me for forgiveness," Pastor David began.

I'm sorry, I did what?

"I told her that it was the gods she needed to ask for forgiveness, not me. She asked me to lead her prayers for her, so I did. We consulted them together, right there actually."

I couldn't see him, and I wondered where his fabrication of events had taken place. That bastard. I was sure my face was the same burgundy hue as the heavy curtains we hid behind. He had stabbed me in the back and was now twisting the knife. I heard my father sigh and a noise that sounded like taking a seat on the creaky wooden pews.

Pastor David continued. "The gods were satisfied with her pleas for forgiveness. She told them that she had fallen in love with another man. My poor Greer had to hear it too."

"No," my father whispered.

I could feel Nathaniel's eyes on me, but I was afraid to look at him.

"I'm afraid so."

The way in which this man lied so freely and managed to pull the wool over all of our eyes was unnerving. I could envision his smirk on his smug face as he besmirched my character. I wanted to punch it off.

"The mystery man was not ready to let Rose go yet and attempted to save her life. Rose had gone along with it at first but soon noticed the error in her ways. She remembered where her loyalties truly lie, her core beliefs. I'm sure that trait was inherited from you, my good man."

My heart was racing. I trusted this man; we all did. The king planted trusted people in the village...I had to catch a gasp of shock from escaping my mouth. I couldn't believe it. I needed to tell him. I stepped forward, but Nathaniel stopped me. He shook his head, eyes urging.

"She drank the god's blood where you're sat, and she passed peacefully holding Greer's hand. He was there for her in her final moments, despite her infidelity."

A pained noise left my father's mouth. Tears fell down his cheeks. Deep sadness threatened my ability to think rationally.

"She told me to tell you she was sorry and that she loved you so much. We buried her last night, and we will hold a vigil tonight to explain the happenings to the community."

Father had stopped his sobbing. "Thank you, David. I would like to place some flowers on her grave and sit with her, if that's okay."

"Of course it is. Go home and wash up and come back this evening. I think you'll like the spot we chose. It's really beautiful during sunset."

I couldn't believe it. What spot? I was right here. I wanted so badly to jump out from my hiding place and reveal his lies.

"I will," Father sniffed. "Thank you, again." He was genuine. He believed the lie.

Sorrow permeated my entire being. Nathaniel rubbed circles on my back that may have well been with sandpaper for all the soothing it did.

"The gods have forgiven us, Joseph," he called as my father made his exit, and with that, the chapel doors closed.

No sooner had my father left than I stormed into the chapel through the back entrance, startling Pastor David. His eyes widened like he'd seen an apparition, but as soon as he caught sight of Nathaniel's giant form, followed by Colm and Sylvie, he dropped his facade.

"You've got some nerve." His words took me by surprise. This man was not the pastor I knew.

When I first started to talk, my parents noticed that I would sometimes stutter. It was more prominent when I was tired. S and R sounds were one I would frequently struggle with. Pastor David would spend one-on-one time with me every Sunday evening and in around a year, he had managed to help me. You would never know now that I had a speech impediment. It resurfaced again when Mother disappeared, but again he took the time to help me. If you were having a bad day or you were worried about something, you could always count on Pastor David to talk you through it and give you advice. He would help anyone in need and had always felt like a leader to us all. To a lot of children, he had felt like a grandfather figure, and he seemed to revel in it. I saw no hint of evil. Nothing but devotion to his people.

"Service starts in an hour, so make it quick and get the hell out of here," he spat.

How dare he! Acting as if we were in the wrong.

"The king's entrusted plant. You fooled me," I laughed falsely.

"I did what was necessary. This community thrives because of it."

"Oh yes, quite the hero," I quipped. The time for niceties had well and truly passed. "You lie to everyone here," I shouted as he moved toward the door and pushed the bolt up into its latch.

"Greer, get the curtains." Greer appeared from a doorway at the back of the chapel and carried out his father's orders subserviently.

"Greer..." I called; sucker punched by his presence. Pastor David had mentioned him in his lie to Father, but I didn't think for a second he was truly part of it, but I could hardly hold myself as a good judge of character.

"Rose." He made a beeline for me, grabbing me in a tight embrace. I should have melted into him, but I couldn't help remaining stiff at his touch. He pulled back, scanning me with uncertainty. "I was so worried. Thank you for returning her. The gods will be so grateful."

I threw my arms around his neck. I was so relieved he was unaware but also saddened at the prospect of all he had to learn about Sandy, about the kingdom of Thane, and of his father.

"Greer, I'm so sorry. I had no idea what was going on, but I came back. I have so much I need to tell you." My hand went straight for the pendant around my neck. 'A rose for a Rose. A gift for my gift.'

He held me at arm's length, and his eyes drank me in like he hadn't seen me in months, not a week. He truly missed me, and to be honest, I had missed him too. His eye roved the length of my body.

"What the fuck are you wearing?" He violently grabbed the hem of the cloak and tugged me towards him.

Rattled by the sudden flip of a switch, I'd never seen him in any other way but gentle. I'd watched him exercise patience while teaching the children. It would make me into a pile of mush and sadden me that we would never get the opportunity to have a child together. I heard a growl from behind.

"Heel dog," he glowered over my shoulder at Nathaniel. "I can smell him all over you." His attention turned back to me. "Didn't take long, did it?"

He broke out into a laughter steeped in arrogance. Who was this man? His entire demeanour changed like he had unmasked himself revealing his true identity. 'The apple doesn't fall far from the tree' came to mind.

"Greer. I…"

"I didn't take you for a whore," he snickered.

"Don't you dare speak to her like that. You will show her respect," Nathaniel yelled at him.

"Shut up, Nathaniel. You are all as good as dead anyway. The king should have had word by now," Greer said.

"You know each other?" I started to back away from them.

"You haven't even heard the best part," Greer revelled at the piece of information that he was dangling in front of me seemingly desperate to reveal. "Or do you want to tell her?"

I watched Nathaniel fill his lungs and wipe his hand along his jaw. He glanced at Colm and Sylvie for guidance, I assumed, but Sylvie lightly shook her head. You could hear a pin drop in the silence that followed, bar the beating in my ears. I was in the company of strangers. That's what they were, strangers.

"No one? Alright, I volunteer," Greer said, just as Nathaniel grabbed him by the throat, strangling his words. His toes swept the floor.

"Stop!" I screamed. Nathaniel released his hold after lingering a few more moments. He loomed over Greer, who was still larger than most men in the village.

"Tell me what?" I asked.

"The prophecy," he began.

"Don't," Nathaniel spat.

"Maybe I can interject," Pastor David offered with an effort to defuse the animosity. The collective tension in the room was so thick, you'd need a sword to cut it. It was obvious that Sandy's guests were reluctant to allow David to disclose this huge secret that they all seemed to be keeping from me but had surrendered to the fact that I would discover it sooner or later. It may as well be now.

David took a diary from his pocket and read an excerpt.

> *Magic blood bears the heir.*
> *A flower of crimson, Twin Souls bound.*
> *With wings and fire,*
> *The king will fall.*

"A flower of crimson," Greer began. "A rose, Rose. Seems you are the chosen one after all."

No, no, no, no. This can't be it. I was saved because they think I'm someone from a prophecy, a vague one at that, and I'm what, supposed to kill the king? Absolutely not.

"Go on, Petal, humour me. What's going on in that pretty little head of yours right now?" Greer smirked at me.

The weight of their stares was like an anvil on my chest. They looked at me like I was a dangerous wild beast or a ticking time bomb ready to go off. I made for the door, still guarded by Pastor David. I was a bull in a furniture shop. I would rip through Pastor David and burst through that door. I'd like to see him stop me.

"Get out of my way!" I screamed at him.

"Rose, you know I can't do that. It's not what's best for the village."

"Well, maybe it is David!" He was no longer my Pastor.

He did not budge.

"Fine," I about turned, and headed to the back door. The last thing I wanted was to cause any harm to my community, to my father when he had seemed so content with the lie that David had spoon fed him.

"Rose, wait," Nathaniel pleaded, but I was gone.

-15-

I came to an abrupt halt, Nathaniel so hot on my tail that he nearly slammed into my back. I twisted to face him. My rapid movements took him by surprise. I was a boiling pot of rage, dynamite seconds from exploding. But the look on his face almost caused my hardened expression to falter. He reached for me, and I stepped back, wrapping my arms around myself in an attempt to hold myself together.

"Rose, it's not what you think," he started.

"Well, I'm getting kind of sick of things not being what I think," I shouted.

"Yes, we do think you may be the one from prophecy, but we discovered that after deciding to put a stop to this madness."

"And you thought, 'Hey let's just not tell her about it.'," I snapped.

"We were going to tell you; we were just waiting for the right time," he reasoned.

"Right," I nodded, while scoffing through a faux smile. "Oh, and you and Greer are already pals. Was that something else you were saving for another time?"

"I promise you; I had no idea..."

"Gods, I bet you were having a good laugh at my expense. Poor, naive Rose. What a fool."

"I wouldn't do that." He looked offended that I could think of him in that way.

"Well, how would I know? I barely know you, Nathaniel! It seems I don't know anyone." I swallowed the lump in my throat. I thought about the way I let myself be led by him. I was such an idiot. So quick to believe and follow this stranger, just like I had with Pastor David and Greer. Have the scraps of moments where I felt a connection all been a clever ploy to keep me close enough to follow but not too close, in the same way that Greer had tricked me into loving him, so that he could make sure 'the flower of crimson' saw out her suicide?

"Don't you understand? My whole world has fallen apart. Those that I trusted, that I loved, have betrayed me." I ran my fingers through my hair. Then, a sudden realisation came to me, "They were Kingsmen? Were there more in the village?"

"I don't know, but it's likely."

I was torn between getting my father and getting the hell out of here, or leaving him in blissful ignorance to carry on his everyday life while I go on a killing spree to take down the bastard monarch and his band of Kingsmen. I couldn't breathe. I dropped to the dirt and sobbed. I sobbed for my father, for my mother, for not seeing through Greer. For the parents that had sacrificed their children to a lie. I sobbed for the ones who had spent their final moments in terror internally but holding it together on the outside for their loved ones. Those that cut their lives short when they had so much more living to do. And I sobbed for me. I sobbed for the little girl that lost her mother, the life that was anything but real, and the betrayal. Oh, the betrayal.

A guttural noise left my throat from the truth that hit me like a punch to the gut. "You had no right to force me into this," the words a breath on my lips.

"What did you say?" Nathaniel knelt in front of me.

"I said you had no right to force me into this. I was happy. I was supposed to die, and I was okay with it," I shouted.

"Well, I'm not! I will never be happy with a life where you don't exist," he raised his voice with a passion I hadn't yet experienced from him.

"You don't even know me!" I bellowed. My eyes prickled, and my breaths were short and sharp, like I was recovering from a sprint.

"I saw you," Nathaniel broke me out of my stupor.

"What?" The word was breathless, barely audible.

"I've been seeing you for years."

As he said it, I saw the weight of his confession leave his shoulders. I sniffed back the last of my tears, and my arse hit the ground of the small courtyard at the back of the chapel with a thud, giving respite to my knees. Nathaniel sat beside me in the dirt. His arm rubbed against my shoulder. I looked up at him. A face I'd started to feel comfortable with. A face I'd begun to trust whether I was right to or not.

"I can't remember the first time, but you were wearing that every time." He pointed to my dress. "Sometimes it would just be a collection of images, like your hair over my eyes, or your hand drawing patterns in my palm like this…" He took my hand and drew a shape that I knew.

"The mark?" I asked. He smiled and nodded once.

"I dreamt that I was too late, and you died before I could reach you," he swallowed. "I dreamt about you at the edge of the woods so many times. Just sitting there talking to yourself. Every time it was from a distance, like I was a fly on the wall." He chuckled at the memory. "Not long after my mark appeared, the dreams stopped. I tried so hard to get them back. I tried to burn your image in my mind, every night before I slept, in the hopes you'd appear but it never worked. I started to really miss you after a while, but then I got my call to the Kingsmen, and well, you know the rest.

"I really believe that it's my destiny to ensure the prophecy is fulfilled. When I saw you at the woods, I couldn't believe it, and then again at the dais. I…I'm not sure what the prophecy means, but I promise I will do everything to keep you safe. I won't let any harm come to you, and you don't have to kill anyone; I will do it for you."

It dawned on me then how hard this past week must have been for him. I thought back to the first time I saw his face and the way he looked at me expectantly.

"You were disappointed?" I muttered.

"Hmm?" He brought his eyes away from his fidgeting hands to meet my gaze.

"The day you took down your hood, the way you looked at me," I began to explain.

"Yeah," he scoffed. "I'd hoped you'd dreamt of me, just like I had you. But you didn't know me, and it really fucking hurt."

"I'm sorry," I told him. I really wished I had known him. It might have saved us from a lot of upset and confusion.

"Do you want to know something?" he said. "The pattern on my cloak, it's for you."

My eyes followed the embroidery on the edges of the cloak. I looked longingly at the beautiful man next to me. He was staring at his hands again, which were clasped in front of him, elbows resting on his knees.

"It's silly, I know, but your hair was red like a rose, and I saw you lay them at the woods one time, and, well, you can imagine my surprise when I heard the pastor call your name," he laughed.

I had wanted to touch him the moment his walls came down, the moment he told me he dreamt of me, I wanted to console him for the disappointment he must have felt, but I was scared. What if this was just one too many mishaps? So much chaos already, and we had only just kissed. I made to reach for him when he got up suddenly, immediately spiking a pang of rejection in my chest.

"We should probably go back inside." He offered a hand and helped me up from the floor.

"Ah there she is." Greer announced my arrival back inside the chapel. "Calmed down now, Petal?"

Oh, that name. What is it about that name that takes me from nought to irate in five seconds? This time, I acted on my intrusive thoughts. I stormed toward Greer, grabbed him by the shoulders, and coiled all my strength into my right knee and pounded it into his balls. He keeled over; pain sliced across his features.

Still hunched and cupping his genitals, he glared up at me through his lashes and laughed through gritted teeth. "Does this mean you're breaking up with me?"

I grabbed my pendant, ripped the necklace from around my neck, and threw it at his face. Violent storms thrashed around my head, whirring in my ears. I wanted to hurt him, to cause him serious damage. I wanted to kill him.

Nathaniel appeared beside me and took my hand, lacing his fingers between mine, bringing me down from the heights that I'd reached. I felt like I'd shot into the sky like a firework. I was like high winds ripping through Sandy, and he was the eye of the storm, the circle of calm while the world around us turned to shit.

The pastor stepped in front of his son. "This is over now, Rose. You must go now," he said. "No one will ever know you returned. The people will live on like nothing happened, but believe me when I say, if you try anything, I will burn this place to the ground, and the Harlow house will be the first I set alight. Do you understand?"

-16-

After leaving the chapel, we spent the rest of the day making up for the time we'd lost. It had taken almost two full days to make it to Sandy and then to turn around to make it this far back towards Thane. The supply tunnel was still off-limits, so we were enroute to another of their discreet thicket campsites.

I couldn't stop myself from looking up suspiciously, checking the trees for any signs of gargantuan spider webs. Colm said that I was easy prey out there alone, that's why the spider had plucked me from the ground. Even a spider as huge as that one wouldn't dare to prey on a group of our size. He assured me I was perfectly safe as long as I stuck with the group. I wondered how much of that was true or whether it was a way to keep me from going solo again. If the latter, he needn't bother. After that experience, I would be choosing the safety of numbers.

Sylvie led the party, and Nathaniel paraded at the back. Colm fell back to walk beside me. I glanced back at Nathaniel in hopes he would catch me looking, but he didn't. Perhaps he had done the same and I'd missed him too. He seemed lost in thought. He'd gone into himself since we had left the chapel, and I couldn't help wishing I knew what was going on inside that gorgeous head of his.

"He'll come around," Colm said, bumping my shoulder with his. I didn't know he had anything to 'come around' from. I felt nervous all of a sudden and wanted to ask Colm, but didn't want to seem too eager. "It's not too far from here. We will all perk up a bit once we've had something to eat," he said.

"Yeah," I agreed, watching my once white pumps kick small stones and twigs on the ground.

"Has Nathaniel told you much about anything?" Colm asked.

"Not much." My eyes left my feet, and I looked at him now. Not much should have been 'barely anything.' I really wanted to know more about what the hell we were doing.

"My father was hungry for power long before I was born. He's the most feared man in the world and I get it. I'm terrified of him too. Pathetic, huh?"

"Not even," I replied.

"He never loved me. I don't even think he's capable of something so wonderful as love." I noticed his eyes glaze. Sylvie glanced back at her Twin Soul and smiled gently. He returned her gesture and nodded. It was beautiful to see how in sync, how aware of each other they were. "I think he loved my mother once. They had their first son over a thousand years ago. There are paintings in the castle of the three of them and they looked so happy."

"What happened?" I asked. He seemed to have gotten stuck in the memory of the happiness portrayed in paint.

"Well, they had a daughter after that and then another two sons, and as time went on the paintings became more sinister looking. They no longer looked a picture of happiness."

"What are your siblings doing about their father?"

"I'm not sure what they would be doing, but..." he paused, and a solemness tainted his features.

"I am so sorry, Colm. I didn't know."

"No, no, it's fine," he cut in quickly. "I never met the older two. They died a long time before I was born. My mother would tell me about them," he smiled. "But never about how they died. I heard rumours that he killed them."

My eyes widened at the possibility. It was blatant that the king was a terrible man, but to kill your own children? Only someone very sick would do such a thing.

"I heard rumours, muttering of staff, whispers from the people of Thane. My eldest brother Jonah was his prodigy. He was raising him to continue our reign once he was gone. But I heard that my brother was able to control all of the elements, it had never been seen before and that scared my father, so he killed him."

A sharp intake of air, I was horrified that he could want to keep his power that badly that he would kill his own flesh and blood.

"Some years later my sister had apparently developed an ability to sway people. To gently persuade them to bend to her will. My father enjoyed this ability and utilised her well until one day she refused to do his bidding. He slew her husband first and as she was dying, I heard, that he stole her power. He took it from her as he took her life." A tear made a track down his cheek.

I couldn't do anything but watch as this man shared such personal stories with me. I wanted to console him, but I was stopped by my reluctance to allow myself to be pulled in. I was still questioning everything and part of me felt guilty for even doubting what he shared with me. It was so convincing; I was sure he was genuine, but I couldn't even trust myself to make that judgment.

"Thaddeus was born while Charlotte was alive, but I never met her, only in the still images in the gilded frames in the castle corridors. Thaddeus developed the ability to manipulate wind which wasn't all that useful to Father as it was quite a common ability, and me, well, I didn't develop an ability and I really struggled to come to terms with that for a while, but surprisingly, my father didn't really care." He huffed through a smile, and I couldn't tell whether he was relieved at his father's lack of care or at his inability to perform.

"Growing up it was mainly Mother and me. She poured herself into me like I was her last chance of happiness. I rarely saw her and Father speak. Father was always wandering around with a lady with red hair." I noticed his eyes flick to my scarlet locks. "She was a nice lady. Always doing little tricks for me or bringing me trinkets from their expeditions. She would say they were from him, but I never believed her. I think she just felt sorry for me. Then one day, maybe ten years ago, maybe more, I never saw her again."

He didn't say it, but I was sure he thought that the red-headed lady had met her demise at the hand of his evil father.

"I think I was about twelve when Mother started to retreat into herself. I started to see her less and less and I was so lonely. When my mark appeared, I couldn't wait to find my Twin Soul." He glanced up at the platinum haired, lithe figure trundling through the thicket ahead of us. "I told myself that I would take them away and we would live a life far from my father. I would love them like mother had loved me in the beginning. But unlike her love, mine would never dwindle. It would be a force, it would grow and feed us both. We would never be hungry. We would never want for anything else." He paused and watched the motion of his treads.

"After almost a year, I hadn't found them, hadn't felt the pull that you're supposed to feel, like they're tugging at the end of a rope that's attached to the both of you. I went to my mother, but she was so shut off from the world that she offered me nothing of use. She told me it was a waste of time looking, and that us Thane's were doomed.

"In my desperation, I decided to go to my father. He told me that if I hadn't found my Twin Soul by now, they were likely dead." He scoffed and rubbed his hand over his face. "I was devastated. I had poured all hope into one outcome, finding my Twin Soul and escaping. On a whim, then and there, I offered myself to my father. I begged him to let me join his ranks. I wanted him to teach me, to show me how to be callous and cruel in the same way that life had been cruel to me."

He surveyed me as though nervous about how I'd react to such a desire. I would not judge a version of him from the past.

He continued. "He trained me, and we grew quite close, well, closer than estranged father and son. He put me in charge of a small unit, he gave me focus and that's where I met Nathaniel, and then subsequently Sylvie."

"That part I do know," I smiled. I wanted to say more. He'd been vulnerable with me, and I strangely got comfort from it. I didn't feel so alien anymore.

"Do you know about the rebels?" He changed the subject.

"Nope," I replied, excited about the change of topic.

"Well, there are three factions outside of ours. Tuck leads the rebels in Fermyn, Alissa leads Brigsbane, and Thoran leads Priors. Each town is equally distanced from Oakenvale; that's the name of the kingdom's capital. That's where Nathaniel and I are from. My father rules everyone and everywhere. Each vale pays their dues, and he allows them to live somewhat freely. Lately, the tithes have become too much. He's got them all in a choke hold. They're running out of essentials. He's bleeding them dry." He lowered his head, and I could tell it hurt him deeply. "The rebellion is growing, and once word of the prophecy spread, we had raised a company of around a thousand members, and at least three hundred of those are fit to fight for the cause, for equality and justice, fight for the right to live happily and comfortably."

He was animated about the prospects of this future.

"Well, now you have a thousand and one." I bumped his arm back and flitted him a friendly smile.

"That means more to me than you know," he grinned benevolently. I wondered if he looked like his father. I couldn't imagine someone with his face being a tyrant. This face betrayed nothing but genuine kindness.

"I know it must be hard to trust us, Red, especially me, the spawn of that monster."

"Colm, I don't think you are your father." I hoped he could feel my sincerity.

"I know it's just…the things I've seen him do while I stood by and did nothing."

"Your hands were tied," I assured him. I didn't know that for a fact, but I could only assume he would have a solid reason to have not acted sooner.

"But I should've done something," he insisted. I could hear the regret in his tone.

"You're doing something now." That was what was important. He put his arm around my shoulders and rubbed his knuckles on the top of my head.

"You're alright, you know," he chuckled.

"So are you." I wriggled out of his grip and caught sight of Nathaniel. This time I caught him watching.

Colm handed Sylvie a paper package fastened with twine and a loaf of bread.

"Nathaniel and I are going to head out to find the others. Make sure you eat. Don't worry about waiting for us." He kissed her on the cheek and headed past me with a wink before making their calling sound out into the wood.

Nathaniel walked towards me, and I opened my mouth to say something but decided it could wait until he was back. He flashed me a smile and followed after Colm. As he passed by me, he covertly hooked his fingers around mine, my arms hanging lax at my sides, and squeezed my fingers briefly without stopping or even looking back. A smile broadened my mouth.

"I know that look," Sylvie teased.

"I don't know what you're talking about," I lied as I glanced back to make sure they were gone. I knew my feelings were written all over my face. My smile was so wide my cheeks ached.

"Yeah, yeah. Come. Sit."

"Can I help with anything?" I offered, although I doubted there was anything I could do to help. The boys were the ones who were taught bush skills. The residents of Sandy didn't see the point in the girls learning that.

"Know how to light a fire?" she asked.

"Erm." Out of all the things she could have asked.

"You can cut the bread," she said as she handed me the loaf and a blade.

"Listen, Sylvie. I'm sorry for the way I've acted. I never meant..."

"No. No need," she interrupted. "There really is no need to apologise. I get it, Rose. I went through it too."

I forgot about that. How self-absorbed to not consider that she too had this happen to her. And look where she was now, happily bound with her Twin Soul, and the freaking founder of a rebellion. It was a good look on her. She was strong and resilient. I hoped that I could be like her one day, instead of this vessel of tumultuous gloop.

"It's just so much to take in. There's so much I still don't know."

"I will tell you everything," she insisted. "Where should I start?"

"The beginning?" I suggested.

-17-

According to the scriptures they'd discovered, the creation of our world began almost six thousand years ago. They hadn't found anything dated before that, as if the world began on that very day. I told Sylvie that when I said the beginning, I didn't mean the beginning of time, but she insisted that it was important to the story.

Jacobi awoke in a place they now called the Deadlands. This was day one. As the name suggests, there was nothing living in the Deadlands. Darkness smothered him like a heavy cloak. He could feel the weight of it, almost suffocating him. He could see nothing, hear nothing, feel nothing but sharp stones and grit digging into his curled-up form. He lay there for hours, for his entire being was new, and he did not yet know what he should do.

Sometime later, a great orb began to form in front of him. It was blindingly bright yellow and painted the sky pink and orange. He moved a hand to shade his eyes as they adjusted to the brightness. He reached out to touch the orb but realised it was not remotely as close as it seemed. As it rose higher, the dark black night gave way to sky blue day. Jacobi pulled himself up to a seated position, his movements stiff and slow, and glanced around at the vast nothingness. For miles and miles around, it was only grey and arid. Huge rock formations with deep crevices made up the mountainous landscape.

Jacobi took shelter from the scorching heat in a nearby cave. His legs wobbled, and his feet hurt from the dry, stone terrain. He found a pebble on the ground, and as he rolled the smooth, cold stone in his fingertips, he felt a pang in his chest. His eyes rolled back, and he began to see someone else—another person lying in the dark. His body new, just like Jacobi's.

Jacobi came back to the present, his hand clutched at his chest. When he moved it away, there was a mark in the centre, and he felt urged to move, even though he had no idea where he would go. He decided to climb the outside of the cave to get a better look around. He turned full circle until his eyes spotted a mountain bigger than any of the other's—it's top smoking like a beacon. He decided that was his destination.

He marched onwards for hours and hours; sweat droplets slid down his forehead and into his stinging eyes, his mouth and nose were so dry, and the air so hot. The mountain was much farther than he had anticipated. He stumbled with dizziness and banged his head on the rocky ground. He saw the man again; his skin was dark, but a chalky layer covered it, dry dust from his surroundings. Jacobi thought he must be around here somewhere. Curly black hair crowned his head; his eyes were deep, dark circles against the whites. What was the man doing? He noticed the same mark on the man's chest, in the same place as his own. He had no idea who he was, but he just had to find this man.

Jacobi got up and pushed on with renewed determination. Darkness came creeping again, and it rained. It washed the dust from his skin. He tilted his head back, opened his mouth and stuck out his tongue, and laughed with joy as the liquid washed over him and hydrated him. The sound of his laughter took him by surprise and despite sounding strange, he enjoyed the feeling the obscure noise brought him.

After a while, it had grown impossibly cold. His body quivered, and his hands and feet were numb, but he kept going, kept driving forward. When it became unbearable, he decided to take shelter in another cave. He dreamt of the man again. This time they had found one another, and his touch drove away the cold and loneliness; it drove away the ache of desperation. They touched one another and embraced each other with lust-filled eyes and panting breaths.

Morning came, and he marched on. His feet were broken and blistered. They wept for respite, but he must find the man. His lips were dry and cracked, and he felt a thirst that he so desperately needed to quench. There was a stabbing sensation in the centre of his torso causing him to hunch over. But he kept on. He knew that all these desperate urges would be satiated upon meeting the man.

Another blanket of darkness. Jacobi lay behind a rock at the base of the tall mountain. He felt sure that he would find the man here, but he did not. Moisture pooled in the corner of his eye and trailed over the bridge of his nose before dripping onto his arm, which he had folded beneath his head. He noticed the dark was not quite so thick this time. It had a glow to it.

He pulled himself up from the ground, dusting off the tiny rock shards that had embedded themselves into the skin of his side, and glanced up at the night sky. There above the peak was an enormous red orb. Jacobi felt like it was a sign, telling him he must go to the top. Intuition told him the orb was the creator, the one who made all of this, the one that gave him life, the Crimson Moon. It ignited a fire in his belly, giving him the push he needed to climb the mountain.

By the time he got to the top, he was crawling. His leg muscles had seized, and his buttocks burned. His knees and his palms were covered in lacerations, but he didn't care; it would be worth it if that man was the reward for the torture his body had been through.

At the top of the mountain, there was a vast pit emitting a heat so intense that Jacobi thought he would pass out. He peered over the lip and saw a bubbling and boiling fiery chasm and thought that that was what he'd been drawn to. He stared and stared and waited. He didn't understand why the deathly heat called to him.

He was preparing to throw himself in when a strangled sound came from across the pit. He looked up, and there, over the other side, was the man. His face worn and dirty, his lips chapped, his eyes desperate. He dragged himself, scurried away from the edge towards the man. His torso was shredded against the rocky mountain. The man also crawled towards Jacobi with the same desperation.

They finally reached one another and curled up, pressing foreheads together. Groans and whimpers left their mouths. They cried and studied each other. Jacobi pressed a hand to the man's heart, and they brought their lips to touching. Jacobi knew in that moment that he would never leave that man, and the man would never leave him.

The skies opened up and dropped soothing, relieving droplets of water onto the men. They lay on their backs and let the rain pour into their mouths and wash over their bodies.

"I'm Jacobi," Jacobi said to his own astonishment. He didn't know how he had formed those words but somehow knew what they meant.

"Adama." To his relief, the man understood and replied.

"Adama," Jacobi breathed. "You are me, and I am you. We will never be apart again, until death takes us from this life."

"Jacobi." Adama laced his fingers with Jacobi's. "You are me, and I am you. I will honour and cherish you until the day we both shall perish."

They spent the night wrapped in each other, saying vows with their bodies. Jacobi took a sharp rock, and after slicing across his own palm, did the same to Adama.

Their blood merged, and as they held their hands over the bubbling pit, droplets fell into the lava below.

When they woke and watched the sunrise, the light cast upon a blanket of green, they heard creatures and saw winged beasts in the sky. The rainwater had collected in the craters and crevices forming lakes and rivers. The Deadlands was teeming with life.

Their lives truly began that day.

Adama had a gift. He would dream about ways that they could improve their existence, like an inbuilt survival manual, and over time the couple learnt to craft and create. They used the resources the land had given them. They built a home, captured and reared animals they had hunted from the woods surrounding them, and Adama became quite skilled at making clothing from the animal furs and pelts.

One morning Adama awoke telling Jacobi of a vivid dream. He believed that on the next Crimson Moon, two infants would be left at the top of the mountain, that they had named the Sacred Volcano, as gifts to them. Jacobi believed Adama to be a dreamer, as he was so desperate to expand their family. Since their union, they hadn't seen the great red orb, but Adama had never failed Jacobi before.

So, on the fourth anniversary of their coming together, they ventured once more up the mountain.

When they got there, even though it was expected, what they saw took them by surprise—two beautiful babes, just like Adama had dreamt—gifts from the gods.

They raised them and loved the children dearly, and on the next Crimson Moon they set off as a family and again found two more babes. This happened over and over until the family had grown so large that they'd managed to create a village.

Jacobi and Adama cherished their lives.

"That is a truly beautiful story," Rose said. But a story was exactly what she thought it was.

"I thought so too," Sylvie agreed.

"But surely that is all it is, a story," Rose told her.

Sylvie silently pondered.

"I was born on the Crimson Moon too," Rose interrupted the silence.

"Really?" Sylvie seemed surprised. "It's actually considered incredibly lucky. I can't believe they were going to take your life on the anniversary of the day your life was given. Wow."

"I wasn't even bothered that it was my birthday. You remember how it was. We were raised to believe it was an honour to be chosen, and they made a bigger fuss of me because I'd been born on that day." Rose paused. Sylvie seemed to be lost in thought. "The day I was born, a girl called Elodie was sacrificed. My parents named me after her: Rose Elodie Harlow."

"Pretty," she acknowledged.

"Yeah. I never met her, obviously, but her parents were always kind to me. They were so happy their daughter lived on in me."

"And how did they feel about the fact that her name was going to die with you?" Sylvie seemed sad talking about the village. I wondered if she missed it. Did she think of her family? I wanted to ask her, but didn't want to pry.

"They were over the moon. They believed that it was because of her that I was chosen. Like having her name was some sort of omen, and that she was able to honour the gods, not once, but twice."

"Madness. It really is a crazy place." I sensed ire in her tone.

"Yeah," I laughed nervously.

"We are going to stop it, Rose, you know that?" Her solemnity was replaced by a look of sincerity. I could see that even though her attempted sacrifice was almost a decade ago, it still seemed to affect her on a deeper level. I suppose she had probably talked it out with her new family, but they couldn't really begin to understand what it was like for us.

"Why did the king stop banishing the unmarked? What made him start to execute them?" I asked.

"I don't know. It started to become a problem, I suppose, like banishment wasn't a deterrent enough. Also, some people got their marks when they came of age, but they could never find their Twin Soul. He decided to make use of those people by turning them into soldiers, slaves, maids, and entertainment."

"Not to be rude, but what the hell do Jacobi and Adama have to do with the king?" I hadn't meant for it to come out that way.

"Well, Adama had the power of prophecy. He would dream of ways they could improve their lives, dream of births and deaths and other significant events. According to Jacobi's diary, Adama had prophesied the last known babes to appear at the volcano. One of them would grow to be evil. He saw the damage that he would do. Jacobi wanted to kill the babies to protect what they had built over the almost four thousand years. They were getting old, and he knew he didn't have much time left in this life.

"From what we could piece together, Adama did not accept Jacobi's plan. Jacobi wanted to throw the babies back into the Sacred Volcano. Adama said that that wasn't who they were and that they would nurture these babies and make every effort to ensure they would not spoil. At the top of the mountain there was a struggle, and in his effort to save the babies from Jacobi, Adama fell into the volcano. Apparently, Jacobi returned to his town with the babies to honour his husband's wishes and then left and was never seen again."

"Those babies?" I had already guessed where she was going with this.

"Yes. We believe they are King Bellinus and Queen Lisandra."

She was deadly serious.

"But then that would make them, like, two thousand years old?" I had heard time again about people being a thousand plus years old, even Colm had mentioned his eldest brother being born so long ago but it was just so...unfathomable. If there was any detail to this whole ordeal that could prevent me from believing any of it, it was the fact that we were supposed to believe that Jacobi and Adama, the first men, lived for four thousand years, and the king and queen were babies that magically appeared on the top of a volcano, two thousand years previously.

"We found diary accounts that talked of a set of Twin Souls that could manipulate heat. They caused the last recorded eruption of the volcano. It wiped out everything Jacobi and Adama had ever created and killed everyone as they slept. Those few that did survive fell in line out of fear. They all moved north and began again, under the rule of the new king and queen."

"So, the king and queen are some two-thousand-year-old, magical volcano babies, and we are going to take them down. Should be easy," I said with satirical spit.

Sylvie laughed. "Nothing worth doing is ever easy," she said.

"Do you think that the prophecy is about me, Sylvie?" I had to admit, I understood the connections even if it was reaching.

"Honestly, I had no idea what the prophecy meant until we turned up to save you, and then it all made sense to me, like the final piece of a puzzle. I think Colm was meant to find me so that I could start this rebellion. I don't think it was a coincidence that you were the first person we saved."

"I'm not a fighter, Sylvie." I really wasn't. I wasn't strong like her.

"I think Greer's balls would disagree." She burst out laughing, lightening the tone once more. The seriousness of our discussion had felt heavy, and I appreciated her uplifting humour.

"I don't think I could kill someone, though," I confessed. Just the thought of it would have me hyperventilating.

"You might not have to be the one to do it. You might just be the key to us taking him down. Maybe it's an idea that you think of, or perhaps you're the catalyst that triggers a whole load of events that brings about the change we all so desperately need," she suggested.

"But what if it's not any of those things, and I do have to kill the king?"

She stared at me for a moment, like she was searching for the answer within me.

"Well, then I think we had better teach you how to use a sword," she laughed.

-18-

"I wonder what's taking them so long," I asked Sylvie.

We finished our food a while ago, in between talking about Jacobi and Adama, the king, and Twin Souls. The bread and meat would be dry and cold now. Perhaps they stopped to eat with the other rebels before making their way back.

Suddenly, Sylvie perked up. She made their call into the air. Some moments passed, but no one replied.

"Hood. Up."

She didn't raise her voice, but her words were clipped. I sensed the urgency in her command and did it right away. I watched as she glanced around camp, mentally taking note of our surroundings.

"Follow my lead."

I didn't need to ask what was wrong. Her senses were clearly sharper than mine; she could detect that someone—or something—was approaching. I thought of Nathaniel. It wasn't that I didn't trust Sylvie to protect me; he obviously did, otherwise he wouldn't have left us alone, unless he didn't expect danger to come calling.

My heart rate started to pick up pace. What if something were to happen to us? What if we were gone when they returned? Sylvie noticed my hands fidgeting and placed a soft grip on top. Her hand enveloped both of mine, and I felt a calming energy sink into my skin.

Sticks snapped under heavy footfall and voices grew louder as they neared our concealed camp. They weren't trying to be discreet, which told me they didn't know we would be here.

"Do you smell smoke?" A gravelly voice asked.

"Yeah, I do, as it happens," someone replied.

A chorus of sniffing. They were close.

"Trent, over here, it's definitely stronger here."

Sylvie grimaced. We had cooked our food over the fire and left it burning whilst we conversed. She had doused it when she had caught the first telling of company.

"Come out, come out, wherever you are," someone teased.

Laughter reverberated around us.

"Shut up, idiots. You're supposed to be soldiers, not petulant children." An authoritative voice boomed at them.

The laughter ceased immediately. We sat stone still. The tension in my body was an ache turning my muscles to stone. I wished, prayed that they would pass by without detecting us.

My prayers did not reach the gods.

I counted seven.

They had pushed through the thick, foliage wall concealing our camp, one by one. Sylvie didn't react, and I tried my best to mirror her image of calm despite the trepidation rumbling around my stomach.

They were all dressed in that black attire that I had come to be familiar with. Kingsman issue; fitted trousers, black combat boots, black button-up shirt, and heavy woollen cloaks. I noticed that none of their cloaks were adorned with a special hem. The thought pleased me momentarily.

It was immediately apparent who the leader was. He carried himself with an authority the others did not have. His jet-black hair swooped back, beady eyes and a hooked nose made him look harsh.

I spotted the fools—one large, one skinny, scruffier than the rest. I found myself comparing these men to Nathaniel for reasons I couldn't grasp. None of them carried themselves like him. He was exquisite, an example of a real man. He stood tall, broad shoulders back, and walked with purpose. He exuded strength and capability. He was caring and polite. I thought about the way he would ask permission before touching me, even non-verbally, he would linger for a moment or two to give me time to decline. He would look at you with a confidence that made you feel safe and comfortable in his presence and that was a gift in itself. He could command any room but also gave others the opportunity to lead. His demeanour oozed integrity and respect. He was calm and considerate. His eyes showed depth, and his smile, that smile, so subtle but so radiant. He would steal my attention from any of these men with ease. There was no comparison.

The leader, Trent perhaps, paced around our camp. He looked under the shelter, using his sword to peel back the canvas, as if to intimidate us.

Long sword, short penis, message received.

He rummaged through our packs and then picked up the meat we had saved for Colm and Nathaniel. He sniffed it first, then began to tear pieces off and put them in his mouth.

Sylvie shot up.

"Put that down!" She ordered.

"No. I don't think I will." His tone full of nonchalance.

"You see, I've been inconvenienced with the task of searching for a fugitive in this very forest. You wouldn't have seen her, would you? Red hair, untwinned and vulnerable." He put on a sympathetic tone with those words, as if I were a damsel and he, a chivalrous knight. "We just want to return her safely so she can face the consequences of evading the plan of the gods and put it right."

I fidgeted nervously with my hood at the mention of my hair colour. The leader noticed. His eyes trailed over the hem, and I saw recognition flash across his features.

"I have no idea what you're talking about," Sylvie snapped, bringing his conspicuous glare back to her. "Put. It. Down."

He threw the meat back into the pan and dusted the remnants from his hands before taking a handkerchief from inside his cloak and wiping his mouth and fingers with it. I noticed Tweedle Dee and Tweedle Dum salivating at the leftovers.

"Perhaps you may be aware of a group of rebels—traitors. It is said they are assisting the fugitive. The king calls for their heads."

He was playing with us. I could feel it. I could see it in the way he looked unbothered by the encounter. He was quietly confident that he had two of the people he was looking for, and he clearly thought he had got us banged to rights.

Sylvie surveyed the camp like she had a plan to act, like we had definitely been rumbled, and she was looking for a way out. Besides the three men in front of us, the other four had fanned out around us. There was nowhere to run. I quietly pleaded with anyone and anything for the others to return. I could see no way we would get through this. Not if they were to remove my hood. They were toying with us. I knew they were. Their glances were too knowing, like an inside joke that they knew the punchline of before he had finished delivering the run-up or like déjà vu, they'd already seen how this one played out.

Suddenly two men grabbed Sylvie from behind. My body reacted on instinct. I reached for her. She shook her head. I stopped in my tracks, body trembling.

Nathaniel, please. I silently begged.

With a man holding each of Sylvie's arms, their leader pushed himself up against her backside, sucking air through his teeth.

"Do you take me for a fool, Sylvie?" He ripped off her hood, revealing her platinum hair.

She struggled as he grabbed a handful of it and ripped her head back to mutter in her ear. "I've dreamt of this moment."

Sneering and chuckling sounded from the mouths of his minions. Two more men approached her and ripped at her clothes. All that remained was her satin camisole vest and knickers. The outlines of her nipples were visible, and I felt the urge to cover her body with my own. The leader reached an arm from behind her and grabbed her breast. His knuckles whitened as he squeezed hard. Sylvie grimaced. My glare widened and I struggled to contain myself, and she read my intentions. She eyed me and gave me a subtle shake of her head, but I could not stand by and let this to happen. I thought of Colm, and the guilt that followed him like a shadow for not intervening with his father. I did the only thing I could think of. I tore down my own hood and unhooked the makeshift hair tie Nathaniel had fastened there. I saw the disappointment in her face, like I'd let her down, foiled her plan. If being the victim of sexual assault was part of her scheme, then I didn't care that I'd ruined it.

Attention turned to me, just like I had wanted. The pervert promptly let go of Sylvie and set his sight on something else.

Me.

He trampled straight through the simmering fire upsetting embers with each tread, his glare fixed on me.

"There she is," he started. "I wondered how far you'd let me go."

That display was all for my attention? I felt sick. I should've revealed myself long before they tore at her clothes like vultures picking at a carcass.

"You're disgusting," I spat at his face.

"Ooh, I love it when they've got a bit of fight in them."

I couldn't wait to knock the smarm from his face. I felt the urge to fight rise in me. I envisioned myself tearing away from the goons gripping my arms, and clawing at his face with my nails. I would gouge his eyes. I would bite his tongue clean from his mouth.

He drew back his hand and knocked my head sidewards with an open palm. A copper tang invaded my mouth. I laughed a wide, bloody grin as I straightened my neck, and I glowered at him. I wondered, did I look as mad as I felt?

My assaulter beckoned two more of his gang. They began to tear at me, the way they had torn at her only moments ago. But I did not make it easy. I thrashed and I screamed, and I told them they were going to die, and I burned them with my words and stabbed daggers in them with my eyes. Their fingers bruised, their nails scratched, but I refused to let them have their way easily. If I was going to go out now, I would sure as hell go out kicking and screaming.

-19-

The thing with men such as these—if men is what we should call them—is that their masculinity is so fragile that they prey on the weaker, using force in order to make themselves feel powerful and dominant. When they think with their pricks, like these arseholes are doing right now, they tend to miss other things going on. Like the sound of knuckles pounding flesh, and yells of pain from twisted appendages, and the cracking of bones in snapping necks.

Another flash of hot pain across my face and I was on the ground with his hand like a vice on my throat. I continued to laugh, because the funny thing was, he hadn't even noticed. He hadn't noticed when her 'damsel in distress' act faded, giving way to a stone-faced killer. He had been so focused on me, just like I had intended, that he didn't notice her overpower two of his men, skewering one in the gut and breaking the other one's neck. He didn't notice the looks on his men's face when the steel blade with floral etchings appeared in front of his neck and sliced across his throat. By the time he had realised it was far too late. I saw the split second of acknowledgement before the glimmering metal stole his life. Fluid spilled like a bloody waterfall from his throat, and I saw the beauty in his demise.

I looked at her, a brilliant warrior, ready to claim her next victim. It was like an immersive performance, and I was her audience. She danced around me, the bellowing, desperate yowls of pain from each man setting the harmonies for her singing blade as she chopped and sliced through all of them. Blood spotted her white skin and hair like a costume of polka dots. She twirled in the air with the grace of a ballerina, leaping and bounding over her fallen enemies. Her lack of clothing exposed her muscular physique. She was remarkable.

She landed with barely a sound as she dipped below the final soldier's blade on her knees, holding the hilt of her own blade with both hands and slashing his stomach. His body crumpled to the floor.

Applause erupted from behind me just like you would expect from the audience after the final act. Alarmed by the abrupt din, I broke from my trance. She had mesmerised me.

Sylvie bowed to whistles and cheers with a wide grin, the opposite of modest. Colm bounded toward her and took her in his arms and dipped her back like they do in a ballroom dance and claimed her blood splattered mouth. I finally tore my eyes away from them to find Nathaniel holding a severed head in his hands next to, who I assume, to be Thoran or Tuck with a strong arm locked around a strangled man. His victim's face like a ripened tomato.

"Bravo, that was a show." Alissa, I deciphered. Her face full of awe and not like she had just witnessed the most brutal and bloodthirsty performance. She was ruggedly pretty. Her raven hair was cropped but long at the back and gathered round her face like feathers. Her face and hands were marked with pale patches, like a beautiful pattern of clouds across her skin. I'd never seen skin like that before. Her eyebrows were dark and thick above huge hazel eyes fanned by dark lashes. She was striking.

"Are you alright?" Nathaniel entered my eyeline, obscuring my view of Alissa. His bottom lip was swollen, and he had a cut under his left eye. Worry struck like a blow to my chest. "You're bleeding," he said with concern etched on his features.

"So are you," I pointed out. My concern dissipated when he brought a partially eaten apple to his lips, taking another bite, leaving a smear of blood on the pale flesh of the fruit. I grimaced at it.

"How can you eat right now? You still have blood on your hands." I winced.

"That's the thing about having to kill others when you have a conscience. There's always blood on my hands, even when I've washed them."

"Looks to me like you're rather enjoying it," I retorted.

"Apples? Love them," he teased. I rolled my eyes. He tossed the apple core and unhooked his canteen from his belt using the liquid to dampen his handkerchief.

"Don't get me wrong, dear Rose, I do not enjoy killing. I kill out of necessity. I kill because I have to, not because I want to. I kill to protect those I love, which is a job I take very seriously." His eye contact did not falter.

He brought the damp cloth to my face, and I recoiled for a moment before I let him continue. The coolness soothed the heat on my cheek from

Trent's assault. I flinched, and he lightened the pressure. His eyes captured mine, ensnaring my gaze. I placed a hand on his to stop him dabbing my cheek, as if the motion was distracting me from falling into the deep inky pools. I was beyond relieved that he was here and in one piece but why in my time of need was it only him that filled my mind. The moment those monsters invaded our camp I wanted Nathaniel. When that harsh faced prick assaulted Sylvie I didn't want Nathaniel to think bad of me for not stepping in. When they began ripping at my clothes, I wondered what kind of feelings it would stir up in him. And when I thought, just before Sylvie had unmasked herself and shown her hand, that maybe we might not make it, I felt utter loss at the fact that I might not get to see him again.

He smiled at me, drawing my attention to his lips, and I impulsively went in for the kiss. He hissed at the contact.

"I'm sorry," I panicked. "What happened to you?" I asked.

But no sooner had I asked than he pulled me to his lips and kissed me hard.

"Never stop kissing me. Even when it hurts." He held me up with his gaze and it felt like the only thing keeping me standing.

"We had a run-in with more of these lot," he waved his hand at the bodies. "Once we dealt with them and reached the others, we made our way back here to find more of them just outside the shrubs there."

"That's them?" I pointed at the severed head next to the limp pile of a man.

"Yes," Nathaniel responded deferentially. He was not proud of his work. As he had said, he did what had to be done.

"How did Sylvie manage to kill them all?" I asked him. I couldn't comprehend it. She had made them look like nothing more than rag dolls.

"These soldiers, although trained, are unmated. None of them have bonded with their Twin Souls," he explained.

"So, she could do all of that just because she married Colm?" I said, matter-of-factly.

Nathaniel laughed at the simplicity of my summary. "Pretty much. Together they're doubly strong, and she is also trained. It definitely gives her an edge."

"So, she could beat you then?"

Nathaniel laughed so hard his shoulders shook. "Yes, but we don't mention that," he grinned.

"Is every mated pair that strong?" He had guided me to sit on a patch of earth not littered with broken bodies. Thoran and Colm had one man by the legs and underarms and carried him out of camp. Tuck dragged one by the hands, his boots leaving streaks in the dirt. By listening to them calling to one another, I'd learnt that Tuck was the one with the beard and no hair, and Thoran was the one with hair and no beard, which made me chuckle for some reason. Sylvie and Alissa were animated in conversation in the corner like a couple of long-distance friends that hadn't seen each other for a while.

"Stronger than those that are not mated, although some unmated soldiers are able to put up a good fight due to training and experience. I've battled mated and won multiple times, actually," he paused, and where I thought I'd see smugness on his face, I didn't. He was not gloating; he was just stating a fact. "Different couples have different abilities, and some don't have any at all."

"What about the king?" I saw a flash of trepidation before he caught it.

"He has many; that's why he's king."

Anxiety started to spread like a forest fire, and what little confidence had started to sprout died. I had begun to think that I might have it in me to at least give it a go. Be the girl in the prophecy, but I realised I did not know my enemy at all.

"He may be powerful, but he is one; we are many." It was almost like he heard my doubts unwind and was trying to keep me from unravelling. "It's not going to be easy, but nothing worth doing ever is."

I smiled at those words. I had heard them before; Sylvie had said the same thing. I wondered if it was a mantra that they all lived by.

I liked it.

Nothing worth doing is ever easy.

-20-

The flagon of pungent amber liquid found its way into my hand again on its third trip around the circle. The 'nectar,' as Tuck called it, caused a more-than-unpleasant burn in my oesophagus, which was displeasing to begin with, but by the third glug, my blood was a flowing warmth travelling around my body, and my throat had numbed to the sting.

"…and that's the reason why Tuck won't come to Brigsbane anymore."

Bellyfuls of laughter bounced around the camp. Thoran playfully spanked Tuck's arse nearly toppling him as he leaned forward for a piece of cheese before laying it on a lump of bread and stuffing it into his mouth in a oner. His action prompted more spirited kerfuffle.

"That's what he thinks. I'm just using it as an excuse because I'm too lazy to travel, am I right, Lis?" Tuck argued.

"I'll say," Lis replied. I caught her eye. "So, Rose, is it?"

"Yes," I replied.

"What's your story then?"

The laughter ceased and a quietness befell the camp and suddenly all eyes were on me.

Where do I even start? "Well, I...er..."

"You don't have to," Nathaniel interjected, attempting to throw me a lifebuoy to save me from my obvious drowning.

"No, it's okay," I insisted, more to convince myself than him.

Maybe it was the alcohol or the fact that we were gathered around a campfire—the perfect venue for storytelling. I told the group about the village and sacrifice ceremonies under the Crimson Moon, which they already knew since that had been the catalyst to grow a rebellion. I mentioned my mother and father and what my general day-to-day entailed. Boring stuff, probably, in comparison to what they do. I told them about the man that I had trusted, our leader and his son, Greer. I noticed a look of distaste on Nathaniel's face at the mention although he had just taken a rather large glug of the amber spirit.

"Ugh. Men," Lis complained.

"Right?!" Sylvie agreed. I'm sure her input was merely out of solidarity. It's plain to see that in Colm's eyes Sylvie was his queen.

There were murmurs of protest around the camp from our male counterparts.

"Well, if the shoe fits," Lis joked.

"We are not talking about you perfect princesses when we say 'men,' just the bad ones, and there are many bad ones." Sylvie explained.

"Oh yes," Lis agreed.

"Well, at least there are a few less today than there were yesterday." The words tumbled from my mouth before I'd had a chance to really think about them. How insensitive of me. Those men had belonged to people. They were someone's brothers, someone's sons. Everyone went quiet once more and stared at me, stunned and slack jawed. The skin of my cheeks started to tingle hot, and I told myself it was from the heat of the campfire, not embarrassment.

Suddenly, heads were thrown back and hands gripped bellies as they all burst into laughter.

"Savage, Red!" Colm laughed. A peculiar compliment, but I'll take it. I was sure I still turned pinker.

"I have an idea." Lis jumped to her feet. "We should train you."

"Yes," Sylvie leapt up too, clapping her hands like a seal.

"Ladies, don't you think we've had enough fighting for one day?" Colm suggested.

"Speak for yourself," Sylvie quipped.

We were like a pack of hyenas, giggling with each other as they tried and failed to teach me how to apprehend someone with their arm behind their back. They showed me how to get out of a chokehold, and then Thoran stepped in and demonstrated on Lis how to flip someone onto their back. They definitely seemed to enjoy it more than they should, especially when they reversed the roles and Lis flattened Thoran. Tuck clapped enthusiastically, his laughter booming. I attempted to try it with Sylvie, but she would not budge.

"It's hardly a fair match, is it, Sylv? You're not just a little village girl anymore." Colm winked at her.

"She can do it with me then," 'Lis' stepped forward with a coquettish persona.

"I think she should do it to Nathaniel," Thoran jibed.

"Oh, I like that idea," Tuck joined in. The three of them like a group of naughty children.

"Come on, guys, don't embarrass them," Sylvie said.

"No. I agree. Come and show me what you've got." I was still me but with a dash of coquette pinched from Lis, and a splash of liquid courage from the nectar.

Nathaniels pupils grew larger and swallowed the colour, and his nostrils flared before he rose from his spot. "I won't go easy on you," he taunted, a picture of confidence but the bob in his throat gave him away.

"Lucky for you, I love a bit of foreplay." I surprised myself with that, chuckling nervously to try to cover the embarrassment that came from my mouth betraying me by blurting my intrusive thoughts. I found myself aroused by my own words. His eyes darkened.

We circled one another, grappling for grip on anything we could get a hold of. Our smiles were playful, but I meant business. I was determined to best him. I faked a move, and he stepped back. Everyone laughed at him for falling for my ruse. We continued to circle in prowling steps. I went for him again, but this time, in his determination not to be fooled twice, he didn't step back. I grabbed his arm, placed my backside against his hip, squatted, and leaned forward, just like they showed me, while jolting his arm. I pulled with all my might and lifted him from the ground…for all of a split second.

"Ohhhh, she nearly did it!" They all squealed and leapt about excitedly.

"Nice one, Red!" Colm slapped me on the back.

"Great form." Tuck shook my shoulder.

Nathaniel chuckled whilst congratulating me with a somewhat patronising hair ruffle that caused a scowl to form on my face.

"Let's go again," I panted.

He seemed excited for us to go another round.

We began our dance again, grasping for purchase. I watched the way he moved, his muscles rippling under his shirt. His shoulders were so broad, housing all of his masculine strength. His stare was so intensely hot I could feel myself melting under it. He was so handsome; it was all I could think about. He was like a lavabee, dazzling me with his luminous rings so I would get close enough for him to sting me. And it worked. He managed to hook his fingers around my wrist and twist my arm behind my back. I sucked in a breath at the pain as the muscles in my arm stretched to their limit. His torso was pressed tightly to my back, and his cedar scent assaulted my senses.

"Boo. No fun," Thoran shouted. "We back the underdog."

I glanced over my shoulder at Nathaniel and smirked like this was nothing. His eyes were greedy.

"You like it rough then?" He taunted.

"I've had it rougher," I countered and twisted out of his grip as the words landed like a weapon, a club perhaps.

I wasted no time as I leapt in the air and climbed up his back like a tree. I wrapped my legs around his waist and placed my left hand on the back of his head, wrapping my right arm around his throat, and tucking my right hand into the bend of my left arm, just like the girls had shown me, and I held on for dear life. Nathaniel stumbled one way and then another while clawing at my arm which only challenged me to tighten my grip. One more sway to the right before he tapped my arm three times in defeat. I dropped from his back landing with sure feet on the ground. He bent at the waist bracing his hands on his knees and panted for breath.

"Yes!" I celebrated, pumping my fists in the air.

"She did it!" Tuck and Thoran high-fived, and Lis and Sylvie jumped on the spot like proud parents seeing their child win the egg and spoon race on sports day. Clapping and congratulations exploded from our audience, but I couldn't look away from him. Nathaniel straightened, rubbing his throat. His fingers trailed over small purple lines, and my sense of achievement died like throwing a bucket of water on a fire.

"Nathaniel?" Gone was the fierce combatant, and now all I felt was guilt for causing him pain. I reached my hand out to him, and he took it gently in his before ripping me forward and straight over his shoulder, tumbling onto my back in the dirt. He landed on top of me, bracing himself with his elbows so as not to crush me.

"Never let your guard down," he teased. The impact had stolen the air from my lungs, but if it hadn't, him being above me like this would have. I felt my core clench and thought of his face hovering above me in a different scenario. He lowered his lips slowly until they were hovering just above mine. "And never feel guilty."

He playfully pecked my forehead before pushing himself back to his feet and bowing his victory to a booing and hissing crowd.

"When everything around me starts spinning, that's usually the cue to go to bed," Lis slurred.

"Well, I should have gone to bed ages ago then," Tuck hiccupped.

"Come on, you two," Thoran sighed and took each of them by the waist, leading them to their shelter. "I'll take the first shift if you want to snooze for a bit, Nathaniel."

"Thanks," Nathaniel responded.

The fire was crackling lightly under a mound of blackened kindling. I was sitting close enough to still feel the heat, but it would soon be cold. I watched the flames flicker, and my eyes grew hot and my eyelids heavy.

"What's the plan tomorrow?" I already knew the plan. I had sat quietly earlier while they discussed it, but it was just the two of us now, and I had to say something to avoid the awkward silence.

"Well, we have more walking to do, which I know you love," he chortled. "And then we should reach the Deadlands before nightfall."

Sylvie and Colm had fallen asleep at the base of an oak. Nathaniel took a blanket and draped it over the pair. "Bet they'll wake up sore tomorrow," he said.

"Quite romantic, though," I mumbled while watching them dreamily. I hadn't meant to say it out loud. I definitely had said it, though. I could feel his eyes on me, but I refused to look. "Night then."

I made for my tent. I wanted so badly to invite him inside for nothing other than company—and maybe I'd let him hold me—but I just wasn't plucky enough. I thought the alcohol would provide me with a false sense of confidence, but it was quite the opposite. I was full of myself when we were fighting earlier. I said things that I never would have said before. I knew that everything that was happening was changing me, and I was starting to feel brave, but just not brave enough to ask this beautiful man to stay with me.

-21-

We were all a lot less noisy and a lot less excitable this morning. I could hear hushed voices, marred with croakiness caused by our enthused chatter and merriment. I would bet there were one or two faces of regret, and I was sure I could hear someone vomiting out there.

I hadn't left my tent yet. At least not until I no longer heard that baulking noise. I was a bit of a contagious vomiter. You know, like when you see someone yawning, it sets you off. Well, when I hear, see, or smell someone vomiting, nine times out of ten, you can bet I will be next in line.

I'd never drunk that type of alcohol before. Liquor like that was only reserved for the men of our village. Sexist, I know. That's something that I've found endearing about my new friends. Yes, they might make jokes, but the respect the men have for their women is inspiring. They don't see them as inferior or incapable. I admired it.

I struggled against the downward pull of gravity and gradually hauled myself up. I groaned as the world spun around me. It had definitely slowed down in comparison to the speed at which it had spun as I'd tried to go to sleep. Tried, being the operative word. I hadn't quite realised how drunk I was until I kissed Nathaniel's cheek before making my way into my shelter for the night. I lay there battling with myself—the devil on one shoulder urging me to invite him in so he could have his way with me, the angel on my other shoulder telling me that good things come to those who wait, and that I should have patience, now was not the right time. There'd been a buzzing between my legs calling to me like a siren, coaxing my fingers to dip into the moisture that pooled there when he'd flipped me on my back. If I wasn't going to be brave enough to invite him in, I could at least pretend he was touching me. My mind replayed the image of him hovering above me in slow motion. I had scorned myself for my inappropriate thoughts. There had only been a slither of canvas separating me from the others.

After miles and miles of trees for days and days, it felt strange to no longer see it ahead of me. The gaps between trunks had become wider as the wood thinned out to give way to the Deadlands. We were almost there. Up ahead, I could just about make out the dark grey terrain, our destination, and it looked bleak to say the least.

"Do we really have to go through there?" I voiced timidly.

"Unfortunately, the supply route will be swarming with soldiers, and if we go around it, it could take weeks," Thoran explained.

Nathaniel rubbed his hands over the beginnings of a beard. He caught me staring.

"What?" he asked.

"Nothing," I stuttered, shaking my head guiltily.

He rubbed over his stubble again, whilst staring me down, challenging me to look away, and it did something to me. I wondered what it would feel like on the sensitive skin of my inner thighs. My eyes widened in shock at my inner monologue. Who was she? Sometimes, I felt like she was her own person, or maybe she was a bolder version of me. Maybe she could teach me a thing or two. I wondered if it was her talking when I'd flirted with Nathaniel during our 'training' under the influence yesterday. If she wanted him, she would have to fight me for him.

Nathaniel was looking at me with intrigue mixed with delight. I started to panic. Had I said that shit out loud?

"Sexy, isn't it?" Colm cut in, saving me from my inner turmoil. I stuttered, my thoughts left me flustered, and I felt as though they could both read me like an open book.

A memory came to the forefront of my mind. I remembered leaving a fantasy-romance novel open on the kitchen table once. The winged warrior had just told the maiden to 'hold onto the headboard,' and I felt the immediate need to clear away my plate and take the story somewhere private, when my dad walked over, picked up the book, and said, "Hey, what are you reading?" His eyes danced over the page for seconds before a state of, shall we say, trauma, took over his whole body. He placed the book down, slowly, then walked away in complete silence. That. That was what was happening right now.

"I keep telling him to leave it, but he insists on being clean-shaven," Colm continued.

"It gets itchy, and it ages me at least a decade, which you wouldn't understand. A decade is nothing to you."

They both laughed.

"Well, I think it makes you look rough and rugged, just how I like them," Thoran tugged Tuck's beard to prove his point.

"I like it," I admitted. Why did I say that? And it such a sultry way.

"Noted," he grinned widely, and my heart tripped over itself.

My head throbbed with every beat of my feet on the ground. I heaved the fresh air into my lungs greedily like it was the tonic to this hangover. I glanced around at the place that had become my new home as of late. I'd never spent time anywhere outside of Sandy, and to think that there was a huge world out there waiting for me. These woods were like a stopgap, limbo, a waiting room on a platform awaiting transport to my next destination. I was nervousness, apprehension, and tension; excitement, wonder, and expectation all rolled into one.

I rubbed my clammy palms on the skirt of my frayed dress and for a moment, all I could feel was a sort of guilt, like I'd let my parents down. The hem was frayed lace, tickling my knees, the once cream fabric a mix of all the shades of the forest. A new addition, a great big green-brown smudge on my back, where Nathaniel had quite literally swept me off my feet.

The impact had been hard, and I was dazed for a moment, but when my eyes had caught up with me, the view was exquisite. When my lungs remembered their duty, oxygen infused with the scent of him had flooded me. It was intoxicating, and if I hadn't already been drunk, I would have been inebriated on lust from my attraction to him. Two lines had appeared between his brows, like I was an equation he was trying to solve. His breathing was ragged and smelled of nectar and need. I wondered, in his dreams of me, had he ever envisioned me under him like that? I thought for a split second of the only man to ever lie with me in that way, and I realised that what I felt before was nothing in comparison to whatever the feeling was whilst pinned under Nathaniel. It was raw and intrinsic.

With Greer, whatever was lacking, I made up for. I read my novels and tried my hardest to mimic the love story. Half the time I pretended he was just like the beaus from the books, rewarding him for the behaviours of my book boyfriends. Whatever he didn't give me, I found in them.

The strain of Nathaniel supporting his weight above me painted a sternness on his face, or was it restraint I saw? In the hard lines and pensive expression, I saw longing. His doe eyes unblinking as he gazed into my soul. Nothing else existed around us while he looked at me like that. I had become all too aware of the fabric between us and cursed its existence. I wanted to feel his skin on mine, but even that wouldn't have been enough. But just before he fell too far, he caught himself, and I was disappointed because I was ready to fall.

"We should probably wait here until nightfall," Tuck suggested. Lis was linking arms with him, resting her head on his shoulder. I noticed he had tilted that side lower just so she could reach, and I smiled at his gesture.

They had decided that entering the Deadlands under the cover of darkness was probably best. We would keep together sneaking from boulder to boulder. We would walk through the night in silence, communicating with hand gestures only. The terrain was unpredictable. None of us had set foot here before and literally were stepping into the unknown.

I joined Nathaniel on a fallen tree. I had to attempt to seat myself three times before I managed to stay put. The trunk was much taller than I had anticipated. Nathaniel chuckled at me and my cheeks blushed.

Could have given me a hand," I joked to redirect him from my discomposure, nudging him lightly with my elbow.

"I knew you could do it," he replied.

His belief in me, even for something so small, the space that he allowed me to figure it out, gave me a warm fuzzy feeling, and I rested my head against his shoulder, just like I'd seen Lis do to Tuck. Part of me wanted to see how he'd react.

I smiled so widely when he lifted his arm and scooped me closer, tucking me into his side. I didn't nearly have enough sleep last night. Maybe I should nap here in the safety of his embrace while we wait for nightfall.

-22-

It was the dead of night, the only light coming from the sliver of a crescent moon. According to the others, these were perfect conditions to move stealthily through the shadow's unseen.

Nathaniel went over the plan once more and warned us—although I felt it was more for my benefit— to keep close, keep quiet, and be alert. I would be between him and Sylvie, and although I had definitely developed a shudder the closer we got to 'go time,' I couldn't have been safer than between the two of them.

Nathaniel's fingers teased my clenched fist open and slowly slipped between mine. I hadn't even noticed my anxious, balled up hands at my side, but that one gesture from him lessened my anxiety.

We had come across all sorts of creatures on our journey across the woods—luckily no Wild of the Woods, not that I believed it existed anymore—but something about this new terrain, a landscape that even my comrades hadn't ventured into, was giving me a really eerie feeling.

I glanced up at the man holding my hand, the faint silver light illuminated one side of his face, and I caught the glimmer in his eyes, and I could just fall into them. They were like deep lakes, the moon's light glittering on the surface, and just like watching rippling water, he brought me tranquillity.

"Lead the way, Mr. Navigator," Colm said to Thoran.

Thoran stepped forward out of the cover of the treeline and gestured with his hand signals that the rest of the group seemed to understand.

Behind him, an amber glow materialised in the air, like a lantern light, and I realised I hadn't asked what abilities my new friends possessed and what kind of power would enable someone to amass light from thin air.

The glow pulsated and I watched with fascination, before it unfurled and erupted, consuming Thoran in a ball of flames. The raging heat blasted through him until he was but cinders on the forest floor.

I heard a scream, or was that me? Or was it the shriek of many steel swords being drawn to attack the phantom amber blast?

"Stay here," Nathaniel ordered, as they all charged forward. Even if I had wanted to run there was no way I could have convinced my legs to obey. They trembled at what I had just witnessed, and the smell of charred flesh made me want to vomit.

Heads whipped from left to right as they scoured the darkness for the source of the fatal flame.

Just then, I heard an almighty yell. Tuck's screams bellowed as he was lifted into the air and tossed into the distance like he was nothing more than a mannequin from Mrs Cromer's haberdashery.

Ear piercing shrieks from both man and beast curdled my blood. My stomach clenched and a hand pressed firmly against my mouth prevented it from emptying its contents.

Blazes blasted and flesh ripped, as I watched from the sidelines, like I was watching a horror production at the theatre. What I would give for my friends to be actors, and for them to be wearing costumes and using props.

Every time the beasts would spit their flames, it illuminated the darkness, like lightning strikes, revealing the true horror that the shadows of night concealed.

I didn't know what to do, but I knew I couldn't let them die without trying to help. I couldn't live with myself if I abandoned them. If I could just get the injured and perhaps drag them back to the woods.

I stepped forward from the cover of trees and Nathaniel turned and spotted me instantly. A flash of flames illuminated our surroundings, his face was dark and glistening, and his eyes were wide with terror. His sword tip sparkled with moisture. He had certainly managed to slay at least one of the monsters.

"Rose, no!" he hollered, waving me back to the safety of the treeline, before a great, scaled beast with enormous wings swooped down and grabbed him by the head with its jagged jaws.

My knees could no longer carry my weight, and I dropped to the ground.

I watched as the beast took to the sky, and Nathaniel's headless body dropped to earth like a stone in front of me. A guttural cry surged from my core and ripped from my throat like the fire-breathing beast. This was my fault. I had distracted him. He told me to stay put and I didn't.

There was a shrill cry next to me as Sylvie stood over a lifeless Lis. Sylvie's face was bubbled and blistered down one side, glueing one eyelid closed. The beast swooped full circle above me and belted out a war cry saturated with victory. This was it. We had lost before the battle had begun.

-23-

"Keep low, and stick together," Nathaniel commanded the group after revisiting the plan once more. "We have no idea what's out there, so keep your eyes and ears open and be quiet." He emphasised the last two words.

"Yes, boss," Colm quipped. "Lead the way, Mr. Navigator."

Thoran stepped forward out of the cover of the treeline and gestured with his hand's commands that the rest of the group seemed to understand.

"Stop!" I screamed as an amber glow unfurled from the thin air behind Thoran.

I threw myself in front of him and pushed him back with all the strength I could gather. He stumbled backward to the ground as the flames swallowed me up. Scorching heat ripped around my sides. Nathaniel's eyes almost popped from his skull at the horror unfolding in front of him.

"Run!" He bellowed as he ducked low and darted right into the blaze and stole me from it.

He dragged us both to the ground to snuff out the flames that still burned on us. He spared no time as he rushed us in the direction of a nearby cave. I waited for the pain to kick in from the scorch that seared my body, but adrenaline was keeping it at bay. I tried not to panic. Tried not to think of the worst.

I matched Nathaniel's determined sprint as we entered the opening of a small cave, just skimming the top of my head. Nathaniel had to crouch low. He frantically swept my hair back from my face, checking every inch of my exposed skin.

"Why did you do that, Rose?" He was shaking my shoulders, his voice a mixture of concern and anger. His eyes filled with tears of frustration. Was he mad because I put myself in danger, or because I risked the prophecy after getting this far?

"I, I..." I wanted to tell him that I'd seen it already. I knew what was coming from the moment Colm told Thoran to lead the way. "I, I'm fine."

I was short with him, as I decided he was mad about the latter. He turned me on the spot and frantically inspected me for injuries, brushing gentle hands from my back around to my front.

"Thank the gods," he sighed as he scrubbed his face with his hands.

"What?" I asked.

"The cloak is fireproof, but I've never really had it tested by a fire-breathing monster!"

"What!?" I pushed his shoulder. "You couldn't have mentioned it earlier?"

I ran my hands up and down my back and around my sides to confirm it. I had been so scared that my clothing had melted into my skin and petrified that when my fight-or-flight mode had subsided, I would be in more pain than I could ever anticipate.

The air around me was a cacophony of metallic clashes and chaotic melee. Screams and screeches pierced my ears. Wings beat like a war drum, and fire ripped through the terrain.

"I have to go and help them."

I grabbed Nathaniel's sleeve, and my pleading eyes locked with his in silent protest. He can't leave me. I saw him die. "Stay here. I'll be back soon."

He left to join the fray, and my stomach swam with nerves. I remembered that I had distracted him in my premonition so I would stay put this time.

I dropped to a squat and wrapped my arms around my head, blocking the sounds of combat from penetrating my ears. I drew deep breaths, in and out, in and out, and the shuddering finally stopped.

Loose strands of hair whipped around my face in a gust of wind. Wind that smelled of ash and carrion. Wind that blanketed me with warmth but not in a comforting way.

A low grumble vibrated the atmosphere around me. I braved a glimpse over the cover of my forearms, and what I saw caused my windpipe to clench and my eyes to pop.

I thought Death would come to me disguised as cherry wine, the sweet liquid coating my throat and inducing a permanent sleep. Now Death stared at me with glowing orbs with narrow slits. It huffed putrid blasts of air from its nostrils and edged ever closer to me, bearing a mouth of ivory daggers. Death was utter darkness closing in on me, and I was powerless to it.

The shadowy beast ran its snout along my rattling jaw, sniffing my scent. Another low grumble caused a small squeak to slip from my mouth. My chest tightened as I locked eyes with my fate. The beast's jagged maw widened, and it roared a deafening shriek. I covered my ears as the sound penetrated them like hot pokers and I dropped to the ground, curling myself into a tight ball as saliva rained down on me.

Some shuffling, thudding, then thumping and I felt the cave around me open up.

I was alone again.

The beast had left, and judging by the fact the sounds of chaos were replaced by the sounds of many beating wings, it seemed the beasts had retreated.

Nathaniel found me lying right where the beast had left me, curled up in a foetal position on the dirt floor of the cave. He scooped me into muscled arms and held me close to his chest, and it was everything I hadn't known I'd needed.

"What happened?" He searched my face for answers.

"I thought I was going to die," I managed. I'd never been so terrified. I'd never felt so utterly helpless. Even in that aranimmanis' web, I had made peace with it.

He drew me close again.

I pulled away, wiped my tears, and straightened myself. "I'm fine," I sniffed. "I'm just so, so tired, and I miss my father."

Nathaniel had come back to me alone, and the realisation snapped me from the hold the beast had had on me.

"Where are they?" I asked, panicked.

Nathaniel walked us to the cave opening and raised his hands to his mouth and made the warbling call. Seconds later, a call came back, and then another.

"Lis is in the treeline over there." He pointed over to the trees from which we had emerged. "I'll go find the others. I want you to run straight to the trees, Rose. If Lis doesn't find you, then I will; just don't move from there. Do you hear me?" I nodded my reply. "I'll find you," he promised.

I believed him, and it gave me the courage to get to my destination. I reached the trees as quick as a flash, scanning between the trunks for any signs of Lis. I didn't see her anywhere, so I did exactly as Nathaniel said and stayed put. I stared into the pitch dark of the Deadlands, willing the others to materialise from the shadows.

Minutes felt like hours. The silence deafening. I could hear my heartbeat pounding in my chest.

Finally, six figures emerged moving ever closer, and fear turned to relief to see them all breathing and walking.

"Come any closer, and I'll cut her throat!"

A cold blade pressed against the soft skin of my neck.

Before anyone had time to react, the beast from the cave returned, landing with a thud in a cloud of dust, and inched towards me with heavy clawed feet and concertinaed clawed wings. Its long neck lurched from its muscular, sleek body. It kept those familiar yellow eyes on me, closing the gap between us stride by stride.

The sounds of swords unsheathing rang out behind the beast.

"Don't be so stupid," sneered the voice, as more creatures shuffled out of the black within inches of my friends.

The beast drew my scent into its nostrils deeply before eyeing whoever was behind me and bowing its head just once.

My apprehender released me and stepped before me.

Instinct kicked in, and I grabbed the scruff of her hooded robe. In my mind I threw my forehead at her nose for the audacity of holding me at the edge of a blade, but in reality, I was not so bold.

Nathaniel charged forward, and the beast shrieked a warning in his direction.

The woman in my grasp hadn't even broken a sweat. I suppose I would be fearless too if I had an army of dragons. Perhaps not an army in numbers, but more than an army in might.

"Fear not. I will not harm you," she nodded to her dragons. "But the wyverns might if they sense evil intent."

Wyverns. Not dragons then.

My eyes scanned the row of wyverns. They were all bigger than any creature I'd ever seen, some more so than others, all equally as terrifying. But there was something about the one that stood closest to me. That one was darker than night and yet stood out like the moon from the stars. It was the embodiment of all of your greatest fears, adorned with scales and claws and teeth. It was curious, and remarkable, and cunning. Its scales shimmered with an iridescence I could just make out in the barely there light. It hadn't taken its eyes off me since it bowed its head at the woman who had just held a knife to my throat.

Nathaniel stepped to my side. "Would you care to explain how it came to be that you were waiting for us?"

The woman replied with an aged crackle to her voice. "They sensed an old enemy…" she said, and I was sure her eyes darted to Colm who looked at her with a puzzled expression.

"So why did they stop?" Nathaniel probed.

"They could smell…*her*." The emphasis on 'her,' she looked at me, the apparent source of said smell.

I sniffed my arms, and although I hadn't bathed for a good few days, I wouldn't say I smelled particularly pungent.

"Well, I'm sorry I offended your sensitive little noses, but I haven't exactly had the opportunity to bathe," I spat at the wyverns, not too different from a bratty child.

To my surprise, a laugh left Nathaniel's lips.

I scowled at him with arms folded across my chest. Yes, quite the impression of a defiant youngling.

"Are you quite finished?" I spat at him this time.

This only elevated his laughter. Colm and Thoran joined in, with unsure tittering, but more out of camaraderie than anything else.

I couldn't help myself. Chuckles began to flow from me, and then the pair of us were staring at one another, laughing our built-up emotions away, like a pair of mad men. Gone was the fear and the sorrow. Gone was the anger and confusion. Well from us at least, confusion was exactly what was painted on the faces of the people standing around us. They were looking at us like someone had told a joke, and we were the only two to understand the punchline. Like, laughter was not the correct response to the situation at hand. They'd be right about that. The sounds of laughter slowly faded away, but our gazes remained. A small smile curved Nathaniel's lips, and I returned the same.

"Do they have names?" I heard Sylvie ask.

"I don't know," the woman replied. "It's somewhat a symbiotic relationship. I heal their wounds, and they let me live here."

Heal their wounds? There's something out there capable of causing damage to something as fierce as them?

"Wounds from what?" I asked her.

"Humans." Her eyes were wide with menace, like the word 'humans' was dirt in her mouth and somehow did not apply to her.

"Wyverns used to fly free. They had a huge territory, vast skies to spread their wings, and plenty of hunting grounds and mountains to nest in, but the king forced them here, in the Deadlands." She gestured around with long, slender hands. "He feared their power, so he locked them up. I know what it's like to be caged. We understand each other."

"You're Megarra," Colm spoke as if the penny just dropped.

"The one and only." She removed her hood, revealing long, frizzy, deep red hair.

My eyes widened. "Your hair!"

"Mmm. I didn't think I'd see another again either." She acknowledged my red locks.

"My mother had red hair," I replied. She breathed a short 'hmm' through her nose.

"Come, let's get you all cleaned up. My house isn't far. A few of you look like you might have some wounds that need tending to, and you all could do with a bath." She wrinkled her nose as if the sight of us disgusted her.

She was right. We were all covered in cuts and bruises, and blood crusted our skin and clothing. Although the others wore black, which soaked up the blood, Mother's ivory gown was changing colour by the day. I surveyed all the stains and pulled threads with sorrow. They had kept it pristine all of these years, and I had ruined it.

"Scram and fetch the water," she ordered the wyverns, "...please." She finished when they grunted their displeasure at the lack of manners with her request.

We arrived at a medium-sized wooden shack tucked under a large, craggy rock after about an hour walk. The wyverns were landing with huge barrels filled with steamy water.

"Baths," she said, gesturing to the three wooden containers in front of us.

"Is the water hot?" Lis asked, an air of excitement in her voice.

"Of course, it's heated by wyvern," she told us, as if all water was heated that way.

"We'll let you ladies wash first," Colm offered, and I could have kissed him right there and then.

I was beyond desperate to wash my body and my hair, and I didn't care that it was outside in a barrel, in front of two other women I barely knew and a horde of fire-breathing beasts.

The three of us immediately began disrobing.

"Goodness, girls, care for some privacy?" Colm laughed and ushered the others inside.

I spotted Tuck lingering in the door frame poking his head out to sneak a peek. I cupped the water in my palm and splashed it towards him. He chuckled and lunged under the threshold.

Megarra returned from the house with a bundle of towels, and a bar of soap each.

I submerged my aching body slowly into the warm liquid. It was heavenly, and it immediately began to soothe me of all the trials we had endured.

The night air nipped at my exposed shoulders, and as though it read my mind, the darkest of the beasts spat a spark at a collection of logs surrounded by a circle of stones, instantly igniting them. I smiled at it with appreciation. It may have been delirium, but I was certain it smiled back at me.

Sylvie let out a big sigh, "This feels so good."

"Doesn't it?" Lis agreed. "I thought I'd caught a tan, but it's just dirt."

She spoke with mock disgust, then giggled as Sylvie flicked water at her with a teasing "urgh."

"How you doing over there?" Sylvie asked me.

"I'm good."

My reply was short, but I really was good. I couldn't think of anything else, but the sensation of the warm water caressing my skin and the soap cleaning away the muck so my pores could breathe again. I felt calm and serene, like I was bathing in a mug of chamomile.

"So, Nathaniel, huh?" Lis started awkwardly. "You guys have a thing?"

Well, I was feeling calm and serene.

"No," I blurted a little too quickly, rousing her suspicion further.

Sylvie's glare widened as she avoided eye contact with me. They'd definitely spoken about us.

"Oh yeah," Lis giggled. "He is rather dreamy, don't you agree, Sylvie?"

"Not my type," she replied.

"Ah, you prefer blonds."

They both giggled.

"I prefer Colm," she corrected. "He's the only man I see."

Lis mocked vomiting noises, setting them both into fits of giggles. It was contagious. I couldn't help but join in.

They both stopped laughing at the sound that slipped from my mouth.

We all exchanged glances.

I felt unsure, like I was maybe not part of the group enough to join in with their jokes. I'd never had a group of girlfriends before. I wasn't sure of the etiquette.

Seconds later, we were all cackling like witches together, quite the coven.

"I like you, Rose," Lis told me.

"I like you too, Lis."

-24-

Wrapped in various blankets and shawls, we sat— some of us at the wooden table in the centre of the kitchen and others on a sofa and a rocking chair in the lounge area of her home—and gulped down bowls of broth Megarra had heated for us.

"So, this is where you've been hiding," Colm concluded.

Megarra scoffed. "What I wonder is why the king's son is in my home with his band of not-so-merry misfits."

"Oh, Meg, you always did make me laugh," he replied playfully.

She glared at him, prompting cackles from them both.

Megarra's skin was white as snow, apart from the deep pink scar that ran from her ear, across her cheek, and zigzagged over her eyelid. Her eye on the scarred side was milky like an opal, unlike the other that glimmered like an emerald. Lines creased her forehead and eyes, suggesting a life spent scowling more often than a smiling. Her frizzy strands were thin, silver highlights shimmered through the dull red.

"I'm glad to see that your scrawny self has grown into a strapping young man, Colm, and I assume that, unlike your father, your moral compass still works?"

"You flatter me, Megarra," he flirted. "What's it been, fifteen years?"

"More or less."

She looked down at her bowl and lost herself in the swirling pattern the grease made on top of the thin liquid. The crew raised a collective brow and shot glances at one another.

"Megarra worked for my father for many years, before I was even a thought," Colm explained from the arm of a chair. He was perched at Sylvie's side while she lay her head against him.

Surprised eyes shot to the older lady.

"You can put your eyes back in your heads. I think it's very clear that the king and I are no longer acquainted. In fact, the king thinks me dead, so if you'd be so kind, I'd like to keep it that way."

Megarra held us all prisoner at her words. A young witch with the power of foresight. It had plagued her in her younger years, so much so that she was unable to separate her visions from reality, so she was imprisoned in her family home for her own good.

Her father was an aide to the king and sought help when Megarra had started to become unmanageable. The king got word and offered Megarra's father a lifeline. The king had access to the best healers, tutors and nannies. He promised the girl would have a better quality of life in the castle. And she did. Megarra thrived, and the king was instrumental in her improvement. She would share her visions with him, and he would reward her with a comfortable lifestyle, not to mention friendship with the most desirable man in the kingdom.

This did not please the queen. The king's affections towards Megarra were somewhat paternal at the beginning, but she aged a lot faster than the king and queen. Soon forty years had passed, and he had barely aged a decade.

Over almost half a century, Megarra's knowledge had helped the king achieve great things, but it was her own research, her own discovery, that would lead to her demise. Megarra had discovered that she could act as a conduit. She could be used as a vessel to syphon power from one body to another. The king used her to harvest powers from many unwilling subjects, his own people, even from his own daughter. This brought the king and Megarra even closer. The queen started to suspect infidelity, although her suspicions were thus far incorrect.

One day, the king called Megarra to his chamber to prove to his hiding wife that the relationship between Megarra and himself was purely platonic, but little did he know, Megarra harboured deep affection for the king, on the basis that he had saved her and had given her a life most people could only dream of. He had called her extraordinary; he had encouraged her; he had saved her from a life of madness, imprisoned in her own mind.

His attentions flattered Megarra, and when he guided her to his bed, she followed. When he placed her gently on the edge and ran soft fingers along her jaw, her lips parted for him in a sharp intake of breath. She gazed longingly at him, and they knew that she was at his whim.

The queen ambushed Megarra from behind the heavy drapes of the four-poster bed. The king pinned Megarra to the mattress, his face creased with disgust, but his eyes showed regret. She knew deep down that he was fond of her.

The queen slashed her blade with fury, slicing the flesh of Megarra's face.

The queen was hysterical. She could not believe that her jealous and rage had led her to be so barbaric. Her hands were quivering, a glistening scarlet.

The king soothed his queen.

How had Megarra not seen this? She had been immobilised the minute she entered his chamber. She had not suspected a thing. No gut feeling, no intuition.

The king beckoned his wife. She sat beside Megarra, who still did not move, despite the white-hot pain searing the gaping wound on her face. Her vision was limited, and she could feel the warm blood seeping down her throat.

The king told the queen that all would be right. She was worried the king would be angry that she had spoiled such an asset as to have a seer at his side. The king told her that he could fix it.

He took the queen's hand and placed it on Megarra's torso. Megarra felt the panic rise through her as she knew exactly what this was. That's when she realised it wasn't her unwillingness causing her lack of fight; it was him. The king had paralysed her when he brushed his knuckle tenderly across her jaw. She knew, because she had helped him to steal that power from the commander's wife. The power of mind control.

Her eyes welled and spilled down her temples. She tried so hard to muster the strength to force his body from hers, but she was spent. She felt her power, her very life, collect in the centre of her torso and drain from her into the hand of the queen. The king had taken her conduit and given her power of sight to his wife, his Twin Soul.

There wasn't a dry eye in the house, as she told us how they disposed of her in the moat surrounding the castle, like they did with many of their victims. Some would burn, some would be used as chuck to feed the many prisoners and beasts kept in the bowels of the castle, and others would be thrown to the allodiles in the moat.

She recalled waking on impact, the shock of the icy water bringing her to. No longer paralysed by the king's touch, she was able to drag herself up the bank on the far side of the keep, and in the cloak of night, she made it to the woods. She had no idea where she was going, but she dragged herself as far away from the castle as she could before she succumbed to the bite of the frigid air.

Megarra sniffed back her emotions and straightened her slump, as if realising how vulnerable she had gotten. And donning her usual nonchalant tone said, "Then the wyverns found me, and I ended up here. Happily-ever-after, isn't that what they say?"

The passing out of kerchiefs, consoling arms across shoulders, and soothing back rubs, Megarra went out for air as the rest of the house came to terms with her story. I felt so deeply saddened for a girl who trusted a king. I myself had trusted a king of sorts.

I took myself away to the room that I'd been allocated.

Megarra's home had three bedrooms. Colm and Sylvie would be sharing the double, I was to take the single, and the rest of the gang were to sleep in the lounge or the wrap-around-porch on various chairs and hammocks. I wanted to argue, wanted to be polite and decline a proper bed when there wasn't one for everyone, but I was desperate for the safety and comfort of a mattress, quilt and pillows, even if these were a little dusty.

I had wafted them before settling on my side with my back to the door watching motes dancing on the moonlight coming through the curtainless window.

I wasn't quite so comfortable being a part of the group 'mourning' session that was happening right now. I heard Colm tell the others he 'would go to talk to her.' Knowing him he would feel some sort of responsibility and offer his apologies as if what his father did was somehow partially his fault. He couldn't be more wrong. It was obvious to me that Colm and his father couldn't be more different.

Knuckles wrapped lightly on the door. I sniffed my watery nose and dabbed the tears that had streamed and left dark spots on the grey pillowcase.

Megarra's story had uncorked my bottled-up anguish, and let it pour.

The latch clicked open, and I listened for footsteps. I hoped that whoever had come by to check on me would see my curled-up form and assume me asleep and leave.

"Can I come in?"

-25-

I didn't answer the question, feigning sleep. I heard the door click shut, giving me the green light to move. I yelped as I spotted Nathaniel inching toward the chest of drawers a few paces from the door.

"I never said yes!" I exclaimed.

"I'm so sorry. I thought you were asleep, and I just wanted to leave this here for you," he replied, flustered from being caught in the act.

"What is it?"

"Well, I washed this," he said as he held up my mother's dress on a clothing hanger.

It wasn't perfect. I don't think it ever could be, but I could see that he had worked hard to remove the blood, grass and mud stains the best he could. His kindness surprised me, and although I could still see many pulled threads and frayed edges, I was grateful that he felt it was worth trying to salvage. Because to me, it was.

"Thank you. You have no idea what that means to me," I told him.

My eyes began to tingle again. I told myself that it was leftover emotion from Megarra's saddening story, but it wasn't. I was overwhelmed by the fact that someone would care—that he would care.

"And I thought you might like to have something a bit more comfortable to wear. Only if you want to," he offered, holding something folded in his hand.

He handed me a black tunic. The smell of it told me who it belonged to. I noticed he had changed from his usual get-up into plum-coloured, loose linen trousers and a fresh black tunic, the laces untied, displaying the crevice between his chest muscles and prominent collarbones. His sleeves rolled up halfway, revealing corded, tanned forearms. His hair was fluffy and had that 'just washed' appearance.

"You shaved?" I pointed out.

Was there something symbolic in it? When he said 'noted' before, I never thought it would mean he would get rid of it. I don't know why I was thinking it had any other meaning than he just wanted it gone. I felt almost rude for commenting.

"Yes," he said, lowering his gaze. "And I washed. The soap smells good," he laughed as he sniffed the backs of his arms. "Anyway, here."

He handed me the tunic but held on to it when I tried to take it, just like he was holding on to my gaze. It looked as though he wanted to say something but was conflicted.

"I should…" he began.

"Turn around," I interrupted.

He paused for a moment before turning to face the chest of drawers by the door. I dropped my towel, purposefully causing it to hit the floor audibly, like I was challenging him, testing him. It didn't take much to know that I was standing totally naked behind him. I watched him in the mirror to my right, and part of me was disappointed not to see him steal a peek, but another part of me was pleased by his decision to respect me.

I pulled the tunic over my head, pausing for a moment, allowing myself to be flooded by his scent. I don't think I'd ever loved a smell more. It rivalled freshly baked bread and spring posies.

"You can turn back around," I announced.

His eyes roamed over me, and something primal flared in him. In a way it felt as though giving me his tunic was his way of claiming me.

"Will you stay with me for a bit?" I asked. I had considered how big of an ask it was after the question had already begun to leave my mouth. It wasn't the same as lying on the forest floor under a canvas shelter in a camp with others around us.

"I...I'm not sure I should..." he stumbled on his words.

Rejection.

Exactly what I was afraid of.

"I understand," I said as I watched my feet shuffle awkwardly. "Thanks for the tunic."

I turned on the spot and strode back towards my bed. I would not show him the tears that immediately pooled at the embarrassment I felt for thinking he would want to stay with me.

A strong hand wrapped around my wrist, stopping me in my tracks. I couldn't turn around. He would think I was pathetic. Hell, I think I'm pathetic.

Nathaniel's warm body pressed against my back as he wrapped one arm around my torso and another across my collar. I leaned my head back into his chest, and he rested his cheek upon the top of it.

"It's not that I don't want to. I just don't trust myself," he said softly against my hair.

Doesn't trust himself to what?

Oh!

My pulse beat double time as I realised what he was referring to. It's me he shouldn't trust. I'm the one who's been leering after the guy.

"Just talking," I suggested.

His chest rose behind me as he stole all the air in the room.

"Okay," he agreed.

-26-

I didn't sleep much last night, and there's evidence of it in the deep grey rings around my eyes.

Despite my body refusing to succumb to my pleas of just one uninterrupted hour, I had stopped trying and made my way out of the house. I wanted to see what morning was like in the Deadlands, as dusk had shown me nothing but bleak.

The wooden porch groaned beneath my feet, causing Tuck to stir in his hammock. I purposefully hadn't worn shoes to tread as lightly as possible. I didn't want anyone to know I was awake. People have a habit of offering company if they know you're alone, as if there's something negative about being on your lonesome.

I disagree.

I think there's something intimate about spending time with oneself. You get to organise your own thoughts and appreciate the sounds that company's voice would conceal. Like the eerie hum in the air, an echo of collective groaning from the sky and the ground and the trees and the creatures all rousing. I sometimes imagined it was the sun yawning as it rose from its slumber below the horizon. Was it all mechanical? Was the god of morn orchestrating it all with a series of levers and pulleys, and was the echoing hum the groan of the machinery?

I could see the beginnings; morning was starting to unfold. You could sense it in the stirring of creatures in nests and dens. I could hear babies calling with empty tums wanting to be filled. I smiled at the thought that even here there was life despite it all looking so dead.

The landscape was made up of dark and jagged volcanic rock that I presumed had erupted from the Sacred Volcano and settled where it cooled. Black porous rock formed peaks and caves. Dead trees and plants still stood like reminders of what once was. In the distance I could see a small section of the woods from which we came yesterday. It must have taken an hour or more to reach Megarra's cabin as we navigated the uneven terrain.

I deeply inhaled the air through my nose. It was a different kind of air here. It was dry and dusty. Below the dust was an underlying herbal scent, like crumbled rocks and sage.

And there she was.

I had naively wondered if she would look different—or if she would still feel the same. I wondered if the sun would even rise here at all. But she did. And as she thawed the land around me, she warmed me too, and I felt a piece of home. It was as though she was following me like a worrying mother, giving me enough distance to make my own mistakes, but there for me should I need comforting. And comforted is what I felt.

Huffs and shuffling came from my right as gigantic sleeping giants, disguised as boulders, unfurled their massive membrane wings and took to the sky. It took my breath away to see them gracefully swooping and circling. They spread their wings wide to the sun as if stretching the remnants of sleep from their appendages as they rode the thermals. They danced in front of the spotlight, performing barrel rolls and loops, rejoicing that the sun had risen another day. I laughed gleefully at the sight.

"Remarkable, huh?"

The interruption brought sadness with it, bursting my bubble of solace. The feeling fleeting when I laid my eyes upon the equally remarkable man who joined me, leaning his hands against the rail that surrounded the porch. Those hands that touched me tenderly, sweeping calming circles on my skin, tucking strayed strands behind my ears, and wiping trailing tears from my cheeks with the rough pad of his thumb last night, while he listened intently to my woes. A man who had been backed into many corners, forced into many battles, and had choice stripped away from him by circumstance, listened to my grievances with empathy and patience. He did not belittle me. He did not try to compare our struggles or tell me that mine were insignificant compared to his.

I had grown up protected and loved, as had he, but the moment he was unmated, his family disposed of him like he was worthless to them. That the only value he had was whatever the king decided.

My father was with me to the end and still loved me deeply even now. I heard it in his voice in the chapel. I hoped weeping at my false grave brought him comfort.

Suddenly, a wyvern landed heavily in front of us, cloaking us with dust. For god's sake. I'd just washed this shit off, and now I was filthy again.

It was the same beast that tried to char me. I would know those eyes anywhere. I swore it had a smug look on its face.

"Hey, what was that for?" I shouted, swiping dirt from my arms. I thought we had come to some sort of mutual tolerance of one another after providing me with a hot bath and starting the fire to keep us warm.

"I think that was for me," Nathaniel said, patting dust from the sleeves of his tunic.

"Really, why? Making enemies out of wyverns doesn't seem smart."

"She's mad about my cloak…" Remorse tinted his face.

"Your cloak? How would you even know that?" I jeered.

"I told you last night it was given to me; I didn't make it myself, nor would I ever." He spoke to the wyvern like he would a fellow human, and my brows lowered as I tried figure him out.

Every day he seemed to reveal another piece of himself that I hadn't seen before. I looked at him perplexed. He laughed at me before that remorse from before appeared again.

"The cloak is fireproof because it has wyvern scales woven into the fabric," he explained.

Now I understood it's anger.

"That's…awful."

"I agree. It belonged to my grandfather, and I had the roses added later. It was made in a time where it wasn't uncommon to use wyverns for…resources."

He glanced up at the wyvern as he gulped that last word like it left an awful taste in his mouth.

The wyvern watched him intently.

I really didn't like the sound of where this conversation was going.

"When the king was unable to force bonds on the wyverns, he began to enslave them. Those that refused obedience were killed, which was most of them. Their bones were used in medicines; they made weapons and jewellery from their teeth and armour from their skin."

I studied the wyvern as she watched him talk. I could see how hurt she was. I wondered if she sensed the scales belonged to someone she knew.

"Wyvern population took a dive. It's really hard for a wyvern to procreate, and when they do manage to lay an egg, it has to be guarded and protected for a long time in order to grow and hatch. The king killed so many and ransacked nests to find eggs to attempt to raise them from birth for easier bonding, but he failed every time. He eventually gave up. Few articles survived over the years."

He directed the next part to the wyvern.

"And you must know that I despise the king for what he did to your families. I will avenge them, and I would never partake in such barbarism. I hold nothing but the utmost respect for you magnificent creatures, and I wear my cloak with honour. And if it's any consolation, my owning such a thing saved her life."

He glanced at me then.

"How do you know she's a she?" I asked.

That wasn't the most important detail to take away from the obscenity of what he just told me, but I didn't think I could hear any more of it without sobbing on her behalf.

"All the ones that live here are. You can tell by the size of their skulls and the spikes."

He pointed to the rather sharp-looking barbs around the base of her skull and the tip of her tail.

"Males spikes travel all the way from the skulls down their backs to the tips of their tails, and their tails are usually barbed. If you notice, these are all partially spiked, and their tails are clubbed. Still an impressive weapon." He smiled at the wyvern fondly.

She huffed from her nostrils in agreement, I assumed, and Nathaniel raised a hand to her.

"How do you know so much?" I asked, watching on with a mixture of fascination and concern as he reached for her. I couldn't be more attracted to this man if I'd tried.

"Books and drawings. These are the first I've seen in real life," he replied. "May I?" he asked the wyvern.

She paused for a moment, assessing his intentions, before she lowered her head and nuzzled into his touch, closing her eyes as she did so.

"I also know she's female because no male could carry such majesty."

She looked at him as if to say, 'You'll have to do better than that to win me over, human.'

I liked her sass. She was a girl after my own heart.

After a breakfast of eggs from the chickens Megarra cooped at the back of the house, we set off to my first training session.

"What's your weapon of choice, oh Chosen One?"

Colm directed my gaze to a collection of weapons laid out on the ground. I rolled my eyes when surveying the selection in front of me. There was a steel sword, the hilt below the hand guard wrapped in black leather strips. I had noticed this one strapped to Sylvie's back. There were two black-handled daggers embossed with swirling patterns, a ball of spikes on a chain that I could definitely see Tuck using. There was a wooden staff and a crossbow.

"I have no idea…None?"

They were all so intimidating.

"Let's just start with our gods-given weapons then."

What did that mean?

He spread his feet apart, bent his knees, and held up his balled-up fists. He laughed as I eye-rolled again. I seemed to be doing that a lot lately.

"Copy me," he instructed. "Knees bent like this, look…elbows tucked."

I did as I was told.

"Good, now look at my hands. Are you right-handed?"

"Yes," I answered, very conscious of how absolutely silly I felt. I knew I looked like the least threatening opponent one would come across in battle. I would be surprised if I wasn't laughed at while the enemy stepped around me to a more worthy adversary.

"Same," he said cheerfully. "Your left hand should be here, and your right here."

I mirrored him by holding my left fist higher than my right.

"You can protect your face with this fist and protect your ribs with this elbow, and then we jab like this."

I could hear him talking, but the beat of my heart was drowning him out as my eyes caught sight of Nathaniel standing on the porch with his face tilted upward, eyes shut, letting the sun's rays soak into his skin, and I felt jealous of the light and the way it touched him.

Colm's large form stepped in front of me, blocking my view.

"Come on, Red. If he's distracting you this much, I might have to leave one of my best soldiers behind when we go to war…"

Elbow tucked, fists in position, right fist jab.

I didn't make contact, but it was enough to startle him. He put his hands up like training pads, and I hit them.

"You punch well."

He gave me an impressed smile and began to move around now, all the while I was still throwing punches his way.

That one was for Pastor David. This one was for Greer. And this one was for the king.

I was starting to break out into a sweat.

"Why don't you tell him how you feel?" Colm suggested.

I felt him watching the strain on my face as I laid into the flesh of his palms, imagining all of the evil bastards that I'd discovered over the last few weeks.

"I can't," I puffed between a one-two.

"Why not?" he quizzed, as if it was that simple.

"Because what if it isn't real?"

I never would have been so careless with my thoughts if I hadn't been so distracted by knocking imaginary Greer's teeth out.

"What do you mean?" he asked.

Well, I might as well carry on now that I've started.

"I was with Greer for nearly four years, Colm, and he managed to fool me for the entirety of that relationship."

Oof, that punch had extra effort behind it. He shook the hurt from his hand. I'm sure the theatrics were merely to humour me.

"Nathaniel's different," he said confidently.

"How so?"

I kept my eyes on my target, imaginary Pastor David, and continued to jab and move. It was a lot easier to be vulnerable whilst demonstrating physical strength.

"Has he told you about his dreams?" he asked.

"Yep."

Pastor David's nose was now spread across his face.

"He was distraught when they stopped. He searched everywhere for you, but the girl of his dreams didn't really exist. He took it hard. It was like you were real and he had you, then he lost you. He was grieving."

I stopped my assault then as the thought of Nathaniel grieving disarmed me.

"When Sylvie and I decided to start the rebellion, he was the first one I went to. He's my best friend, my brother. I trust him with my life. He was ready to give me everything, but part of me knew that he saw it as an opportunity to start looking for you again. Before I had my first mission to run supplies to your village, we had no idea anything else existed outside of Thane. That information gave him new hope, although he never said it, but he was motivated again."

"Well, I didn't know that. He should have said. He was an arsehole when we first met."

Colm chuckled, "He was probably just scared. He had known you for years by that point, and you had no idea who he was."

I pondered on this for a moment and remembered his expression when he had lowered his hood, and I'd called him handsome. He had looked so disappointed at my reaction, and I'd accused him of being an egotistical ass or something along those lines. I'd first realised it back at the chapel, when he had told me about his dreams and I still felt just as guilty now as I did then, even though it wasn't my fault.

"You know the night you met us, he hugged me and whispered, 'It's her,' in my ear, and I knew exactly who 'her' was."

Colm's words reached into my chest and clutched at my heart.

The adrenaline and vexation I had felt in our sparring session had transformed into an impulse to apologise and console Nathaniel.

I looked over to the porch.

He was gone.

-27-

Colm approached me with the sword and passed it to me. The unexpected heaviness tugged my side down as the tip of the blade butted the dirt. He shot me a tight smile, took it from me, and handed me a simple dagger, like he was having me try on shoes for size.

"Slash, stab, poke. That's all you need to know with this one."

His light-hearted tone took away from the sinister acts that he was demonstrating.

"Much better." I tossed the hilt between my hands and rolled it over my fingers before palming it again. I could work with this.

"Neat trick." Colm's brows were raised in thought. "Do you want to try the staff?" He tossed it over to me, and my reflexes surprised us both.

It felt just as comfortable in my grip. I swirled it from palm over knuckles, revelling in the nostalgic whooshing noise.

"How do you know how to do that?" he enquired with a kind of giddiness at his discovery of my talent.

"I used to twirl batons in our dance group. We practised every week and would perform in the town square. I started just after Mother...left us. Father thought it would be good to have something to focus on. I haven't done it for a while, though."

I grinned proudly as I flipped the twirling staff in the air with my right hand, caught it in my left as it came back down to earth, then twirled it around my back to bring it home to my right hand once more.

"Hey Lis, get over here. Think we've found her weapon," he hollered over his shoulder.

She grabbed another staff. "Why don't you show me what you've got?" she challenged with a cunning grin.

"But I don't..." I began before she came at me with rapid attacks that I tried my best to defend myself against. It was so fast there was no way I would be able to counterattack.

An audience started to gather around, and I felt the pressure build in me. Wyverns swooped and shrieked overhead at the commotion below.

Frustration rose as my staff kept clipping the floor, causing me to stumble and not execute my blocks correctly. She clipped my hip bone, and searing hot pain emanated from the impact.

"Come on, Rose, this isn't one of your recitals," she taunted.

"I'm trying my best," I whinged. "It's too long, and I'm too short!" I shouted as I threw my staff to the ground and plonked myself in the dirt, wrapping my head in my hands.

"Oh, Red. A good workman never blames his tools," Colm chuckled.

"Not helpful, Colm," Sylvie scorned, like she was keeping her child in check.

A huff and that familiar scent of rotten flesh, but this time I looked up, not out of terror, but curiosity. The wyvern nuzzled my arms, and my palm fell to the side of her neck. It was cool to the touch. I brought my other hand up to touch her. Her chilly skin soothed my blistering hands. She bleated pleased noises in her throat and hoisted me up from the ground.

"Thank you, Sable," I murmured.

"Sable?" Lis questioned.

"Yes. That's her name," I replied with a confidence that stunned even me.

"You're giving wyverns pet names now?" she scoffed.

"No, that's her name," I asserted.

"Oh, did she tell you that herself?" she retorted in a tone steeped in sarcasm.

"Yes."

I knew how ridiculous it sounded. The creature didn't speak, but talking was not the only way to communicate. Plants communicated through root systems underground. Kind of like when you placed a taut string between two paper cones, and you hear each other from either end. Our bodies talk in the form of expressions and gestures. Music talks to us, evoking our emotions, and equally, if you listen carefully, you can hear all kinds of messages in the silence.

Despite that, I questioned my sanity.

The black beauty picked up the staff with her teeth, a quarter from the end of it, and with a single chomp snapped the end clean off and nudged it towards me.

I picked it up and twirled it a couple of rotations. It was the perfect adjustment.

We locked eyes for a moment, Sable and I, and my chest tingled with a sense of understanding. I felt her faith in me like ripples on a lake. I couldn't see the ripples, but they were there, like soundwaves I suppose, but I could feel them as though they were a physical thing, absorbing into my being and uplifting me. Her encouragement was all I needed to continue.

We spent the rest of the day, Colm, Lis, and I, working my hands into a bloody mess of bruises and blisters. Lis had rapped my knuckles with her staff more times than I could count, and the cracking of our weapons colliding during duelling had reverberated in my now severely aching wrists.

We spent hours back and forth. Colm corrected my stance, pausing play and physically pushing and bending me into position like I was nothing more than clay, and Lis amended my posture by whacking me with the weapon to whip me into shape. I protested at first, but they said it was for my own good, and they were right. Every mistake I made was made only once or twice before I corrected myself milliseconds from error.

Lis was a pro. The staff was nothing like twirling batons. The art of twirling had made me comfortable with handling the pole, but that's as much as I had gained from it. Lis moved the staff in fluid movements, striking and thrusting at her invisible enemy.

Colm grabbed a sword, and they simulated a duel. My heart was in my throat. I knew they wouldn't hurt one another, but it looked so aggressive. She spun and swung the staff, slashing and stabbing. She caught him with a jab to the stomach, which accelerated their aggression further. Powerful grunts and yells rang out as their weapons clashed.

"I thought you were supposed to be showing Rose how to use that thing, not beat the shit out of each other."

Nathaniel approached the sparring ring that Colm and Lis had drawn in the dirt with the points of their armaments. They moved boldly in a half circle, at opposite sides, whilst staring at one another fiercely, like two opponents about to fight to the death. It made for excellent theatre. When had I become entertained by the idea of violence?

The fighting ceased, and their aggressive scowls switched instantly to deviant expressions like a couple of troublemakers.

"For your information, I reckon she could best you, brother," Colm teased.

"As much as I don't doubt that I think she's worked hard enough for today."

Had he come to rescue me?

"Tomorrow then?" I suggested.

He laughed, "I like your spirit."

I woke with agonisingly stiff hands. I couldn't bend my knuckles. I complained while trying to clutch the handle of my mug of steaming dandelion tea. Meg took the cup and held it to my lips. I embarrassingly took a sip, dribbling it down my chin like an infant that was unable to feed itself. I quickly glanced around to make sure no one else was there to see how pathetic I was.

"Let me take a look," Megarra offered. "Oh, it's not too bad. I can fix that."

She brought a bowl and rags to the table.

"Vinegar," she said as she dabbed the liquid onto the fissures on my skin. I sucked air through my teeth at the sting.

"This will disinfect the wounds," she explained, although I already knew.

An image of Mother dabbing vinegar on my scraped knees as a child flashed before my eyes.

She then opened a caddy of plants.

"This will itch like mad, but I promise you it will help the pain in your joints."

She began rapping the branches of stinging nettles along the backs of my hands and wrists. I fought against the desperation to scratch the affected skin clean off.

"There," she announced while placing her weapon on the table. Not a staff in the hands of a warrior but equally as painful. "I assume you're not going to rest them today?"

She smiled, already knowing my answer.

"You assume correctly," I confirmed.

She rewrapped my hands with fresh strips of fabric. "I admire your tenacity."

I studied her face for a moment and tried to guess her age. Did witches age different to regular folk? I remembered she had aged much faster than the king. If like the people of Sandy, I'd say she was maybe sixty-five, not too much older than Father. Her skin was quite lined, which I suppose wouldn't be helped by the dry, dusty climate she lived in. Her chin curved slightly from her jaw, creating a scalloped appearance. The scar over her eye and down her cheek was almost the same colour as the lengths of her hair and puckered at places. You could tell how deep it must have been, and for what little resources she had to mend it, not to mention the wyvern's lack of dexterity, she hadn't done a bad job at all.

Her eye had been really badly affected by it. I felt sorrowful when I met her other eye, sparkling emerald green; it was dazzling and quite youthful, and to have had two of them! She would have been so beautiful before the cruelty of her circumstances got its claws in her. I wondered if that eye shone brighter to make up for the other one that was nothing but milky scar tissue. It reminded me of who did this to her.

"I have to keep going if I'm going to stand a chance at defeating the king," I said, almost like an oath to her.

She paused at my admission.

"Can I offer you some advice?" she asked.

I nodded my reply.

"What is for you will not pass you by. If it is written that you are the one that the gods have chosen to take down that monster, then so it will be."

Was that her way of telling me I didn't have to try so hard?

"You know about the prophecy?" I mused.

"Child, I'm the one who told of the prophecy…"

-28-

After lunch, I met Nathaniel in what had become our training arena, which was just a bit of flat open ground not far from the front of the house. He was there in the casual attire he seemed to live in now, getting accustomed to the feel of the staff. Compared to Lis, it looked clumsy, and I wondered how much of Colm's statement was said in jest. Everything about him seemed so faultless, and the idea that he was an amateur at something sent giddy tingles across my appled cheeks.

He turned to face me, like he sensed my approach before I'd even set foot off the porch. His hair fluttered around his face in the same breeze that stole the air from my lungs. He was utterly perfect, and I was in trouble.

I had only managed a few paces before I felt the ground disappear beneath my feet.

The sudden upward movement caused my stomach to flip. Sable had swiped me by the shoulders with her talons and whipped me up into the sky, as if I were no more than a hare and she an eagle. She drove us higher and higher.

I announced my terror with howling screams. My body was boneless, and any minute now I felt as though I'd lose consciousness. There was a moment of weightlessness before she released her grip, and I plummeted, rotating through the earth and sky. My arms and legs were frantic in their search for something to grab onto. I tumbled in my free-fall, blood gushing to my head. My hair whipped my eyes, stinging with tears. A blur of grey, then blue, then grey. Terror consumed me like a monster with huge jaws.

Suddenly, my ribs crunched as I collided with a solid surface, and astonishingly, I hadn't exploded on impact. I scrambled to get myself upright, if I could even tell what upright was.

I was on Sable's back, and we were still not in the safety of solid ground.

The wind battered me as I struggled to balance myself. I managed to straddle a gap just below her wings where her back dipped slightly. Too afraid to sit straight, I laid flat, wrapping my arms and legs around her as tight as possible, and closed my eyes, shutting out the world that blurred by.

"Sable, please take me down. I'm begging you," I groaned through gritted teeth.

Sable shrieked and banked left, coaxing another scream from me. Her body so wide that my arms and legs burned from how taut my gripping muscles were.

She tucked her wings and darted back down to earth like an arrow before we came skidding to a halt in a cloud of dust.

I heard feet pounding the ground in between my coughing and spluttering, gasping for oxygen in the dense cloud.

"Rose!"

Nathaniel shouted my name, but I didn't move a muscle. I'd literally been scared stiff.

"What were you thinking?" he shouted at Sable, I assumed, since this was not my doing.

More footsteps hurried towards us.

"Is she okay?"

I heard the concern in their words. I must have lost my voice somewhere in the sky and left it there because I no longer had the ability to speak.

Sable began to shimmy, like a sodden dog shaking the rain from its coat, like I was a piece of debris that had gotten caught between her spines whilst flying.

Colm laughed that hearty laugh. I heard Sylvie's coy giggles too. Even the wyvern made a noise in her throat like she was joining in.

"That's right, make fun of my terror," I croaked as my voice fell from the sky and re-entered my larynx. I supposed it was a peculiar sight but laughing at my trauma was mean.

Nathaniel peeled me off the back of the crouched wyvern and carried me toward the house with everyone else in tow.

"Pretty impressive though, Red. You've just done something that the king tried and failed at for decades. This is monumental," he celebrated.

Hmm. He was right. Although, I couldn't really take credit for it, and I'm sure it didn't look all that impressive, and it sure as hell didn't sound like I had achieved something outstanding. My ego did feel boosted, a little.

"Put me down. I can walk myself," my pride snapped, as I wriggled out of Nathaniel's grip. I just flew on a wyvern's back. I'm sure I could walk to the house.

One step, two steps...

My jelly legs betrayed my ego.

Immediately, Nathaniel had my right arm, and Sable's head wedged under my left. I noticed the pair scowling at one another. Were they fighting over me?

Over chamomile tea, I sat and listened to excited accounts from the eye-witnesses of my abduction—that's what I was calling it. I was taken against my will.

Nathaniel's face was stern. He was not impressed with Sable's behaviour in putting my life at risk. The others were talking about it like it was the most spectacular thing they'd ever seen. My anger dissipated hearing what they saw. Where I was a mess of congealed, boneless flesh, they saw a strong warrior commandeering a wyvern. I liked the picture painted even though I knew it wasn't the truth, but who was I to correct them?

Sable had avoided me for some days now, as though she thought I would be furious with her. And I was to some degree. She should have asked my permission to pluck me from the ground and hurl me through the air. I mean, I probably would have said no, but that's my choice to make. I didn't notice any of them in the skies whilst training, nor did I hear their shrieks and bleats that I had grown accustomed to. I sort of missed them.

One night, out on the porch, after hours of pole-arm practice, I heard the familiar heartbeat-like pulsing of wyvern in flight. They landed away from the porch, refraining from covering us all in a layer of fine dust. I was glad to see they'd brushed up on their landing etiquette.

Sable padded over slowly, barely visible with the dark inky sky behind her. As she got closer, I could see she carried something in her jaws.

"Are we celebrating something?" Megarra asked. "I've never been treated to a whole osailuros before. Grab that, you two."

I recognised the deceased creature Sable had dropped at the foot of the porch. It's feline physique, exoskeletal skull, and curved, spiked antlers. It didn't seem so intimidating in the clutches of the wyvern's maw.

Thoran and Tuck went to collect the carcass, when Sable screeched at them in disapproval. She flicked her head at me.

"It's for me?" I asked.

She bowed her head once.

"Is this your way of apologising for the other day?"

Sable nodded.

"Thank you, Sable. I would like to share it with my friends. Is that okay?"

She side-eyed the gang before nodding and taking off.

"I've been with them for years, and I've never seen them act like that," Megarra exclaimed, gobsmacked.

"Maybe you should try being kinder to them," Colm jibed.

"I'm kinder to them than I am to most, I'll have you know," she returned.

The pair squabbled playfully about the difference between kindness and cordiality while I watched my wyvern join her pack.

Later that night I called Sable. I wasn't sure where they retired at night. For some reason I thought they'd be curled up near the porch like yard dogs. I should have known better than to think they'd act like an obedient pet. Maybe they perched in branches like owls. Although the tree would have to be gargantuan, like a giant redwood. Did they hang upside down in caves like bats, or have huge nests on craggy cliffs like eagles? I noted that as something I would like to be educated on. I could probably ask one of the others. Nathaniel seemed to know a bit about them, but I never did rely on word of mouth as my only source of information. I loved to read books or observe with my own eyes. Maybe he would share his reading material with me one day.

Sable landed in front of me, her gaze expectant.

"Thank you for my meal. You spoiled me."

I crouched to grasp a slippery, exposed bone and heaved to her the huge portion I had saved. A hind quarter, a big juicy rump, and thigh. I didn't pre-cook it as, one, it was too big, and two, I assumed wyverns weren't accustomed to cooking their food. Although it crossed my mind that they did have the ability to cook by flame. I bid her goodnight and left her to tuck into the osailuros leg.

We spent the next few days training hour after hour, and yesterday we were able to get through an entire afternoon without Lis cracking me authoritatively to correct my errors. I was near perfect. I knew how to sweep someone off their feet, much to Thoran's displeasure, and I knew how to use the staff to defend myself as much as to disarm an enemy and break bones. I also brushed up on my combat skills and practised using a dagger in a bag of bundled-up rags.

I felt energised, powerful, self-assured, and brave.

Nathaniel and I were sparring out front.

"Megarra was the one who told the king the prophecy," I puffed between jabbing and blocking.

"She told you that?" Nathaniel replied with an air aggravation.

"Yes?"

I went for the jab and hit thin air where Nathaniel had stood seconds ago.

"Where are you going?" I called to his back as he strutted to the house with purpose.

"We need to talk to her," he shouted without turning around.

"Can we talk?" Nathaniel asked Megarra abruptly, interrupting her from unhooking dried, smoked osailuros meat from the drying rack.

"Of course," she obliged eyeing us suspiciously whilst taking a seat at the kitchen table.

"What do you know about the prophecy?" he enquired.

"Child, you'll have to be more specific. There are many prophecies. All that we are and all that we will become is already written."

I noticed a flash of impatience ripple across Nathaniel's features before he caught himself. I could tell he didn't have time for her cryptic speeches. Anyone else, he may have coaxed the answers from in a less than pleasant way, but Megarra had been kind to us, and Nathaniel was a man of honour.

"The prophecy that led us to this one here," he gestured to me. As his gaze met mine, his tension melted away and he siled softly.

He continued, "you know? Magic blood bears the heir, A flower of Crimson…"

"Ah yes, the last prophecy on my lips," she spoke as she lowered her gaze before busying her hands folding the pile of washed rags in front of her. "Magic blood bears the heir. A flower of crimson. Twin Souls bound. A girl with wings and fire. The king will fall." She recited the words with an ominous tone.

"What does it mean exactly?" Nathaniel enquired.

"What does anything mean?" she countered.

Nathaniel sighed, steepled his fingers, and rested them under his chin, as though praying to the gods to grant him composure before continuing. He opened his mouth, no doubt to reiterate the question in another form, as if asking it a different way might provoke a different answer.

"There's more to it than that," she interjected before his words breached his lips.

Neither of us spoke. We waited for her to divulge.

"You only have part of the prophecy," she said before taking a deep breath.

I was feeling a little nervous now.

"Deliver them from the mouth of hell. What's pure will spoil. Rolling heat will devour. Babes of wrath. Eternal night.

"Magic blood bears the heir. A flower of crimson. Twin Souls bound. A girl with wings and fire. The king will fall.

"I do not claim to know the answer; I am just the vessel from which the prophecies flow."

She shrank down in her seat. It was barely noticeable, but I glimpsed it.

"Well, I *was* the vessel." Her emphasis on 'was.'

She took her folded pile of rags and left the table.

"That was odd," Nathaniel uttered.

"Mm."

The atmosphere in the room had changed the moment she left. Sorrow projected from her skin, and she left it here with us at the table.

"Sylvie told me the story of Jacobi and Adama," I began. "The beginning of that prophecy very much sounds like it could be the one Adama saw about Bellinus."

"It does," he agreed. "But then that prophecy didn't come from her. It had already been spoken."

"True," I acknowledged. "Perhaps it didn't originate from her, but she could have been repeating something that she had read. Or maybe the prophecies appear to different people at different times, so they are not forgotten."

Nathaniel rested his elbow on the table and his chin on his fist. "What good would that be though if the prophecy has already passed?"

Good point. There would be no use in the first part of the prophecy coming to Megarra almost two thousand years after the event had happened.

"Maybe the second part is the counter to the first part. Maybe Adama had seen the first bit only, and when the second part was forged, both parts came to Megarra."

"That could be right," he shrugged. "I suppose if they had returned the babies to the Sacred Volcano..."

"You mean murdered innocent newborns?" I scoffed with distaste.

I knew what vote I would've cast.

"Semantics," he responded. "If they had murdered the *innocent newborns*," he paused for effect. "I guess the second part of the prophecy would have been different."

"Maybe I wouldn't exist then. There would be no need for me."

I laughed to cover the twisting in my stomach at how flippant life could be. One tiny alteration and you could wipe out someone's entire future.

"Hey," he wrapped his warm hands around mine and dipped his head to meet my gaze. When I didn't look at him, he lifted my chin with his finger to bring us level. "Please do not think the only use for you is to fulfil a prophecy. You weren't created to correct someone's mistake. You were made from love."

Made from love.

My eyes glazed at those words that my father so often said.

Nathaniels expression softened. "You may not have existed in this life, but you would have been someone somewhere, and I would have hopped worlds and breached dimensions to find you."

-29-

"I'm going to miss this place," I told Sable. "It's the truest experience I've ever had."

There was an undertone of indignation in my words. I still hadn't really addressed the scope of everything that had happened since that day, a month or so ago. It was as if nothing before then was real. Like I was born on that day, and everything before that was a past life. I had been reincarnated. Obviously not in the physical sense, but I did feel like a different person now. It was now time to look forward. I would probably need to debrief when it's over. I couldn't fathom the fact that any day now this would be it.

Sable looked at me like she understood.

"Do you like living here?" I asked.

"It's safe."

"There's a lot more to it than meets the eye, that's for sure. There's something beautiful about it." I pondered.

"You should see it from up there. Keep your eyes open this time?"

"No, no, I don't want to see it from the sky, thanks. I like the ground." I stamped my feet in the dirt for emphasis.

"You can trust me."

"It's not that I don't trust you; I'm just…not brave enough."

"You are one of the bravest humans I know."

"I'm really trying to be…"

Great, I'm having an imaginary conversation with a wyvern. I really am going crazy. And crazier still, she's giving me a pep talk.

Sable tilted her left side down in an invitation to get on.

"I can't," I whispered, trembling.

She stared at me with an intensity, willing me, and I submitted like it was something I was supposed to do, all the while wondering whether she held the power of hypnotism, as I methodically began to climb.

She was patient with me while I acclimatised myself on my perch at the dip below her wings. I glided my fingertips over her smooth, cool scales. The movement along her silky skin soothed my nerves.

I clenched my thighs and wrapped my hands around one of the spines along her sleek neck.

"Is this okay?" I asked.

She huffed, and I took it as a yes. See, the pep talk was all in my imagination.

"I'm ready," I told her, and then I filled my lungs with air and courage as I braced myself for lift-off.

Her wings beat the air in time with the pounding in my chest, and we began to rise. A few strong pushes against the downward force of gravity, and we were flying. This time I was not ripped and jerked about. There was no stomach flip and blood rushing. It was smooth and gliding, filled with butterflies of excitement and thrill. It was sure and steady. Her wings spanned impressively either side of her magnificent body. I felt her muscles ripple with every flap of her wings.

"Hold on."

She banked left and elegantly swooped us back the way we came and over the house, which was now a tiny square below us.

The terrain had lost its bumps and looked like an even blanket of grey from up here. I could make out the larger of the caves as we flew toward the greatest formation of the Deadlands, the Sacred Volcano. The wind caressed my cheeks and ran its fingers through my hair. The air up here was so fresh and crisp.

I could see the dense treetops for miles around in all shades of green, like a sprawling lawn. It was breathtaking. White fluffy clouds had come to meet us. I braved holding on to her with just one hand and danced my fingertips through the cool nebulous mist.

Suddenly, we were engulfed with fog, and I wondered how she could see where we were going. My pulse started to quicken as I could no longer tell up from down.

"Sable…" My voice wobbled in warning.

A flash of red caught my eye to the right of me, then a crack like thunder. She hovered for a moment, flapping her wings to keep us in the sky before taking a nosedive. I held on with white knuckles, and the plummet stole a scream from my throat.

We emerged from the clouds to utter carnage below in a place that I had never seen before. The night sky lit up with orange flames as wyverns torched stone buildings and armour-clad soldiers boiled alive in their tin-can garments.

A whistle pierced the air as a huge bolt shot through the sky, impaling a red wyvern, whose limbs went limp before tumbling from the sky and smashing into the ground.

I heard men cheer, but their celebrations were cut short with one final act before its life ended. A swipe of a barbed tail demolished the wooden structure from which the bolt was shot. I whooped internally at that tiny consolation.

In every direction, man and wyvern battled, buildings blazed, and the smell of fear and singed hair and flesh was putrid in the air. Mammoth stones hurtled across the landscape, colliding with winged bodies that dropped like dead weights from the sky. My wide eyes shot from side to side at the horror everywhere I looked.

Just then, we lurched upward to avoid a boulder. Sable steadied us with a few strong strokes of her wings, and that was when I saw him. On his head was a crown, and his fist was clenched, his focus on that of an indigo wyvern. Its throat was aglow, and I could see that he had forced the flames to backfire within the wyvern's own throat, and the creature was now burning from the inside out. The king's face painted a picture of smug insanity. He was enjoying it.

We ventured back through the cloud, swapping red war for white mist, and howls of defeat for rushing winds, and we landed back at the Deadlands in moments.

"What was that?" I hollered at her, my mind still reeling. We were there. It felt real.

"I showed you what was, so you could see the importance of what will be."

"How did you do it?" I choked.

"You are special, Crimson One."

"Special how?" I squealed, exacerbated by the many times I had been told I was 'special' or 'chosen.'

"You will free us all."

Before I could ask her to show me how, I was greeted with faces of awe upon our return to earth.

"That was really something," Lis gushed.

"You're a natural up there, Red," Colm enthused.

Their words sounded echoey. I felt like I was trapped between two worlds.

I watched Sable take to the skies without me. I must have looked like a fish out water as I tried to form a sentence. I was completely bowled over. My face was still frozen with terror, but no one seemed to notice.

"Megarra has kindly ordered, I mean organised..." Colm laughed at his intentional mistake that referenced the ongoing tennis match of back and forth about Megarra's treatment of her winged acquaintances, "...the wyverns to take us to the kingdom, which we are very grateful for. This will cut our travel down dramatically and means we can conserve our energy for the battle ahead."

He talked like quite the leader and carried himself like one too.

I felt a warm touch at the small of my back. Nathaniel looked at me with pride, like he was witnessing the prophecy come to life. The one to be heir. A queen to conquer the king.

The girl of wings and fire.

Tuck attached the last weapons pack to Petra, a charcoal wyvern who blended in so seamlessly with the landscape. She was smaller than the rest. Lis would be her rider.

I was already seated on Sable's back while I waited for the others to settle into their respective modes of transport.

It was foreign to us all, but, of course, Nathaniel took to it like a natural. I watched him intently as he leapt onto the wyvern's back end and pushed off to swing his leg over to straddle the back of Anala. Sable and Anala were similar in size and build, but Anala sported a remarkable flash of scarlet red on her underbelly. The same colour mottled the scales along the ridges above her deep rouge eyes, which looked almost like eyebrows. It gave so much character to her sweet face.

Nathaniel talked to her in low tones while stroking the side of her neck and along her shoulders. She leaned into his touch, and he smiled at her response. I wondered what he could have said to her. Could he communicate with her the same way Sable had with me?

"You feel deeply for him." Sable transmitted her words to me, and I could hear them, not like a voice to the ears, but more like an internal dialogue spoken with a voice much lower and wiser than mine. I don't think it's something I will ever get used to.

"Is it that obvious?" I tried to push words back to her without saying them aloud, but she didn't respond.

"It's been a pleasure, old Meg," Colm called down to the witch standing in front of her home. Her face was full of hope and loss, like a mother sending her children off to their very first day of school. She didn't reply, as though she couldn't find the words. She just waved back at him astride a large grey wyvern, Sable had informed me was named Ilmari. Sylvie sat in front of him, plaiting her silky strands, securing her hair readying for flight.

I nodded my readiness to Nathaniel, although ready may not be the right term. I felt nothing. Not the hope or loss that Meg displayed, nor the excited energy that some of the others had, nor the nerves, nor the cool composure that Nathaniel was modelling.

Gods, he was so handsome.

I glanced around at all of us on the backs of these magnificent beasts. We had all achieved something that the king could not. This thought ignited a little spark of conviction in my belly.

We glided through the air at a steady pace. The skies were clear and vibrant blue. A swarm of birds took off from the treetops below, cawing at us disgruntled, as though we were in their territory. I huffed a laugh at their courage to protest creatures as large as our companions. I closed my eyes, and I let myself really feel the serenity of the air stroking over my skin and around my neck. I breathed it in and let it wash over me.

'What will be is already written,' is that what Megarra had said? I was just a pawn in a game the gods played, and the next move was up to them. With that knowledge, I could take action knowing that regardless of what I did, the intended outcome would always come to be.

Flashes of red stole my sight. Agony ripped through me. A woman screamed. A copper tang, blood. A scent of sweet milk. A man's voice singing lullabies. Eyes of deep velvet brown and honey. "You are me, and I am you." Bellows of pain. Metal dragged along stone. Beasts screeching, fire roaring, people cheering. A castle. And a red-headed girl with a crown. A handsome man that smells like cedar and smoke and feels like home. "I adore you." Blood dripping down the wrists of joined hands.

I come to as if waking from a dream, but I was not asleep. Residual pain lingered in my torso, and I could still smell the blood and feel the horror. I looked over at Nathaniel, who already had his eyes on me, but these were knowing, like he saw it too. It was there on his face for just a second. I was sure of it. I saw it playing out in the glimmer of his eyes, but when I looked harder, all I saw was worry.

"Are you doing okay over there?" he called with uncertainty.

No, he did not share my vision, because if he did, he would know I do not feel okay. I couldn't even find a reply. I just stared at him, trying hard to separate what was real and what was not.

He was real.

I focused on him to tether me to reality.

"Sable?" My voice trembled. I only spoke her name, but it was loaded with questions.

"I cannot tell you. You need to think for yourself."

"Was that a prophecy? Am I a seer?" I hadn't realised I'd raised my voice until I glanced at the furrowed brows surveying me. What was it with everyone talking in riddles?

"It's the future."

"But it doesn't make sense," I groaned. "It was just flashing images and sounds."

"Rose?" Nathaniel called. He was becoming restless with my lack of response.

"Think, Crimson One. Search deep."

It was all so fast, like flashes of lightning; if you're not looking in the right place, you miss the forks. The blood, the crying, the singing. My brain was spinning so fast I got motion sickness.

"Rose?" Louder this time. I heard the panic in his voice at my ignorance.

"Don't focus on what you don't know. Focus on what you do know."

What I do know?

I closed my eyes and steadied my breathing, and I thought. I thought hard. I could almost feel the cogs turning and my brain tensing with the overload.

What do I know?

I know those eyes were his. I know those hands were ours. And that voice saying the words, 'I adore you,' was from my mouth. I looked at him with welling eyes as a deluge of unexplainable sensations flooded my body.

His eyes were already on me, watching me.

Something new pounded in my chest and hummed in my veins. No, not new; it was there before but magnified now. My hairs stood on end as a kind of magical electricity buzzed on the surface my skin. My body called to him in waves of energy, like the rippling lake, like Sylvie's magnet analogy. I finally understood it. I wanted to dismount Sable and walk the airspace between us so that I could reach him.

"I wouldn't advise that." Sable, the voice of reason.

Nathaniel's expression transformed from worry to realisation, as though I'd described these sensations aloud or maybe it was visible as much it felt physical. He was reading me like an open book, and it was knocking him for six.

His chest rose and his throat bobbed. His eyes glistened with understanding.

"Thank you for joining me," he shouted over. His cheeks dimpled, as he smiled profusely. "I've been waiting a very long time, my love."

I was overcome with emotions. I wept tears of elation and newfound belonging between laughter.

His lips did not move, but I heard his voice. *"You are me, and I am you."*

I giggled in disbelief through the tears as the wind whipped my hair and my heart pounded, rivalling the beating wings of my wyvern.

"I love you," I thought. It was the only thing I knew to be wholly true in its entirety. I thought it as much for confirmation to myself as to tell him.

"I love you too, Rose Elodie Harlow," he shouted back.

We landed mere seconds before I dismounted Sable and mounted Nathaniel. I climbed into his arms and wrapped my legs around him, and kissed him with an urgency that said I'd been waiting too damn long for this moment. He tasted like cinnamon and fate, and it was living and dying.

Our foreheads pressed together as we caught our breaths. I wanted to test our connection to see if I was imagining it.

"I love you."

I didn't need to confirm it to myself this time. It was as true as the air in my lungs and the blood in my veins. It lived in me. Had ventured through me and taken root inside my chest. I could feel it like it was woven into my very being, like an essential organ. It was innate. I wanted to tell him over and over as if the words would never be enough.

"I love you," he sent back with the widest grin, dimpling his cheeks deeper than I'd ever seen. It was such a pretty smile.

"I can't believe I can hear you," I laughed, astonished.

"Finally," he replied with a sigh. *"You never responded again after the first time at the river."*

My eyebrows wrinkled as I tried to recollect the memory.

"Home," he said.

I raised a hand to my mouth in astonishment as I remembered.

"You said that out loud," I countered.

He subtly shook his head.

"That was so long ago."

My eyes tingled with emotion, it felt almost eerie.

"Yes," he laughed.

"Have you been able to hear me all this time?" Oh, gods. It's like had read my journal or something.

"Not all the time. Just sometimes. Mainly when you're looking at me, and if it concerns me," Nathaniel explained, and I didn't miss the mischief in his gaze.

"Oh, gods. That was personal," I cringed. How many times had I internally voiced my opinions of this man? How many times had I ogled him? The tent! The night we drank the nectar! My eyes widened at the memory.

"What happened in the tent?" he probed with a smirking mouth.

I slapped his shoulder as he maintained his grip around my waist.

"You don't have to be shy around me. I love you."

I smiled at those three words like a cat that got the cream.

"When you two are finished, we have places to be," Sylvie interrupted.

I had forgotten they were even here and what we were here to do. My mind was distracted by my visions and what they meant, and my heart seemed to have grown twice the size and was battering the insides of its bone prison.

I shot Nathaniel a questioning look.

"Can they hear us?" I asked, panicked.

"No," he laughed. *"They cannot. This is something only for us."*

-30-

The wyverns left us north of the capital in the woods on the edge of Brigsbane, Alissa's home, and Priors, where Thoran grew up. We weren't supposed to arrive until tomorrow night after a planned trek of roughly twenty-four long hours with very short stops in between. We would then sleep the night in a tavern in Brigsbane before waking for battle brief the next morning. The rest of the rebels were gathering in Brigsbane tonight for a final meeting before travelling to the capital in small groups so as not to arouse suspicion.

Brigsbane was one of the biggest towns in the kingdom, second largest to the capital, Oakenvale. Some of the wealthiest lived on the borders between Brigsbane and Oakenvale. Their stately homes with neat lawns and private gates were mostly perched on the Upperlands nearer to the capital. The people who inhabited these homes were ancient lords and ladies, who were most vital in maintaining the king's reign, or their offspring, homes passed down to them through generational wealth, carrying on their parents' legacies.

They rarely left their hilltop commune. Positioned up high on a clifftop that looked down on the valley into the capital. Much like their self-professed statuses, they saw themselves above the others. They didn't mingle with the regular folk of the kingdom. The only use the affluent had for the normal folk of Thane was to hire them to cater to their lavish lifestyles. The staff were underpaid and treated poorly. They were taxed tremendously, and they struggled to make ends meet.

The streets were narrow and much of Brigsbane was dilapidated. The majority of the rebels resided here. They were fed up with their patriarch and wanted to live freely. Those that had not joined the rebellion turned a blind eye to the plotting.

"I bet they'll be in the Three Cocks," Tuck suggested.

It was eerily quiet.

Candlelit windows were a glow in the dusk.

In Sandy the evenings were spent socialising, dining outside and evening walks. Brigsbane seemed abandoned and I wondered if it was the norm or whether the residents were in hiding.

The only noises were the flapping of awning being caught by the breeze and barking of dogs in the distance. A cat jumped from a ledge upending an empty milk churn. The clatter startled us all and echoed through the dark alleyways. I was glad to see that I wasn't the only one disconcerted. Sylvie had placed herself in the safe grip of Colm's large arms and I thought it peculiar that someone as deadly as her still needed comforting after being spooked.

Nathaniel stepped behind me and enveloped me with strong arms and his woody scent.

"Feeling left out?" he whispered into my mind while nuzzling his chin into the slope of my shoulder.

"No," I huffed, playfully elbowing him in the side and wriggling out of his grip.

I loved that he curled himself around me, but I didn't want people to think I was weak, especially not the other rebels. I was supposed to be a prophecy. I could not allow myself to be seen to be scared.

Nathaniel shot me a smile that told me he could see right through my brave girl act.

Considering the size of the town and the fact that we had been walking a good twenty minutes I would have thought we'd have met someone by now. The place seemed abandoned until we got closer to the crooked terracotta building with exposed timber beams adorned with a bar sign picturing three proud peacocks. The hum of chatter burgeoning the closer we got, and when we entered the open-plan salon, it was so loud you couldn't hear yourself think. A mixture of high-pitched cackles and alto bellowing, a sea of bodies wearing browns and blacks and greys, all blended together like one constant din and one enormous mass. Tens of different conversations filled the air in the bustling building. It was so full that the addition of us extras would break down the walls that already seemed to be struggling to contain its many occupants.

Nathaniel took my hand and linked us to the others, and we weaved as one long line, snaking in and out towards the back of the tavern until we reached the bar. Colm climbed the wooden platform and leaned over to rattle the rope of the bell that I knew, from back at the village, meant last orders.

He raised his hands to his face and warbled. The racket ceased immediately, and heads turned synchronically and warbled back at him. Who knew such a strange noise could have such a powerful effect?

A scraping of table legs against the floor, and a massive man rose from the crowd in the booth in the far corner. He had long chestnut hair with a vibrant carrot-orange beard.

"Ey up, I thought we weren't meeting you until the day after tomorrow." His voice boomed with an accent similar to Lis' but a lot deeper and thicker.

"Slight change of plan, my good fellow. We arrived early, so we thought we would meet you here," Colm replied jovially.

There was some discontented murmuring. A change of plan seemed inconceivable.

The mass around me began to stir when they noticed me. Whispers of, *'It's her. That's the girl.'*

Nathaniel pulled me in front of him protectively, shielding me with his body. I noticed he no longer linked us to the rest of our friends but had still kept my hand in his.

I felt so small, so vulnerable, and the nervous buzz in my chest started to intensify. I was anxious to meet these people, I suppose like anyone would be meeting someone new. But now, I felt scared, frightened that they would not accept me, that they might be hostile towards me. That one small movement of Nathaniel putting his body before mine flipped the narrative for me. I now felt at risk of harm. A bead of sweat trailed down my lower back. There was a real lack of air in this place, and it smelled of sweaty men and stale ale.

"Hey, it's okay. No one's going to hurt you," Nathaniel reassured me. "If you wouldn't mind, can you release your grip a little?" He chuckled ever so slightly.

We both looked down at our joined hands, my knuckles white and locked stiff. His usually tan skin had started to turn a shade of purple. I tore my hand away and wiped the moisture that had built on my palms on my trouser legs.

"There's someone we would like you to meet," Colm announced.

More murmured conversation, as he crouched and reached a hand to me. I shook my head frantically. I didn't know what to expect, but I wasn't ready to be paraded as a saviour to the people that had modelled their choices based on the belief that I existed.

"It's better to do it now and in one go. We will address everyone at once," he whispered to me.

Was he expecting me to speak? To address them like I was their queen, and they were my subjects. I felt sick.

Nathaniel laced his fingers with mine once more. "Hate to say it, but he's right. I'll come with you."

I had no choice.

"Come on, Red." Colm's tone was merry, but I knew he was nervous. There was a lot riding on this going right.

My back to the bar, Nathaniel pressed himself against me. "I've got you."

He hoisted me up onto the platform before climbing up himself.

From up here I could see our surroundings better. The door that we had entered was in front of me. The staircase to the left led up to a gallery landing with lots of doors with numbers on. Round tables and chairs littered the floor space stuffed full of drinkers and their tankards. The walls were wood-panelled and decorated with paintings. Portraits of a man holding a rifle with two dogs, a painting of an elk in a forest, and a man holding some sort of golden bird's upside down by the feet. They looked dead. There were sconces on the walls, and above us a huge chandelier hung from the ceiling decorated with cobwebs. I wondered how they were able to light the candles way up there.

"Thanks, brother. I'll take it from here," Nathaniel told him.

Colm smiled nervously before shuffling away.

"Stay. In fact, all of you, stay." Nathaniel gestured to Sylvie and Tuck, Thoran, and Lis to get up on the bar. Colm pulled Sylvie up. Thoran assisted Lis, and Tuck jumped straight up from a standing position and landed with a grunt beside us all before slapping Thoran and Lis playfully on the buttocks with a "ha-ha."

They stood with straight backs and heads high. I looked at them all. Thoran with his black quiff, cropped around the back and sides. He had permanent dimples, even when he wasn't smiling. Tuck's beard hung down to the centre of his chest but was always well-groomed. He oiled it daily, which meant he always smelled of rosemary. Lis, with her shaggy wolf cut and beautiful, patterned skin. Twin Souls, Colm and Sylvie, ethereal and otherworldly, and Nathaniel—my heart, my Twin Soul. They were a family, and I really wanted them to be my family. If we were to win this fight, would this moment right here be encapsulated by an artist's paintbrush and paint and adorned in a frame on the walls of this tavern—the base for the rebellion. It should be, I thought.

"As Colm said, we arrived earlier than we expected. We arrived by wyvern, would you believe!"

If I thought the murmurs were loud before, then this was strident.

"*Wings and fire.*" I heard several times.

"It's true," Colm interjected, supporting his friend's claims.

"Our sources were right," Nathaniel continued. "I went to the village, and I saved her moments from death. The girl with blood-red hair, born under the Crimson Moon. This, ladies and gentle, or not so gentle, men…," the crowd laughed, "is Rose Harlow. We believe she is who we've been waiting for."

He looked at me while he spoke those last few words, and I knew it was because he had been waiting the most.

The tavern erupted in cheers and heavy hands slapping tables. Ale sloshed from their vessels as chairs teetered.

"Did you want to add anything?" Nathaniel whispered to me.

"Absolutely not." I frowned.

"Before that day, Rose knew of nothing outside of her village, so as you can imagine, it's been very overwhelming for her. She has been incredible, she has trained hard, and she has come with us, despite us being complete strangers to her. But I believe in her. We believe in her. We will try to come around and talk to you, but please respect her boundaries and treat her with the courtesy she deserves."

There were some raised eyebrows and funny faces being pulled as the crowd calmed and took to their seats. I know it wasn't his intention, but he made me sound almost high maintenance.

The barkeep let us down on the side of the bar intended for bartenders only. I thanked him. I was grateful to not have to get back into that sardine can.

"Sorry if I said anything wrong. I didn't mean to talk for you." Nathaniel had held me back while the others merged into the throng.

"It's fine. You said what you thought was best and all with good intentions."

I was grateful for his lead. If I was expected to address an audience anytime soon, I should probably ask for his guidance. He seemed very comfortable with it which surprised me as it seemed communication wasn't his strong suit, in our first few days spent together at least.

"I can't imagine how hard this is for you." He rubbed soothing strokes up and down my arms.

"I have you here. I'm fine."

Our eyes lingered for a moment before he smiled in acceptance of my answer.

We wended through the crowd to the far corner where the large man sat.

"Maurice!" Colm greeted him with that manly backslapping hug thing that I'd seen him do before.

"Prince!" the large man exclaimed, equally as happy to greet Colm.

Maurice nodded his head to me and told his company to shuffle round to give us room.

"Rose, Maurice is a key player in this rebellion. He's been holding the fort while we were out looking for you," Colm explained.

I smiled nervously at him.

Maurice sat back, stroking his long beard, assessing me with sunken eyes hidden behind brows as bushy as his facial decor.

"I can't express how happy I am to see you, Miss. I almost can't believe my eyes," Maurice said wearing a calm, sort of relieved, but in awe, expression.

"Me an' all," came a voice from a rather thin man to our left. "I mean, no offence, but you're just a girl."

Ah, so not happy to see me but more 'can't believe his eyes.'

"Don't start, Colin, the prophecy says..." Maurice sighed.

"I know what the prophecy says, Maurice," Colin interrupted.

Maurice sat up straight then, and I saw the full size of him.

Colin's voice began to wobble with intimidation. "We are taking a huge risk here. I just expected our saviour to be a little more…"

"A little more what?" Nathaniel spat.

"Never mind," Colin sighed before leaving the group.

"Sorry about that, Miss. We are all a bag of nerves. This has been a long time coming. Many of this lot will lose their lives in the coming days, and now you're here; it just feels a bit more real."

"The tone has definitely changed in here, that's for sure." A barmaid came to the table with a tray of mugs foaming at the top and placed them in front of us with a slosh before collecting the empty ones.

"I know Gwyneth. We thought we would have one last hurrah before things get ugly, but I think most of them still thought tomorrow would never come," Maurice replied.

"Well, I'm very glad you're here, Rose Harlow." She smiled at me genuinely. "On the house." She nodded to the drinks.

I don't know what I was expecting to find here, but I know the sounds of merriment that we had entered to were no longer so jolly. There was nervous chattering and quick glances. My stomach was an ocean in a storm, and my confidence was a fishing boat trying so desperately not to capsize. I needed some courage.

I picked up a tankard, brought it to my lips, and gulped and gulped. It was a damn sight better than the 'nectar' we'd shared around the camp. I slammed the vessel on the table and swiped the foam from my lips with the back of my hand. The whole table stared at me in silence before Maurice's shoulders started to quiver, and laughter burst from his bearded face.

He slapped the table, stood up, and shouted, "Whatever happens tomorrow, we will not go down without a fight. We take back our freedom or die trying. Who's with me?"

The bar erupted into *'yeah's'* and cheers, and *'hear-hear's.'*

Maurice held his ale out in front of him and bellowed a low, deep note from the depths of his puffed-out chest until others stood and held the same position at their respective places around the tavern.

Then they all broke out into song.

> *"There once was a girl with hair red as the moon,*
> *'pon wings she would fly, not a moment too soon,*
> *The delicate flower will chop off his head.*
> *She'll storm the castle and kill the king dead.*
>
> *We searched far and wide to finally find her.*
> *And come tomorrow, with us rebels behind her,*

*We'll follow her gladly; she's the one the gods chose.
She'll give us our freedom, the gift of a rose."*

Clanking and cheering followed their performance. I couldn't stop myself from being led on by their infectious spirit.

More and more trays full of ale made their way around the tables. There was a happy buzz about the place.

Many had come to say hello, and now the ale had relaxed me; I was finding it easier to converse. I listened to their stories and laughed at their jokes. I heard awful accounts of families ripped apart by the mad monarch as he took what he wanted without a care for his people.

It was obvious the kinship here was strong. These people were from all walks of life. Some lived comfortably, some struggled to survive, some were Kingsmen, some were slaves, some were mated, and others weren't, but they had all come together to bring down the king in the pursuit of freedom and equality.

As the evening went on, the crowd had filtered out, some going home to eat and sleep and spend time with loved ones, others on to other taverns. We stayed put and basked in the warmth of camaraderie.

Nathaniel still had my hand in his under the table.

"Where's the lavatory?" I asked Lis. I had managed to drink two tankards full and that was it. It was much harder than it looked. Maurice must've emptied five since I'd been at the table, and Gwyneth had just handed him another.

"Just over in that back corner," Lis pointed out. "Do you want me to come with?" she offered.

"No, no, I'll be quick," I replied.

They didn't have to worry about me doing a disappearing act from a pub in the middle of Brigsbane. Where would I go? I didn't feel the need to run. Not unless Nathaniel was with me. I go where he goes. That's my new mantra.

The ladies' room had three cubicles and what looked like an old trough meant for cow feed as a sink, with a metal faucet protruding from the wall above.

"Who does she think she is?" a voice said after the door creaked open and closed.

"I know! I mean, I know she was going to die, but at least her people didn't suffer for it. They rewarded them for their sacrifices. My Terence did the last supply run. He said there were all sorts of things. He took some of it and brought it home for us. Made a big pot of stew to last us a week."

"Lucky you! We've been watering down our stew pot this week, so it'll last us a bit longer."

"Little Miss *'I had a perfect life until a handsome stranger came and swept me away.'* Did you see the way she looked at him? Strangers, my eye. Didn't seem to take her too long to get herself acquainted."

The posse cackled.

Another chimed in, "What do we get for our sacrifices, eh?"

I stayed in the cubicle as quiet as a mouse until the coast was clear to exit.

Back at the table another round of drinks was in, and I couldn't stomach another sip. The first drink was refreshing, the second was okay, but by the third I was completely sick of it. Not to mention after hearing what

Colin thought of me and now the women in the cubicle, I'd gone off the idea of socialising or engaging in niceties.

Nathaniel flashed me a smile as I sat, and he returned my hand into his before settling back into the conversation.

"What will we all do when it's over?" Maurice asked the group.

I noticed Colm and Sylvie across the table. Their faces lit up like they knew exactly what they wanted the future to be like. They were all teeth and fluttering lashes before nodding to one another in agreement.

"Well," Sylvie began.

"Sylvie and I would like to start a family," Colm finished speedily, before they both laughed with watery eyes. You could see how much it meant to them.

I looked at Nathaniel and wondered what he thought. Did he see himself married and starting a family? It was certainly not something I had planned.

"What about you, Miss?" Maurice asked.

"I...I hadn't really given it much thought. I've never had a future to consider. I should have been dead already," I replied with a nervous huff of a laugh.

A few silent moments ensued before Maurice replied, "Well, the possibilities are endless, and you could have anything your heart desires."

I was certain his eyes flicked to Nathaniel for a split second. It was that obvious then. It's what they were all thinking, that belonging to a man was my only desire.

"Well, we are going to spend our last night..." Tuck began the sentence sandwiched between Thoran and Lis. He ended it, whispering to them only.

"What do you say, Rose? Fancy joining us?" Lis suggested.

Joining what? He never finished his sentence.

Nathaniel's gulp of ale burst from his mouth in a splutter. He grabbed a cloth Gwyneth had taken from the waistband of her apron whilst clearing away our empties and began to dry himself and the table.

"Lis fancies herself a girlfriend," Thoran explained. "She reckons there's too much masculinity going on here," he said twirling his finger between the three of them to the tune of devious laughter.

Lis fluttered her eyelashes playfully at me, and now I understood the dynamic of this trio.

"I am flattered," I began. And I was. "She definitely turns me on the most out of the three of you." I did my best sultry voice. The flirtatiousness gave me a thrill. "But..."

"Ugh, there's always a but," Lis sighed playfully.

"Yeah, there is," Tuck chuckled, and judging by the yelps from the pair at his sides and his arms disappearing from around their shoulders, I assumed he grabbed himself a couple of handfuls of his implied 'but.'

"...I'm all about the masculinity too."

My voice seemed to be loaded with suggestion, and the direction of my gaze confirmed exactly who was in my thoughts. He knew it too. The corner of his mouth curved as he blinked fast and gulped at the imagery I was sending him. I was unsure if it was possible, but his reaction told me the message was received.

Colin piped up from the end of the table. He had perched a chair right at the corner despite the lack of space and the fact that nobody seemed to want him there. "Masculinity?" he tskd. "I heard you were fucking Greer, and that twat is nothing if not a pussy."

"Watch your mouth." Nathaniel reacted immediately.

Chairs screeched and chests puffed.

Despite his smaller stature, Colin squared his shoulders and stood firmly in front of Nathaniel with a confidence that took me by surprise.

My face burned red. I could feel it, and the sympathetic looks from others at the table made me act rashly.

I slid my chair back and got to my feet while clutching that third mug of ale, which was probably flat and definitely warm, and poured it over Colin's head.

"Oh, come on, can't the bitch take a joke? She's too sensitive," he spoke. He was addressing everyone around the table. "We're gonna lose if she's supposed to be the one who…"

His words were cut short by the sound of fist against flesh.

I didn't see who did it. I was already on my way upstairs to room twelve, according to the key the bartender passed me, as I stormed by the bar.

-31-

"I can't do this, Nathaniel."

He had followed me up the stairs to my room and had found me slumped with my back against the door, defeated. I had tried to unlock it, but the key wouldn't turn, and I gave up, far too easily.

"Can't do what, Rose?" He probed while he grabbed the door handle and the key that I'd left in the lock and wiggled it around.

The lock clicked and he held the door open for me to enter, closing it and locking it behind him.

I was in a cell. Granted it wasn't iron bars and damp stone stinking of human excrement. This cell had furnishings, drawers, a bed. The window was glass and although we were on the second storey maybe there was a foothold or two to assist me on the way down

No.

This wasn't something I could run away from. They found me before. Would a prophecy rat me out again if I were to evade my destiny?

"I can't be your hero. I can't kill someone. I don't want to be a queen to these people."

The words tumbled from my mouth with no mind for my sharp tongue.

His jaw tensed and I wondered what words he had quashed. His eyes urged me to go on, but his mouth remained still. He knew that if he spoke, he would interrupt my flow, and I would put a lid on it, and bottle it all back up.

His awareness was one of the things I'd grown to love about him. He knew when to back off, he knew when to intervene, and he knew when to show support in subtle ways, like a brush of the knuckles, a firm hand at the base of my spine. This time it was large hands on each of my shoulders. Velvet heat radiating from them, covering my cold words.

"When were you going to tell me that you were my Twin Soul?"

Anyone would think I was mad at the fact, and the way he looked at me, like I'd just knocked the wind out of him, told me he had sensed the same from my tone.

"When did you first know?"

I didn't mean to yell at him, but I was just so embittered.

Everything was moving as fast as my plummet from my first flight with Sable. She had lifted the tavern from its foundations, and it was whirling through the sky.

My responsibilities were to take care of my father, to pass on our teachings to the younglings and to give my life to my community. I owed them that. They had raised and nurtured me collectively and it was my duty to return the favour.

I had tried. I really had. But navigating through the smoke and mirrors was like finding the exit of an endless maze.

"The day I saw you at the woods," he admitted, and the tavern stilled.

I thought about that day. I'd gone there to make peace with my fate and ask for Mother to be there, waiting for me to join her on the other side. I remembered the dark figure in the woods. I thought it was Death, making sure that I didn't back out of my arrangement with the gods. I didn't fear him. As he ran through the trees, I instinctively followed. I recalled feeling the tether, and he must have felt it too. And his reaction had been to run away from me.

"Why didn't you tell me?" I griped and my voice wobbled with despondency. "You must have heard my words as I begged the gods to let mother meet me. You must have heard me talk about Greer. Was that it? Is that why you ran? Were you disappointed in me for sharing myself with someone else?"

"No," he snapped, as though the very thought preposterous. He sighed and his expression softened. "You just had so much that you had to come to terms with. I didn't want to pressure you further."

He walked away from me and ran his hands through his hair, and I immediately felt awful for scorning him. He had accepted that he wasn't to be twinned, sent away from his family, and recruited as a killing machine. It must have knocked him sideways to find me there unexpectedly.

"It was so hard not to tell you straight away. I'd dreamt of you for so long, and there you were, right in front of me. I'd convinced myself that the reason for the dreams was because it was my destiny to help you to fulfil your destiny. But then, I saw you, and it hit me right here." He tapped his chest, right where his heartbeat beneath, as he said those last two words. "It took everything in my power not to blaze through that village, through the kingdom, and destroy them all for doing this to you."

"They didn't do anything to me. They didn't know any better. I was so happy. Life was easy. I was cared for and loved."

Did knowing this make him feel any better? How many times would I repeat the fact that I was happy, I was loved? Was it to convince myself that it was true, to prevent me from picking it apart and finding the flaws that I had been blind to. "I lived my life knowing that everyone in it was feeling as good and happy as I was. I had a purpose, and I know it was all a lie, but I didn't know any different. Ignorance really is bliss," I scoffed a laugh. "Even if there was no afterlife, I would have died thinking I had done something great. And now I have to kill a king and advocate for a bunch of strangers, some of whom have been very rude to me. I have no connection to these people."

Maybe Colin was right. Maybe I was a bitch.

"Sure, some of them are a bit rough around the edges. They've lived hard lives. But there's more to them than that. There are good people here, Rose, and they're worth saving too."

I dropped my head in shame. I was tired, and I felt guilty for thinking for a split second that anyone wasn't worthy of my personal sacrifices.

"Rose?" Nathaniel hooked a finger and raised my chin so that I was looking up at him. The desperation in his eyes begged me to let go with him. "I am sorry that this has happened to you. I am sorry you feel so overwhelmed. I want you to share it all with me. Please don't shut me out. When you're sad, angry, desperate, nervous, happy, excited…I want it all."

"I…" Conflict caught in my throat.

The way he looked at me completely disarmed me from the internal battle that was ravaging my brain. He ran a thumb along my cheekbone, and his hand came to rest at the side of my face. Fingers laced in the hair at the nape of my neck, and I'd forgotten what it was that I was about to say.

"Listen to me," he pleaded, his eyes bore into mine. "This is bigger than us, bigger than your village, bigger than the whole kingdom. You are a part of a world full of beings, Rose. The gods chose you to free us all. You can bring that happiness and love that you felt growing up to everyone. You still have purpose, and the goal is the same. Except this time, you get to keep your life."

I searched his eyes for a hint of a lie, but all I found was integrity.

"How do you know?" I whispered.

"Because I will never let anything happen to you."

I've felt love before.

The love of my parents was wholesome, and nurturing, and unconditional. My love with Greer gave me tingles and butterflies, but it just touched the surface. I was desperate for more. But this, the way this man made me feel. His love penetrated my skin and washed through my entire being in waves. It drenched me until I could absorb no more. I still had butterflies, but there weren't just a few; there was a whole colony living in my body.

I felt alive.

I felt it course through my veins. I felt invincible and courageous. The words were there on the tip of my tongue, and yet they were not nearly enough to describe my feelings towards him in this moment.

I locked my eyes with his and implored him to feel the sincerity of my words.

"I adore you."

They came naturally. Truer than anything else that I knew. As true as north. As true as the sun.

His breath caught in his throat as he gulped. Moisture crept from the corner of his eyes and coated his waterline. He widened them and blinked it away quickly.

His voice crackled with raw emotion. "You have no idea," he breathed.

He placed the lightest kiss upon my lips and placed his forehead gently to mine. "I adore you."

-32-

"Wake up, Rose!" Mother's voice compelled me.

I jolted awake in the arms of the man who whispered promises to me with lips and tongue, over every inch of my skin through the night. I had asked him to stay with me. He removed his weapons and boots in reply. He stepped out of his trousers, folded them up, and placed them on the console next to the bed. I stared at him, rooted to the spot, uncertain of the next move.

"Do you sleep fully clothed?" he enquired, although I could sense a playfulness to the question.

I shook my head but kept my position at the other side of the bed.

I still wore the tunic he had let me borrow, and a pair of breeches that were far too generous at the waist. I had grabbed a bunch of the surplus fabric and tied a knot in it to keep the trousers from falling down. The only clothing Megarra had to spare were a few kirtles that she had scavenged, and all I had was Mother's wedding dress, none of which were suitable for travelling by wyvern, unless I sat sideways like the ladies on horseback in the books I read.

My gaze followed him as he made his way around the bed to meet me. The rhythm of my heart was like the gallop of horses. He reached under the back of the tunic, my breath held in anticipation. With a quick tug he unknotted the bunched-up waistband of the breeches, and they fell in a pool of fabric at my feet.

And still, I did not move.

Even as the lack of covering on my legs sent a chill of prickles over my skin, I kept my eyes locked on him expectantly.

He brought himself around to stand in front of me.

"You are so beautiful," he breathed.

The tiny hairs on my skin all stood to attention at his proximity. A shuddering breath escaped my lips.

"I've never felt this way about anyone," he confessed, while he tucked my red locks behind my ears. "You get under my skin and burrow deep into every cell. You light up the darkest parts of me." He kissed me tenderly, and my eyes closed with the indulgence. "Let me show you how you make me feel."

He picked me up out from my pooled breeches and into his arms, and I instinctively wrapped my legs around his middle. His fingers delved into the cushiony flesh around my hips, and he groaned as he luxuriated in the way I rocked into his touch. The friction of my core against his torso sent shockwaves of pleasure through my body. He breathed those three words into my mouth and kissed from one corner to the other, drawing my lips in and scraping the skin with his teeth.

He laid me down softly in comparison to the passion with which he groped and devoured me and paused for a moment as he settled between my legs. Heat radiated from the apex of my thighs, and I searched his features for a hint that he had felt it.

He pressed himself to me.

"See how you make me feel," he sent from his mind while his mouth found that sensitive spot on my neck, just below my ear.

I tilted my hips, crushing my core against the swell of him. He sucked air between his teeth and his jaw set. I began to reach for him between us, when he caught me midway.

Suddenly, my arms were above my head, pinned by both of my wrists captured in his large hand.

"This isn't about me," he whispered in my ear.

His warm breath sent shivers down my spine. He pulled back and gave me a look that said, *'Do you understand?'*

I held his glare before deciding to obey, relaxing my arms into their new position above my head, and I curved my fingers around the iron bars of the bedstead.

He wouldn't let me touch him. He didn't want to be distracted in his mission to worship me.

He unbuttoned my tunic partway and peppered the skin between my breasts with kisses while muttering, "I adore you," so my heart could hear it.

His teeth scraped my hardened nipples through my shirt in reward for their reaction to his touch. He delved under my clothing for bare skin and buried his hands into my back, curving my stomach up to meet his mouth.

I craved him deeply, desired to feel him entirely, but something about this felt just as, if not more, intimate.

Kneeling between my legs, he wrapped his solid arms around me and hoisted me up into position in his lap. My fingers found their place in his cropped hair at the nape of his neck. We stared at one another, panting breaths into each other.

"I love you," he swallowed.

"I love you," I smiled.

"I want to give myself to you like Jacobi did to Adama," he whispered. "You are me, and I am you."

Heat filtered into me where our bodies pressed together, and my heart fluttered at the sensation.

"Let's give ourselves thousands of years, because one lifetime with you just isn't enough."

My eyes began to sting with awareness of what this moment was.

"Will you bond with me, Rose Harlow?"

He gazed amorously, bursting with affection and desire.

I began to nod, small at first, but more exaggerated as the prospect of being bonded to him sunk in. Being his wife. Being his Twin Soul.

"You are me, and I am you," I repeated to him.

I couldn't manage the words out loud for the laughing and crying between kissing him and burying my face in the soft skin of his neck, inhaling him.

This was love.

This was happiness.

Ignorance was not bliss.

This was.

◆◆◆

The background noise of men sharing ales and belly laughter still echoed up the hall hours later. I admired their stamina. How they managed to consume so much liquid, I will never know.

I thought of all the stories I was told, the way Maurice greeted me and sung his ditty, and when the punters joined in with him, like a massive jolly choir. The sound so powerful it armed me with faith.

I thought of Gwyneth serving our ales and telling me she was glad I was here. I thought of Colm and Sylvie's faces when they shared that they wanted to start a family. All of those moments would not be ruined by Colin's comments and the women in the lavatory.

It took me a minute or two to realise that those noises were not belly laughs but were furious roars. Glass was smashing, not clinking with cheers. The raucous was no longer merry but aggressive. Have they really drunk themselves into a stupor and knocked ten bells out of one another? I knew tensions were high, and my mother would always tell me, 'You put the devil in your mouth, he'll steal your brains,' but now really wasn't the time to fight within our ranks.

Nathaniel stirred next to me.

"What's going on?" He sat up, rubbing sleep from his eyes. It was hard to care about whatever they were doing when I saw this version of him. And to think that I would get to see this version of him forever.

"Someone's fighting, I think," I scoffed.

"Ugh, not again," he sighed.

"They make a habit of this, do they?" I tilted my head, brows creased.

"Boisterous alpha males and alcohol is the perfect mix for a cock measuring competition," he chuckled.

He stretched his arms upwards and twisted his back left and then right.

"I've never slept so well," he declared.

"It was barely a nap," I laughed.

"Exactly."

Suddenly, our door burst open, and I clutched the blankets at my partially naked body.

"We have to go, now!" Colm's eyes were bursting from his skull, and the fact he didn't make a witty remark about our situation told me he was deadly serious. "They've taken her. The bastards have taken her."

Utter despair wrinkled his features.

"Who? What's going on?" I probed.

"Sylvie!" His hand clutched his sandy-coloured strands. "She went to use the bathroom, and I heard a tussle. I went in after her, and the place was smashed to bits. She was gone. Then they started piling through the tavern. I will die without her," Colm spewed in a state of pure panic.

"Who started piling through the tavern?" I asked.

"Kingsmen!" They both stated.

"Shit! I'll get my gear on and be down before you can say, 'kill the fucking king.'."

Nathaniel's assurances to Colm startled me. I hadn't heard him speak so aggressively before. He hastily gathered his clothes.

Colm nodded. "I can't lose her, Nathaniel." His stare was wide and serious.

"You won't," Nathaniel asserted.

He really meant it when he said he protected the ones he loved.

"Oh, Rose, we were supposed to give you these together. Sylvie had planned to help you get into them, but Nathaniel will have to do it." Colm's voice wavered as he handed me a bundle and a pair of boots. He dashed out of the room and came back a moment later holding a weapon, similar to the staff I'd practised with, but this one had a sharp dagger tip on one end and small barbed spikes at the other. It was just the right size. "We had hoped you would be able to get a feel for it first, but you'll have to learn as we go. War has already begun. We leave in five."

Before I could even thank him, he was gone.

Nathaniel had managed to dress while Colm was talking. He had on his usual black attire with the addition of a black leather vest, and he fastened his cloak in its rightful place around his neck.

I admired him.

"As much as I love the way you are looking at me right now, I'm going to need you to get dressed."

He concealed a flattered grin making sure to stay with the seriousness of the situation.

"Oh, erm," I was flustered. Rather inappropriate of me to be lusting after him right now but it was connatural.

"May I?" he asked while holding two empty hands in front of him.

I nodded despite not knowing what he was asking consent for.

He fastened the buttons of the tunic that he had so delicately unbuttoned only a few hours ago. He handed me some fitted leather trousers, and I wriggled into them. They fit perfectly. When had they had the time to get these for me?

Next, he strapped a smaller version of his leather vest around my torso, fastening it with buckles at my sides. I sat on the edge of the bed and put on the thick, knitted boot socks he had given me.

"Whatever happens today, stay close to me and talk to me. *I can hear you, remember."* He placed a boot on my left foot. "And don't do anything you aren't comfortable with." He put the other boot on my right foot. "One last thing." He picked up the material that had bound the rest of my clothing together and shook it out. It was a cloak. He fastened it around my neck with a brass pin, strapped a dagger to my thigh, and handed me my weapon. He studied me for a moment before using the tie from my clothing bundle, gathering my hair to the nape of my neck, and securing it.

He brought his lips to the slope of my shoulder and kissed me softly while breathing me in deeply.

"You haven't said anything," he pointed out.

"I'm scared," I admitted.

"You are brave, you are strong, you are dangerous, you are mine… You are me, and I am you."

There were those words again. He recited them over and over like a mantra during our time together. I let them replay in my mind this time and committed them to memory.

"I love you," I told him. It was all I could say. It was the only emotion I could be sure of right now. The only feeling that wasn't changing, wasn't up and down like wyvern flight.

"Ready?" he asked.

Was it too late to say no?

The bar was empty by the time we arrived downstairs. The doors were swinging off their hinges, and the brawl was in the street. I felt his worried gaze on me as I took in the chaos around us.

He spoke. "This is our destiny. The prophecy brought us together, and it will see us through this. And whatever happens, we will go through it together. I believe in us!"

-33-

The soldiers wore a red serpentine sigil on the front of a basic steel vest covering dark blue tunics and breeches. No chain mail, no helmets. Just average men, like Father or Mr. Morrison, our neighbour. They were fighting for their lives; I just wasn't sure their fight was with us.

What did the king dangle in front of them to get them to fight for him? Whom had he held hostage? What had he threatened them with that they would put their lives on the line to protect him? Surely, he didn't need them to protect him, the all-powerful king, so what were they here for?

Bodies lay in bloody puddles on the street, most of the victims wearing the King's Army costume, a small consolation, I suppose. Were they familiar with the orchestrators of their demise? Did they drink together in the taverns, or trade eggs for potatoes at the market on Sunday?

Metal clanged, and it drew my attention to the soldiers and rebels in combat ahead of us. I could smell the copper tang of blood in the frigid air, frigid with Death's icy breath, as he dragged souls to the next life.

A roar from the right, and a bloodied soldier was charging toward me. My instinct told me to duck. Nathaniel swung his sword over my head, striking the soldier down. I dared not look back to see the outcome.

We carried on into the fray of swinging arms and clashing metal. I followed Nathaniel, clutching the back of his cloak, as he fought to clear a path through the crowd. He punched at faces with his free hand and shoved them to the ground with a boot to a torso. He blocked attacks with his blade and slashed and stabbed at the relentless onslaught.

I was his shadow; he was my shield. I kept as close to him as possible, avoiding, ducking, and spinning away from attacks. I had to use my pole-arm to deflect a sword or two, but I hadn't had the courage to use the deadlier ends. The ends that could really inflict damage.

"How are we doing back there?" His voice entered my mind like a soft touch.

"Okay," my voice trembled.

"You're doing great," he assured me, as he grunted and clashed with another attacker.

He may not realise it, but those words really did boost my confidence. If only little by little. I stood slightly taller, not crouching as low behind his huge body. His broad back still shielded me entirely.

We reached the end of the street. I glanced behind at all of the fallen bodies that littered the alleys. Streets, that I imagined, during the day were filled with busy people, children playing hopscotch, mother's shopping for produce, men on their way to work. They all belonged to someone. They all deserved to live.

Nathaniel turned my head back to face him. "Look at me. You're doing great."

He forced my focus. I panted to catch my breath. My adrenaline had my heart beating double time.

"Nathaniel," Colm shouted from the middle of the town square.

We ran toward him, weaving in and out of clashing soldiers and rebels. I spotted Lis in a ready stance, grinning like a mad man at an oncoming attacker. He didn't even get a hit on her before she skewered him on the end of her sword. Tuck and Thoran were nearby, working together to defeat a group that had advanced on them.

Suddenly, I was tugged backwards, only a few more paces from Colm and the others. I screamed as I twisted myself around to face my apprehender. He snarled at me whilst playing tug of war with my cape with a low-pitched giggle, like it was a game we were playing.

Before I could think, I raised my right arm with force, and my spear tip impaled the man's gullet. Surprise burst in his eyes like I'd cheated, like I'd broken the rules of the game we played. He hadn't seen it coming. I hadn't revealed my hand until the last second. Hell, I didn't even know what move I was going to make.

Nathaniel spun me back to him. It had all happened in seconds.

"Rose, are you okay?" He was frantic. "I'm so sorry, I didn't mean to…you did so well."

Regret diffused from him for his lapse in judgement. It had taken some seconds for him to realise that I had no longer been behind him, and in that fraction of a moment he could have lost me due to his own negligence. He pulled me into an embrace as my arms hung limply at my sides.

"I'm sorry. I'm so sorry."

"I'm fine." I tried to assure him.

In all honestly it was kind of a blessing. It forced me into action. I couldn't stick to him like a limpet to a rock for the whole battle. It could be the death of him. That very thought awoke something in me. Unlocked the memory of the premonition. The one that I had locked away in a box. One that I did not ever want to relive again. I could not let him die because of me.

"I have an idea," Nathaniel exclaimed as he began climbing the sides of the bandstand in the town square, leaving me in the safety of the others. When he reached the roof, he warbled, louder than before and bellowed, "STOP! EVERYONE STOP!"

The chaos died down, and the clanging petered out, and attentions turned to Nathaniel.

"I don't know what lies King Bellinus has told you about why we war today. The truth is there was a prophecy, and that prophecy told the king that one day a girl with red hair, born under the Crimson Moon, would end his reign and bring freedom to the people."

A hum of discussion filled the air. I saw faces of confusion dressed in shiny silver and blue, and nods of confirmation from our comrades.

"That day has come, and Rose is here with us today."

I waved awkwardly from the bandstand between Thoran and Tuck. I wasn't sure what else to do at my introduction, although the colour of my hair was probably a giveaway, and I realised the awkward wave was absolutely unnecessary.

"There are almost five hundred of us across the kingdom that have decided enough is enough. It is time for the tyranny to cease."

The Kingsmen talked amongst themselves before Colm stepped forward to back Nathaniel up. "Please do not take this with offense, but you will not beat us here, so join us. King Bellinus does not care for you; he does not care whether you live or die. You are disposable to him," Colm called out to his audience. Some were bloody and bruised, and some hobbled with injury.

"But what makes you think that you can beat him?" someone called out.

"We might join you and die for it," another said to a chorus of agreement.

"You will die today if you fight against us. You may as well fight with us and stand up for your right to freedom. No more tithes…"

The soldiers liked the look of that suggestion.

"…no more hunger. You can feed your families…"

"Yeah!" The majority shouted. Fists pumped the air.

"…we are all equals. No more dictatorship!" Colm yelled.

The crowd erupted into cheers as the exhausted soldiers' weapons clattered to the ground. I saw the Kingsmen and rebels shaking hands and patting one another on shoulders and backs. I grinned proudly. It was an inspiring sight.

"You are more than welcome to rest, or go to your loved ones, or even go to the taverns to drink, or you can join us on our march forward. The choice is yours," Nathaniel offered.

"They've taken the princess to the castle. They used us to delay you," a soldier shouted.

"Good. That's exactly where we are headed."

I filled with pride watching Nathaniel command the crowd. It would have been easier to slay those men and make our way to the castle, but he was a good man. His kind nature wanted to give these men a chance, and in doing so, he gave them the option to choose their own destinies. I was in awe of him. Him and Colm both. Men like them were the type of men that should be at the helm of the kingdom.

-34-

Our march up the hill towards the Upperlands was inspiriting. We moved like a legion of warriors with determination and purpose. The blend of the brown and black leathers of the freedom fighters and the navy and red uniforms of the Kingsmen was a symbol of what we hoped to achieve, unity. We were all equal and working together. We were a group of individuals marching towards a common goal, and in order to do that, we had a king to take down.

We could smell the smoke before we saw the flames. The row of mansions up ahead was bathed in an orange glow. Raiders looted the houses while vandalising them, breaking down doors, ripping down fences, and smashing windows. You could see them running from house to house with booty carried in arms or sacks.

I noticed the immediate tension in our ranks. The Kingsmen were conflicted between ingrained duty and righteousness.

"I do not speak for everyone, but this is not our goal," Nathaniel addressed us, but I suspected it was for the benefit of our newest additions.

"However, desperate people do desperate things. Look closer at what they carry."

I saw many vases and platters and paintings, but the majority of them were carrying crates of food and potato sacks or bales of materials. Looking closer still, I saw gaunt faces with perturbed expressions, many of them children. These people were obviously desperate. Moral or not, part of me cheered them on.

The path snaked through woodland, and it felt as though we were once more back in the woods between Sandy and the Deadlands. It didn't feel as dark or dense, and these woods didn't have so many eyes, unless they were all hiding from the sheer mass of us.

We marched around the perimeter of Oakenvale before we spilled out of the forest and into the streets. In the darkness, it must've looked as though the forest had grown legs and was creeping into town.

There were no lights on, nothing to be heard. The town was sleeping, as you would expect at only a couple of hours past midnight. It felt eerie, and I'd expected the place to be swarming with soldiers, just like Brigsbane had been.

The castle towered over the town like a stern, all-seeing guardian. It was a granite-stone authoritarian, reminding the kingdom that no one could so much as bat an eyelid without the monarchy knowing. The closer we got, an intense feeling of doom started to batter at the walls of courage I had built.

"I'm nervous too. It's okay to feel that way. It's because it means so much."

I nod at his words and used them as materials to fill in the cracks of the walls to reinforce them.

It had started to rain, and puddles of red had collected around the cobbles. Broken weapons scattered around the floor, our procession picking up any bits that may be useful and storing them on their person. Some took armour, and others took extra baldrics and scabbards to store surplus weapons.

"Seems the others have made quite the impact," Colm said as he glanced around, no doubt looking for casualties that were part of his brethren.

My gaze caught a slumped body of a soldier against a shop front with an axe embedded in his skull. My stomach clenched, threatening to empty its contents.

"Try not to look. Keep your eyes ahead. We can mourn them later," Nathaniel's calm voice entered my mind.

"I feel it so deeply, and I don't even know him. I can't bear to think about what it would feel like to lose any of you," I admitted. I hadn't told him, but I already had a pretty good idea of what that felt like.

"I know. But we can't let ourselves think like that right now," he replied.

I had wanted to hear more comforting words from him, but those were the right words.

I took a deep breath and snatched myself away from the oppressive heaviness that was threatening to hold me back, like an intruder inside me, pulling and snapping at my heartstrings—I had to stop it.

Its presence stole my attention away from committing Nathaniel's face to memory. He would be my motivation to keep me moving on through this nightmare. The grassy plains leading up to it were vast, and as expected, the drawbridge was raised. What I hadn't expected, though, was the haunting silence. It was like turning up when the party was over, and all the guests had gone home.

"I don't like this," Lis expressed.

"It's an ambush. They will burst out and surround us any minute now," one of the soldiers said shakily.

"Do you know that for a fact?" Nathaniel asked. "What can you tell us?"

"No, I was just speculating," the short but stout man stuttered a reply. "We weren't told anything other than to storm the tavern and draw you all out while they took the girl...for which we are truly sorry." His eyes met the ground.

"No apology necessary," Colm replied. "Well, my wife is in there, so I'm not waiting any longer, ambush or not."

He began to stride forward.

"Colm wait..." Nathaniel wrapped his hand around Colm's arm.

I was staring into the darkness as they discussed their next moves, and I was sure I could see movement. It was like watching black ants swarm an apple core in the dark, with the moon the only source of light.

"Nathaniel." I tapped his arm. "There's someone out there." My voice was a whisper.

Everyone studied the shadows with squinted eyes.

"She's right. Draw your weapons."

No sooner had the sound of metal unsheathing rung out through our group than the shadows lifted like a blanket. Rows upon rows of soldiers ran forward in crouched positions, bawling like a foghorn sounding the start of war. The closer they got; I realised that the soldiers that had ambushed us in Brigsbane were just regular people conscripted to be deployed for the sole purpose of delaying us. They were not trained Kingsmen like Colm and Nathaniel. The ones in front of us wore the signature black uniform that Nathaniel modelled so flawlessly, reinforced with a black chainmail, black leather vests and various helmets ranging from smooth head coverings to extravagant pieces that bore fierce visages.

The first ones reached us in seconds with a smash of their shields. We braced our bodies as our feet drove into the mud. The cries of the wounded rang out, but there was no time to think of which side they belonged to. These men were definitely stronger and larger. Their vests were padded, and they wore spiked shoulder pads. I used my height to my advantage, swooping low and driving my spear upwards into soft torsos.

"My love, talk to me," Nathaniel fretted.

"No time," I grunted. *"I'm a bit busy."* I ducked and weaved, pommelled and sliced with both ends of my weapon. It was light and well balanced and was made for these hands. It was like an extension of my own body.

The ground began to rumble with what sounded like the heavy footfall of thousands more soldiers, and for the first time since we engaged with these troops, my courage faltered.

"More troops?" I asked Nathaniel, with alarm.

"No. Maurice."

I ducked beneath a spiked ball and sliced my dagger in the underarm of its wielder and caught sight of rows of soldiers disappearing from in front of me, like the ground was swiped out from beneath their feet, their yells going from loud to barely audible to nothing.

"Maurice did that?" I shrieked.

"Earth magic," Nathaniel grunted, whilst throwing a man over his shoulder onto the polearm of a soldier behind him.

As we got to the crevice in the earth, it closed over, allowing us passage. I still stuck out a foot and tested its viability before stepping on it. I had learned my lesson when it came to things not being what they seem.

We charged towards the next line of soldiers, who stood there without drawing their weapons. As we clashed with them, it was like running head-first into a brick wall. My pole reverberated up my arm, sending pain through my shoulder. I yelled out in agony. The tip of my spear head had snapped off. Shit.

"I'm fine," I sent through our bond to Nathaniel before he could react.

"You better be," he replied. He knew exactly how I was since he was right next to me, holding his own shoulder, rotating the pain away.

"This is a distraction," he shouted. "Stay alert."

"What are they doing?" I asked. It was creepy the way they were standing there, staring forward, unreactive, like a line of life-sized toy soldiers.

"They're shielding," he replied. "Colm, what are we thinking?"

"We keep a bulk here in the middle and take a group either side to try to get around. I'll take the left; you take the right." Colm commanded.

"Received," Nathaniel replied, then he shouted the orders to those to our right, and those that were behind were told to stand their ground poised for the shield to drop.

Our group began running the line. Nathaniel bent and picked up a helmet from the ground, inspecting it before shoving it rather forcefully on my head. I adjusted it so the metal nosepiece didn't obscure my vision. My face was exposed apart from my forehead and nose. It sat on my head like a bobbed wig made of steel.

"If I have to wear one, then so do you," I protested.

He tried to challenge me by staring me down, but he thought better of arguing and grabbed himself one mid-run. By now many of the others had done the same.

A horn sound rang out, and I knew it could only be the signal for something bad.

We had made it to the large wall that separated the town from the castle grounds, making the climb upward. The shield had not expanded this far.

Suddenly, the drops of rain became leaden like ball bearings and pelted those of us on the wrong side of the shield. Those who had not made it onto the wall were screaming in agony as the rain pelted their skin, leaving welts the size of golf balls. I watched in horror. Those who had stayed on the field wailed and dropped to the ground, curling into tight balls. Some tried to hide under the bodies of the fallen. Others grabbed scraps of armour, and our cloaked members covered themselves and others to shield from the flesh-piercing rain.

"We can't stop," Nathaniel ordered, and we all followed his lead to the other side of the shielded Kingsmen.

We pounced from the wall, taking our foe by surprise, and began our assault. I used the spiked end of my pole like a club, smashing knees and taking feet out from underneath the enemy, before plunging my blunt blade into any exposed soft parts or leaving them to my associates' prerogative.

These men were so much taller than I was, and I had learnt that it was far easier to take their legs out first and, somehow, I didn't feel bad about it. The soldiers we had met before that had now joined our ranks looked as though they'd been coerced, but these men, they looked like they were proud to be defending the king. These men didn't look desperate. They looked hungry for violence. They were clean and fed and bedizened with ostentatious armour. No doubt they benefitted from heeding their sovereign.

The shield soon dropped, and the rain returned to a drizzle, and our soldiers were united again. There were so many more of them than us, but we could not let that make us falter.

"Nathaniel." A large woman with a nose ring and braided hair approached us. "Dante said it's time to tunnel."

Tunnel?

"Stay with me," he told me as he grabbed my hand, and we about turned and ran back down the hill like we were retreating.

I heard confused murmurs, and I was certain the word 'cowards' was hurled at us. There must have been only a hundred of us left, and I had no idea how many more Kingsmen.

Once at the bottom of the hill, I felt the air thicken. I looked up and saw no stars in the sky, no light from the moon. I felt no rain. We were under a blanket of shadow, just like they had been on the escarpment. The ground trembled, and a trench opened up before us.

"Jump," Nathaniel yelled, and the command echoed up the line.

We landed with a thud, and Nathaniel led me in the same direction Colm and the others had travelled when we had split earlier. I was worried about them but couldn't allow myself to dwell on it. The shadow was a lid on the trench, and we plunged into complete darkness. There was no noise except the panting of breathlessness and the shuffling of feet.

"Where are we going?"

I could not see a thing, and if it wasn't for Nathaniel's grip on my hand, I wouldn't know what way to go to get out of this maze. I was certain we were going uphill. I could feel the burn in my calf muscles from the incline.

"We are going under the army to the top," he explained.

"We can do that?" I huffed, surprised.

"Yes, Dante is at the front tunnelling."

Over the course of the last few weeks, they had explained the abilities that the Twin Souls possessed, but seeing them demonstrate their powers before my own eyes was mind-boggling and completely baffling and pretty badass.

We exited the tunnel just in time to witness our troops, who had breached the surface ahead of us, snatched from the ground and expelled through the air by an invisible force. The rush blew strands of loose hair back from my face, as my cape billowed behind me. Their screams ended with a thump, as their bodies smashed the ground. If we had exited a few moments sooner, we would have been with them. My legs buckled at the thought and Nathaniel steadied me.

We had tunnelled, bypassing the chaos on the hill up to the castle.

"Hydros now!" Someone shouted as water rose from the moat like a looming aqua monster and washed the fighters downhill.

"Our people are there," I cried out.

"I know," Nathaniel answered. "This will not harm them as such. We have geos waiting for them at the bottom to bring them up to us."

We waited with bated breath to see if our people would rise from the rush of water. Coned silver helmets peaked, fingertips emerged and stretched skyward, and bodies scrambled up out of the swell. Red and blue soldiers, black and brown rebels, and all black Kingsmen, swamp-green scales on black clawed humanoids with elongated serrated snouts. My gut clenched and forced a fearful yelp from my mouth. Screeches permeated the air. My eyes darted around the cluster of bodies, trying to pick out the creatures. I counted six so far.

"RUN!" I screamed to the people at the bottom of the hill.

They clambered to their feet, the ground a slippery slope of congealed mud, blood, and gunk from the moat. They charged up the hill, enemies no longer concerned with challenging one another. Screams echoed as people disappeared from the crowd; gurgling and tearing sounded between the roars of desperation to survive.

The men, although some incredibly strong, were at a disadvantage in the slippery, boggy terrain that the hydromancer had created. The clawed appendages of the amphibious monsters gave them the upper hand. They moved much faster disabling all victims regardless of their strength and stature. A group of both Kingsmen and rebels managed to bring one scaled beast down as I looked on with horror.

A shrill cry to my left pierced my ears. One of the monsters emerged from the bank of the moat and dragged a lady to the ground, tearing into the soft flesh of her torso to the soundtrack of wailing and gurgling.

Nathaniel acted quickly, swung his weapon, and sliced the creature's head off with his blade. He grabbed me away from the edge before searching the riverbed for others.

Several spears were embedded in the floor of the moat, standing tall and bowing towards the castle, decorated with the skeletal fragments of who knows what. Fish flapped around gasping for air, and the muddy moat bottom squirmed with creatures left uncovered.

"We need to go back down and help them," he told me, before his eyes widened and glowed orange. He tucked me to his body before whipping us around, trading places with me. He roared as a flaming arrow collided with his back.

"NO!" I screamed.

"It's okay," he grunted. "Wyvern scales."

He reached over his shoulder and pulled the arrow out. The impact had not penetrated him. It had embedded itself in the leather vest under his cloak. Relief flooded me, it hadn't reached his skin, but the sound he made told me it would leave a dark bruise. More flames peaked through the crenels of the battlement atop the castle.

"Find cover," Nathaniel yelled to those around us.

Our army dispersed in all directions. Some disappearing into trenches and appearing further away.

The bowmen released their arrows. They came down on us like fiery rain.

Nathaniel pulled us to the ground, covering my body with his. I heard the thuds and the sucking of air through his teeth as he winced at the arrow strike.

Tears of worry streaked my cheeks. I tried to hide it, but a sniffing sound gave me away.

"Hey, I'm good, okay? Don't worry about me."

As if he was trying to soothe me right now when he was the one being pommelled in the back with flaming arrows.

"That's like telling me not to breathe."

He laughed at my admission.

"We need to make a move while they are reloading," he instructed me.

"Where to?"

"The moat," he said.

"What? Why?"

The place was a death trap.

"There's a hidden passage directly under the drawbridge. We just need to hope that a geo meets us there."

He grunted and panted this time as the arrows rained down a second time.

"Nathaniel?" A voice boomed from outside of our protective cloak.

"Maurice?"

"Aye. I'm gonna burrow down into the tunnel and up into the gatehouse and lower the drawbridge. I need you to get up onto the battlements and take out those archers."

On the next break, we scrambled into the moat trench and waded through the thick stodgy mud. My feet weighed a tonne as I struggled to lift one in front of the other. Every squelch smelled of pond scum and decay. The ammonia stung the back of my nose, and I really did not want to lower myself into it.

We'd found our mark.

Maurice forced his arms outward, and with the backs of his hands pressed together, he drew them apart. His face creased with the effort, as if his hands were really pushing the mud. He strained as the earth parted like he could really feel the weight of the soil and rocks as it moved. We progressed inch by inch, and Maurice grunted and grappled with the burden of the dirt.

We'd gone as far as we could go.

Maurice pushed the large slab of stone above us like it was nothing more than a loft hatch.

"I'll get to work on the bridge. You two go get those archers," he commanded.

Nathaniel grabbed my hand as we ran up the stairs. The staircase wound around and around like a helter-skelter. Thin slitted windows let in what little light was outside, but it was so dark I could barely make out each tread. My hand grabbed for a rail or something to push off on our incline. My thighs and calves were burning like acid.

We broke through the battlement and were met with a surprise attack, as Lis leapt through the air with her sword above her head to strike down on us. I saw the moment recognition stole the ferociousness from her features. Nathaniel captured her mid-air at her waist before setting her on her feet and ruffling her hair playfully.

"I could have killed you," she exclaimed.

"I would have given you a good battle first," Nathaniel laughed. "Catch up later. We've got work to do."

"No need. We took care of it." She crossed her arms across her chest smugly.

No sooner had she held that pose than a soldier picked himself off the floor and charged at us with his broadsword. I admired his tenacity in thinking he could challenge three of us.

Lis was poised to counter his attack, but before he could reach us, he stopped mid-motion and suddenly sprung backwards, like he was on a bungee cord. A big blond beauty with a blood-splattered face and a toothy grin stood in the spot the soldier had been.

"Nice of you to join us!" Colm jested.

I peered around the battlement at the fallen soldiers. The same ones responsible for raining fire on us were now slumped against the wall or flat out on the battlement floor. Some were even hanging over the edge of the embrasures, and only their legs were visible.

Just then a pounding echoed around the staircase behind us.

We backed away from the door, anticipating what it would give birth to.

Soldiers burst out in formation behind their leader. Row after row filed in, blocking the only exit from this godsforsaken place.

Their commander was a huge unit of a man, fully clad in silver steel scales complete with a wyvern head helmet. He exuded arrogance, and I wondered, had I finally come face to face with the king?

-35-

"Thaddeus," Colm addressed the frontman.

"Brother," Thaddeus replied monotonously as though we were nothing more than an irritation.

The rain poured down on us, drenching the two brothers staring daggers at one another, the air thick with the tension of unspoken words.

"I'll be honest, I wasn't surprised to hear of your betrayal. Especially after matching with one of Father's village pets," Thaddeus spat whilst giving Rose a once over with a curled lip.

"You watch your tongue, Thaddeus," Colm ordered through a stiffened jaw.

"Or what, Colm? You'll do nothing. You always were the weak link of this family. Mother babied you far too much." The bitterness in his voice caused his nose to wrinkle.

"I was a sick child. She did what any good mother would," Colm returned.

"Father should've terminated you the minute you were born."

My mouth gaped at the suggestion. How cruel to say such a thing to a sibling.

"Father is a monster, Thaddeus. You know this. He does not care for us or Mother. All he cares about is power. Help us put an end to him. Help us free the people."

Colm tried to reason with his brother.

"And have us follow this red-headed village scum as our queen?" Thaddeus made a face as though he had tasted something awful.

Nathaniel jerked forward, but I stretched my arm across his body to stop him. Thaddeus laughed as he caught me.

"I see she has you under control already," he addressed Nathaniel.

"Let me kill him," he pleaded with me.

"Patience, my loyal subject," I jested, although it did not lighten the mood as I had hoped.

"Where's Sylvie?" Colm shouted at his brother.

"That doesn't matter anymore. She's as good as dead," Thaddeus replied without an ounce of care for his sister-by-bond. "Father has probably drained her already. Don't you feel yourself fading away yet?"

I glanced at Nathaniel, but he shook his head. Thaddeus was lying. His goal was to cause Colm to act rashly.

"What did you do?" Colm stormed toward Thaddeus, drawing his sword from its scabbard.

Thaddeus did the same, and both blades clashed in front of snarling faces in a brotherly feud.

Droplets of rain fell from their brows, furrowed with pure aggression.

We began to edge forward using their feud as a distraction.

They had double our numbers, we had to get an advantage somehow.

Our attempt did not go unnoticed.

An energy burst from Thaddeus sending us flying into the arms of our comrades behind us. The rain splattered the ground around us, and I realised that someone had managed to shield us from the force of Thaddeus' aero attack, lessening the damage it could have afflicted.

I looked at the droplets and wondered if any of our hydromancers could weaponize them like our enemy had when we were making our way up the plains.

Tuck jumped up from the ground with two balled up fists out in front of him before pulling them back with force. The soldiers fell to the ground on their backs, as if Tuck had just ripped a black tablecloth out from beneath their feet like one of those magic tricks, but this time the crockery and wine glasses toppled, but that was the aim.

A tall blonde with cropped hair and masculine features who I'm sure Colm called Julia, whirled their hands in a circular motion, gathering the moisture in the air and throwing it onto the downed soldiers, sending them back down to the ground again.

Thaddeus was strong and fast as he marched towards us, resisting the assault of the battering rain. He pointed his palm towards the hydromancer and sent Julia over the walls of the battlement with a swiping motion.

Everyone stopped and could do nothing but watch as the screams faded, signifying the start of another brawl.

Two sides roared as they ran at each other on the battlement. Bodies tore through the air, howling, as they were lifted from the ground and tossed like they weighed nothing. Metal clanged and fists pounded flesh.

All around people were defending what they believed in, and it was time for me to join my family on their mission for righteousness, and I found my first target. He was tag-teaming Lis with another soldier, both grinning and giggling like they knew they'd have her two to one.

Cowards.

I waltzed over and tapped one on the shoulder, and as he turned to face me, I wiped the smarm from his face as my knee struck his groin—a Greer special. I ripped off his helmet as he doubled over and smacked the back of his head with it.

"You bitch!" he growled. He ran at me, hands ready to grab, but I ducked just in time and swung the spiked club end of my polearm around the back of his skull with a head-splitting crack.

"Badass," Lis cheered.

A pivot, and I already found myself face to face with another attacker. He grinned with his tensed fingers out to his left before launching a hefty block of stone towards me. Geomancer. I pivoted back, and it skimmed me between the shoulder blades, knocking the wind out of me. The contact shook me, but I recovered quickly, even more irate than before. I grabbed the hilt of my dagger and waited for him to close the gap, then thrust it into the flesh where his neck sloped down to his shoulder. I did not enjoy the noise bubbling through the gash it left.

"Careful, please," Nathaniel reminded.

"I got this. Don't let me distract you," I replied, more of a plea, as a soldier caught him in a grip around his neck. I thanked the gods for preventing me from witnessing Nathaniels death by my distraction, as he

spun quickly to free himself, twisting the soldier's arm behind his back at an unnatural angle. The crunch I heard pulled a yell from the soldier's gut.

My eyes shot about for another enemy to defeat. Between us we had managed to reduce their numbers by at least half, and all of those who had become important to me were among the survivors, still battling through.

My gaze drifted back to Nathaniel taking on not one, but three soldiers. The way he moved so gracefully but with so much force. He drove his attack home. He was so manful and gallant. His brawn and vigour ignited a spark in me, and I felt the urge to stride right up to him and claim him here mid battle. I surprised myself that I could feel turned on in the midst of such life-threatening atrocities.

In my peripheral, I spied the glint of a blade coming for me. I countered it with my staff and sliced the attacker's throat with my own blade. I noticed Colm paused in awe at my ruthlessness.

"You're phenomenal, Red!" he called to me.

"I had a great teacher," I shouted back.

"I reckon you could teach me a thing or two. The student has become the master," he cackled.

The huge grin that painted his face was quickly erased by widened eyes and a look of complete terror.

A feeling of weightlessness brought with it awareness that I was rising from the ground, my arms and legs in a tight grip, like being held by a giant fist. I turned my head to find Thaddeus sneering, holding me in with a force I was unable to wriggle free from, and I knew then at any moment I'd be going over the side of the parapet just like Julia.

"Rose!"

In my thirst for blood, I had become separated from Nathaniel, who was now on the far side of the battlement. He instantly bounded into a sprint, but there was no way he would reach me in time.

"No, Rose!"

I could hear the beginnings of a sob catch his throat. I couldn't look at him any longer.

Fear trembled through me, but I refused to show it to Thaddeus. I smiled in the face of Death. He snickered at me until something behind me caught his eye. I turned my head in time to see Colm dart past me, running full throttle at Thaddeus, clashing his shoulder with Thaddeus' midsection.

"No!" I screamed as he tackled Thaddeus over the battlement wall.

I slammed into a merlon as the grip around me released. I rolled myself into the crenel, frantically searching for Colm's landing spot. I found him...speared through the torso by one of the spikes protruding from the moat bed.

A deep, guttural roar ripped from my core and tore from my mouth as my hands fisted my hair.

"Colm!" Nathaniel bellowed from my side.

A vociferous, earth shattering-scream escaped me as he called for his best friend, breaking my heart further.

The stones beneath me began to shift and crack. Another howl of indignation, and the rain and the earth and the wind and the fire from the beacons were a whirlpool of forces in the airspace above us. I released the painful grip on my strands as an assault of the elements crashed down on us all. Screams of agony perforated my eardrums as burning bodies stumbled by, arms flailing. The smell of singed hair and flesh stung my eyes as desperate victims threw themselves from the battlements to escape the hell that had rained down on us all.

Suddenly, time resumed its normal speed, and I remembered my people were on this rooftop with me.

Shit.

In my anger, I lost all regard for anyone else.

Behind me, perplexed expressions on wandering rebels as they took in their surroundings. They were unharmed, apparently shielded, and I wondered, despite my absolute loss of control. Had I been the cause of the chaos that had unfolded up here on the battlements? The cloud of fury that pelted the parapet. Had I managed to simultaneously protect my people from my wrath? Relief and deep exhaustion buckled my knees.

Nathaniel caught me in his arms. "We can talk about this later, but we have to get off this roof before it collapses," he urged.

Just then, a familiar beating sounded in the air. The war drum thrums of wyvern wings. We scrambled back to the edge and glanced out at the glorious sight of the serpentine, winged creatures that our enemies had the audacity to wear as their sigil.

They were on our side.

They torched the plains as soldiers dispersed like insects.

Sable approached the battlement with a rider upon her back.

"Meg!" I exclaimed. "I thought you could never set foot here again?"

"I'm not on foot, child. I'm flying," she chuckled.

I could not describe how glad I was to see them.

"Meg, Colm is down there." She cast her eyes to follow where I was pointing. "You have to get him back to the Deadlands Meg. I can't leave him there. This can't be where it ends for him."

I locked eyes with Sable. *"Please save him."*

She blinked at me. I trusted her with everything I had left.

I glanced down at Colm once more, his face already starting to pale, a line of stark red blood curved around his cheek from the corner of his mouth. My eyes began to sting as the weight of what I had requested of them slapped me in the face. It was the type of slap that would wake one from a nightmare, but I was still in one.

"Rose, we have to move," Nathaniel urged, pulling me from the edge toward the door, his face wet with tears of sorrow.

"Please find a way to bring him back. Promise me," I cried out to them as he dragged me to the door, knowing full well that no one had the ability to bring someone back from the dead.

"I will do everything in my power," Megarra humoured me, but the look in her eyes told me she knew that there was nothing she could do.

Every survivor from the battlement had made it to the bottom of the winding stairs in one piece whilst the stone platform and turrets crumbled.

Nathaniel kept me back at the bottom. He didn't pause before pressing his lips so firmly against mine it calmed my erratic heartbeat and tremors. It stopped my mind from racing, thinking about Sylvie and Colm, thinking of all the soldiers that had just had holes punched into them by leaden rain while being pommelled by rubble and burnt alive by a flurry of elements that I'm almost certain was a product of my unbridled temper, but at the same time was completely unfathomable. I had never displayed power before. Maybe it was all coincidence.

Nathaniel's splayed hand straddled my lower back, and heat throbbed from it, sending tingles over my skin like a million feather-light touches. I parted my lips, and his tongue swept over mine, catapulting me into a frenzy of need. His other hand lifted my thigh and wrapped it around his waist as he pressed his hard length against me.

"Of all the days I have lived, none of them have fulfilled me more than the days I have spent with you," he breathed into my mouth, his lashes wet from grief, stuck together as though they'd been dipped in black ink. "You're a fucking queen, Rose Harlow, and I'm going to spend the rest of my days worshipping every part of you."

-36-

Lis, Thoran, Tuck, Nathaniel, and I searched room after room in the castle, avoiding the brawls, trusting our brothers in arms to take care of our enemies, whilst we searched for the head of the beast, and when we found it, I would gladly decapitate the monster.

"This would be a lot easier if Colm were here," Thoran claimed with a hint of sorrow in his voice.

Colm's wild-eyed expression flashed across my memory. It was frozen there. I'd never seen that one before. His sharp lines housed usually soft features. Laughter lines wrinkled his vibrant eyes where his cheeks would be lifted by his constant smile. His sandy hair was always askew due to expressive hands and his jovial lolloping. But this face, the one that had embedded itself into my brain, was contorted with anguish, creased with exertion as he sprang into action with so much regard for me and so little for himself. He knew his wife was in this castle. His mission was to save her above all else, so why did he sacrifice himself for me? Maybe he never intended to go over the wall. Maybe he thought he would detach himself from his brother sooner. Maybe Thaddeus held on to Colm to accompany him to the grave. Had he realised his fate in that split second? Did Colm regret it? Did he regret saving my life in that moment before...?

We moved in silence, and I would bet that all our heads were filled with thoughts of Colm, but we couldn't let ourselves be held hostage by the grief, not while Sylvie was still out there, and not whilst this prophesied nemesis of mine was hiding somewhere in this castle.

The deeper we got into the belly of the fortress, the more the battle sounds faded. It was like standing on a narrow ledge, taking tiny shuffling steps to get to our destination. With bated breath, we inched forward careful not to slip up, not knowing what we would find around each dark corner.

The throne room was frigid stone with an orange glow from the sconces on the pillars between narrow, arch-shaped windows.

A contrast of cold and warmth, the room was vast, and although we crept, our collective steps bounced off the walls.

Huge tapestries hung, navy blue with that red wyvern crest. My eyes scanned the various wall hangings and wall-mounted weapons until they settled on the arrangement at the far end of the hall. A huge chandelier dangled from the ceiling, housing thick candles dripping with spent wax. A large arched window framed an incredible view of the sunrise, painting the morning sky amber and rose casting the enormous throne and the person standing to the right of it in shadow.

My heartbeat stuttered for a moment. The shaded beings should have stolen my attention, but my eyes had completed their loop of the room as I took it all in and landed on the final, most hideous part of the decor.

A swirl of emotions, a bitter taste on my tongue, and a rush of disgust for the disturbing decoration. Its eyes were familiar, but there was no glow there. Scarlet scales and an ever-open mouth of jagged teeth, the wyvern's face was frozen with a ferocious snarl, its head mounted on a wooden plinth above the throne, like it was a medal or a trophy of a hunter.

"Magnificent, isn't he?" a voice croaked from the shadows.

It was sonorous and gravelly and fattened with pomp.

We edged closer until our vision adjusted to the dim room, and for the very first time I cast my eyes on my enemy.

"I'm sure he was," I replied, biting my tongue at all of the words I wanted to say. I knew they would fall on deaf ears.

"Did you enjoy your welcome party?" he teased.

"Not very king-like of you to sit on your throne while others fight your battle for you," I retorted.

"Quite. But I'm exactly where I'm supposed to be."

"You're not as impressive as I was expecting."

That was putting it politely. This man in front of me had garnered so much fear from his subjects. He was notoriously cruel, and his power was unmatched, so why did the man in front of me look so frail that he would need help to even get up from his high-backed chair made of bone and swords?

"Well, I am two thousand years old, Rose Harlow."

He offered his excuse to me. It was a little underwhelming, to be honest. I had been riled up to the point that I was imagining all the ways I was going to do it, and seeing that wyvern head mounted there reminded me of the horrors Sable had shared with me on our flight. I'd never felt so certain that I could end a life happily and without regret until I caught sight of this feeble-looking man.

"You look just like her," he laughed scornfully.

I looked around to the others expecting that he was talking to one of them, but his eyes were still on me.

"Who?" I snarled, impatient to his riddles.

"Your mother," he answered, as if it were obvious.

"You don't know my mother," I scoffed.

"Don't I?" he replied, with a knowing smirk lifting one corner of his mouth.

"It was you? You took her from us?"

My brows furrowed with disbelief. He was lying.

"No," he bellowed as he slowly straightened from his slouch in his royal chair. "She gave herself to me."

"No." I raised my voice this time, mocking the way that he had said no to me.

I stunned him with my outburst. He wasn't used to disdain being dealt his way.

"You're lying. She wouldn't have done that. She didn't know about any of this."

She wouldn't. She was a villager. She was born and raised there. She didn't know about the king or that anything existed outside of the village. If she had she would have done something, told my father. Unless she did try to do something and confided in Pastor David.

Horror tingled my scalp.

"A mother's love knows no bounds," he remarked, but it sounded more sarcastic than genuine.

He wanted so badly to pique my interest, for me to ask the questions he wanted me to ask. I was falling into his trap in the narrative that he was trying to create, and I couldn't help myself. I needed more proof of his lies.

"You're a liar," I screamed as I began to march to him, glaring at my tormentor, as I was reminded of all the mothers love I'd been deprived of.

A slight raise of his hand, and he threw me backward. I landed on my arse on the spot that I had been standing in. I was getting sick of arrogant royal pricks throwing me around.

Nathaniel helped me to my feet to the sound of swords being unsheathed.

"Don't be ridiculous. None of you are a match for me. Put down your weapons," he belittled.

My friends held fast, refusing his command. "I said, put down your weapons," he yelled.

And still, they did not move.

"If we are no match for you, as you say, then it should not matter that we hold weapons," Thoran argued.

"Suit yourself," the king replied lightly.

But before the expressions of victory had fully formed on our faces, lightning bolts of pain shot through my body. My muscles tensed at the strain and burned with the torment. My jaw clenched so hard I thought my teeth would break. The grunting and panting coming from behind me told me we were all experiencing the same pain.

Suddenly, it stopped, and I looked back at my friends, recovering from the torture we had all endured. Reddened faces creased with exertion and beads of sweat speckled their faces. I had to be careful; I didn't want them punished because of me.

"Again, I ask that you put down your weapons."

His voice was calm, as if what he had just done to the five of us had had no physical effect on him whatsoever.

We exchanged agreeing glances, before our weapons clattered to the ground.

Nathaniel kicked his dagger towards the king in anger.

The king responded with an eyebrow raised, then laughed. "Where were we? Ah, yes, your mother was a powerful woman. She had heard a whisper on the wind of a prophecy. Quite a useful power, to hear whispers. It's the same power that told me you were coming."

He paused.

If he expected me to buy it, then he was wrong.

"She claimed that she was the subject of the prophecy, and that she had come to kill me. Silly me," he laughed. "I didn't even question her about the prophecy that had haunted me for years. I saw her red hair and believed her lies. It's funny; she actually thought she could do it. She completely underestimated me. She was right there, right where you're standing now."

I glanced at my feet and imagined her here alone, how scared she must have been to discover all of this for the first time and to travel all of this way and face a fiercer version of the monster before me.

I could feel her presence like a ghost in the room.

He wasn't lying.

Why did she come here?

"She started muttering some garbage about cursing me to death, but I put a stop to her before she could finish. I got great pleasure from watching her life drain from her eyes."

A tear escaped regardless of how hard I tried to keep it from falling. I kept my face as neutral as possible to prevent him from seeing how much the truth tore me up inside, but I failed.

"You're a monster," I screamed at him.

My temper was building, a storm gathering force.

"No!" he bellowed back. "I'm a god!"

His voice echoed around the chamber.

Nathaniel placed a supportive hand on my shoulder, tethering me to the spot.

"You see, your mother knew that her precious daughter was the one the prophecy spoke of, and she thought she could manipulate me into believing her to be the one, in order to protect you. I'll give her credit where credit is due; it did fool me for a while. Your mother was a witch, child, and I absorbed that witch for what she did to me."

I could see his temper rising. He was the most animated he had been so far. Animated with rage and fury that reddened his face as the words left his mouth covered in spittle. He wiped his dewy lips with the sleeve of his robe before resuming his slumped posture.

I slipped Nathaniel's grip and made for the king again.

Fuck him.

I would finish what my mother couldn't.

He raised his open palm and lifted me from the ground before slamming me back down.

"Rose."

Nathaniel collected me from the flagstone floor.

That time the attack seemed to be only on me.

He crouched beside me. *"No more. Just be patient. We need to wait for the right moment."*

His words confused me. The right moment? When would be the right moment to kill a king that should already be dead if length of life was judged on how worthy you were of living?

"With your mother's power, I heard of another prophecy. It told me that I could achieve total immortality if I were to possess every power, every ability, and guess what? There is only one that I do not have. Until today…"

His smug grin only widened as we exchanged perplexed glances. None of us possessed anything the king would need.

"Wait for the right moment," Nathaniel repeated like he knew that what was about to come could provoke me into making a mistake.

Did he already know?

Or was it so predictable that I would act so rashly.

"Sylvie," the king beckoned.

Sylvie emerged from behind the throne, stone-faced and glassy eyed.

Lis gasped from behind me as Tuck and Thoran held her back from striding forward.

The kings' eyes flicked towards them and an expression of approval at their restraint seemed to impress him. Or was he disappointed that he didn't get the chance to abuse his power.

Sylvie's focus locked forward and would not meet with any of ours. She was no longer in her battle leathers. The sleeves of her gown draped from shoulder to wrist and fluttered while she moved. The material looked fluid like water in a crystal blue hue.

"Sylvie here is kindly helping me to achieve my destiny," the king announced.

I glanced around at the slack jawed faces of betrayal. A tear trailed down Lis' cheek and Thoran looked like he was warring with himself about the appropriate action to take.

"She is my missing piece," he continued. "Can you believe it? Destiny is a peculiar force, and I love the way she serves me. I now understand why she led my son to Sandy. My daughter-by-bond has the power of rejuvenation!" he coughed, as the sudden surge of excitement became a little too much for his frail frame to manage.

Rejuvenation?

That was one of the rare powers. That's why she looked so good.

"Give that power to me, Sylvie," he commanded her. She began to move towards him.

"Wait," I shouted.

She paused.

I couldn't accept that she would go through all of this and willingly side with that piece of shit. She wouldn't betray us. All of this was because of her. But most of all, she wouldn't do this to Colm.

"Sylvie, I don't know how he is making you do what he wants, but you have to know something. Colm's dead."

She turned her head to me stiffly with her statuesque face and deathly glare, and I saw it.

I saw the tears well in her eyes, and a line etched the space between her brows for a millisecond.

A yelping noise left the mouth of the person to the right of the throne, and I looked to her for the first time like she had almost been invisible throughout this whole ordeal. If not for the crown on her head, a much simpler band in comparison to the king's metallic head piece, jagged with what I assume to be the spines of the very wyvern on the plinth above him, I could pick her out of a line up as Colm's mother from their likeness alone.

The queen wore an expression identical to Sylvie's.

She looked half the king's age, which I knew was down to my mother's curse.

I could see how I had missed her. Her hair was greying, dull as the drab clothing that adorned her thin frame. The remnants of her sandy blonde youth still clung to some of the strands. She was a mousy-looking woman, but more than that, you could tell her face was once kind, was once lit up by the same jovial and carefree charisma that Colm displayed.

I allowed myself to weep for a moment at his loss.

The king was controlling her. He was controlling them both. There was no other answer. The queen had stood stock still at his side in the shadows and hadn't reacted to anything thus far, until I announced the death of her son.

"That traitorous scum does not deserve our sorrow, Lisandra," the king sniped.

Sylvie reached out her trembling arm to place her hand upon the king's. I could see how hard she was trying to fight against his hold. I had to stall.

"Thaddeus is dead too," I blurted out.

I had no idea of the impact those words would have after meeting the man himself not so long ago on the battlements, but my arsenal was sparse. I had to try something.

The queen stumbled out of his hold and brought a handkerchief to her mouth to catch a sob.

The king paused for a moment, and I saw cracks in his facade. He quickly gathered his composure.

"Did you do this on purpose?" he addressed the queen. "Do you hate me that much that you would give me such weak children?" he scowled.

I noticed the queen cower as though she was used to this man not just causing harm with his words but physically breaking her with his hands.

Sylvie's knees folded, and she dropped to kneel at the foot of the throne, her hand still grasped by King Bellinus. He inhaled deeply, sighing with satisfaction as she began to squeal with agony. I could see her soul slipping away and revitalising him before our eyes.

"What do we do?" I asked Nathaniel desperately.

I was done waiting for the right moment if that moment came after watching the bastard take Sylvie's life from her.

"Watch the queen," he advised calmly.

I looked at Queen Lisandra as she furtively dipped to the ground while the king was occupied with Sylvie, concealing an object in her hand, before promptly returning to her position by his throne.

I noticed she did not have her own throne. My beloved would never stand. He would sit beside me, my equal.

The flames in the sconces danced higher, their light flickering around the room.

"Behave, Lisandra," the king ordered his wife. I could sense no love in his tone.

"I don't think I will."

Her voice shook with nervousness as if she had done nothing but obey him her entire existence and this act of freewill was foreign to her.

I wondered had it really been her that slashed at Megarra's face those years ago or had the king controlled her then too.

He turned slowly to find her poised with Nathaniel's dagger at the vulnerable skin of her throat, her knuckles white with the force with which she grasped the hilt.

The king's eyes widened in shock at his wife's threat.

"What is she doing?" I asked Nathaniel.

"Without his Twin Soul, his powers will fade, and he will eventually join her in death. I guess she has nothing left to live for," he explained.

And with that, she plunged the knife deep into her neck. Blood oozed from the wound, coating the blade and dripping along her fingers.

"What have you done?" King Bellinus breathed.

And as if to bestow a hint upon me, Nathaniel's sword glimmered in the flickering flames on the stone slabs ahead of me.

My impulses took hold, and I lunged for it, sweeping it from the ground, closing the gap between the king and I in a few stealthy strides, and drove it into the bastard's heart.

He clutched the blade where it stuck, lodged between his ribs.

Water pooled in the corners of his crinkled milky eyes.

"Witch," he snarled, before he morphed into stone.

What the fuck?

Confusion took over me, freezing me in a daze.

Nathaniel tried to pull me away.

"Rose, it's over. Let's go," he pleaded.

"What…" I mumbled. "I don't…"

"I don't know, but the castle isn't going to hold much longer."

And he was right. The whole time we had been in here, the battle had continued. The clashing and clanging, bellows and groans, bangs and thrums, blood spilled, and flames licked.

Mortar and brick dust trickled from the ceiling, bringing me back to my senses. I began to pull frantically at the sword entrapped in the solidified king.

"Leave it," Nathaniel begged.

"No," I insisted, as I tugged with all the strength I could muster.

"I don't need it, if it means losing you."

He pulled at me to let go of the hilt of the murder weapon.

"No," I repeated, firmer this time.

Tears of frustration rolled down my cheeks as I jerked the sword frantically. "I want to keep the sword that killed the king. I want it as my trophy, just like him and his wyvern head."

Nathaniel looked at me, and a flash of worry shimmered across his face. He put his hands over mine and pulled. A few sharp tugs, and the sword was free.

"There's your trophy." His words were short. He was angry with me. "Now let's go. Sylvie, can you walk?"

Sylvie didn't respond.

Huge stones were falling from above us now.

"Come on," he shouted, as he grabbed Sylvie.

Lis was encouraging us with beckoning hands while Tuck and Thoran held up the nearly collapsed threshold.

A rock the size of the mounted wyvern head smashed to the ground, separating me from Nathaniel and Sylvie.

Lis sprinted towards us.

Another smash to my other side.

"Rose!"

I heard Lis scream my name before blinding pain struck my forehead, sending me to the hard stone floor. The room spun and my hearing muffled like I was underwater. I was drifting downriver, and I surrendered myself to the current.

Blood rippled in front of my eyes.

"Rose."

The voice bubbled around me.

"Rose."

Clearer this time.

My vision started to focus, and the blood that had rippled before was not blood, but her hair. Red braids upon a face that looked familiar but different. She had ebony skin, kind eyes, and a dimple on her chin. She had the face of my mother but worn, aged.

"You must get up, Rose. This is not the end."

She gave me her hand and I took it, wrenching me from the ground.

I glanced around to get my bearings.

I saw Tuck and Thoran at the far end of the room holding up the doorway.

I looked back to my mother, and she was gone.

This is not the end.

My leg felt like spikes had been hammered into it, and I could not put full pressure on it, but I ran.

I ran with the power of my mother, the power of Nathaniel's love, and the power of the girl that killed the king.

-37-

I barely remembered our flight back to the Deadlands. I drifted in and out of consciousness. My adrenaline supply ran dry once I'd clambered onto Sable's back. Sheer exhaustion hit me like a tonne of bricks. I was hungry and thirsty, and my entire body was one cramping muscle. I felt numb, as if I'd felt so many things that my ability to feel any one thing had faltered. I went from love and camaraderie in the tavern to brutality and murder on the battlefield in the space of one night. I exerted my body in a way I'd never experienced before and hoped to never experience again. I had been locked in fight mode, and at times I scared myself with how eager I was to annihilate our enemy.

I watched someone I had grown to love die before my eyes, then witnessed his mother slit her own throat, burdened by the loss of her children, to bring an end to her husband's reign of terror.

I was punched and pommelled by fists and weapons, and a castle almost collapsed on me.

I had maimed and murdered people.

I had killed the king.

"Sleep, child." A voice encouraged me.

Like a spell, I succumbed in the safety of the dip of Sable's back, between her wings.

Resting against Nathaniel, I slept.

Even in sleep, I was haunted by the images of battle. I watched everyone I loved die, all of them skewered on the pikes protruding from the moat bed.

Sylvie and Nathaniel either side of Colm. Lis, Tuck, and Thoran to the left of them. My father was there, his mouth gaped wide, and his arms dangled. Meg's wiry hair was strewn, obscuring her face.

And most shockingly, Sable.

Her head had been ripped from her body, like the mounted head in the throne room, and the pike protruded from her mouth, pushing her tongue to hang out over the side.

The moat began to fill.

As the murky water reached their limp bodies, their eyes and mouths snapped open, and the most horrifying, ear-piercing screams tore from their throats.

I turned and cried for help.

When I looked down, I was holding the hilt of Nathaniel's sword with both hands, and at the end of the blade was the king.

Bellinus wrapped his hand around the steel and sunk it into his own stomach. He walked towards me, the sword sinking further into his body. He seemed to be enjoying it; he was smirking.

When he could walk no further, he took a dagger from his belt and plunged the knife into my gut.

◆◆◆

My eyes flickered open to catch dust motes dancing below the beams of a ceiling I recognised. I was in the room I had stayed in at Megarra's home. I let out a hefty sigh as I sunk further into the mattress.

The window was open. I could feel a breeze floating through, licking the sweat from my night terror. I knew it wasn't real. I knew it was my subconscious being cruel, terrorising me.

I was a murderer now. I probably deserved the torture.

I wouldn't allow it. I would take that nightmare as what could have been. I would let the visions humble me, to remind me to be grateful that we had managed a different outcome.

Someone stirred beside me.

Nathaniel sat on a chair next to the bed with my hand in his, his forearm a pillow for his heavy head. He stretched out his hunched-over form and rubbed the sleep from his eyes.

He wore a wistful look, one that said he was unsure how to interact with me right now, and it scared me. He smiled pensively and drew a breath like he had been holding it until I woke. His fingers cautiously caressed the side of my face as though I was the fragile one, yet he looked like he was at breaking point. His brows were low, and his eyes were missing their usual sparkle.

"Want to talk about it?"

His voice had a roughness as if he had kept a vow of silence until he was certain I was okay.

His weary eyes searched mine, and I was suddenly overcome with emotions. I cracked as the dam gave way, and out spilled weeks worth of trauma.

He stroked my hair and leaned in closer but never took his eyes off me. Soft kisses peppered my hair, my forehead, and the tears that streaked down my cheeks, wetting his lips.

He pressed his head to mine, and I breathed him in.

The scents that I grew up with; Mother's hair, the morning coffee on Father's breath, the herbal scent of Mother's fingertips, the air in the village that was crisp and clean and carried the scent of freshly baked goods but sometimes reeked of animals, especially on mucking-out day. They were just that, scents I grew up with, smells I would always be fond of.

But this one, the way he smelled, that was home. I sniffed the final tears away and revelled in the feeling of letting go of all my woes. I felt far less heavy. I'd grieved appropriately for those I'd loved and those I did not know but deserved more than a passing thought. I grieved for the centuries of poor treatment of both humans and creatures of the kingdom, the whole kingdom, however wide that may be.

And I grieved for me.

The girl who had done unthinkable things and been changed in unimaginable ways. I made a promise to myself that whatever may come next, I would do my utmost to make sure it was right and just.

I noticed Nathaniel dab his face in a way that was secretive, trying to play it off as an itch, but I saw the streaks within the dirt, like little streams running through hillsides.

"What's wrong?" I asked.

He was holding back, and the cracks were starting to appear.

"Nothing," he replied.

He flashed a small smile, but the flare of his nostrils and the rapid blinking of his lids told a different story.

"Please, don't hide from me."

That was all it took before his cover was blown.

"I killed her," he whispered while swallowing a lump in his throat.

"Killed who?" I probed.

We had injured and killed many soldiers on the way to the king. I didn't feel too great about it either, but he was more acclimatised to that life than me. He had said he killed as was necessary; to protect those he loved. He scrubbed his face with both hands, and I noticed that he was still so filthy. His stubble was back and at least three days' worth of growth.

"How..."

But before I could finish asking him how long we had been back for he interrupted.

"I killed the queen."

The confession spilled from his quivering lips. "I killed Colm's mother."

He wrapped a hand over his mouth as though the words held much more weight when spoken aloud.

"No," I objected.

I dipped my head to meet his lowered gaze. He met me halfway.

"I was there Nathaniel. She took her own life."

"I gave her the weapon. I willed her to do it," he sniffed.

"Nathaniel, no."

I cupped his face softly and he nuzzled in, pressing his hand against my own to keep it in place.

"Lisandra chose to end her life as it was the only way to stop Bellinus. But ultimately, the death of her children led her to make that decision."

He shook his head in disbelief.

He thought I was wrong.

"I didn't deviate from the plan. I used the love that she had for Colm, just like we were supposed to, I made sure my knife landed close to her, and I willed her to do it."

A memory flashed across my mind.

The details of what had happened were still cloudy, but I remembered this... *'Watch the queen.'* He had said it so calmly and with such certainty, like he had foreseen it.

"Are you a seer?" I asked, a prickling sensation rippling the back of my neck.

He shook his head in reply.

"So how did you know she would do it?"

"I didn't."

"Exactly. You killed Lisandra as much as I amassed a cloud of rage above my head then used it to annihilate those people on the battlements causing it to collapse."

Neither thing was plausible.

I wouldn't allow him to carry this burden, to take responsibility for something out of his control. I cared too much to let that happen.

"Actually, we should probably talk," he said, his expression solemn.

I wasn't ready to have such a conversation.

"Can it wait?"

-38-

"He's excited to see you too," Nathaniel confirmed, as I scraped half of my hair back from my face and fastened it at the back.

I was back in comfy pre-war clothes of a simple tunic and loose trousers, ready to meet the others downstairs.

According to Nathaniel, I'd been out of it for a few days, and they were all a ball of nerves anticipating my waking.

The bump to my head had left a tender lump and the large splinter of wood that had been lodged in my lower leg he had removed and stitched meticulously, cleaned and changed the dressing daily. He had said it was at least a foot long but when I assessed the wound it looked slightly worse than a scratch. He too was surprised at how quickly I had healed.

He had stayed by my side in case I decided to come to in the middle of the night, and refused all offers of a good meal and hadn't even bathed, which I could certainly smell. Blood was still encrusted on his clothing and skin.

He had washed me from top to toe. My skin smelled of citrus, and my hair had been tentatively combed and oiled.

In taking care of me, he had abandoned himself.

"I do want to see them, but can we do something first?"

I left him standing in the bedroom watching me leave with a puzzled expression while I nipped across the corridor to the bathroom.

Floral paper browned with age hung from the walls. There were black spots in the corners where the damp had infected the paintwork. A huge half barrel sat in the centre with various towels hanging over its ledge and the privy in the corner. An ornate, oval mirror hung on the wall, and I had to double-take at the girl who walked by.

Was that me?

My reflection had maybe a decade on me.

When I'd left Sandy, when I was taken...I'd been full of youth. My eyes were bright like the sun that had browned my skin.

The girl staring back at me looked as though she had lived hard. Her skin was ashy and dry. Her lips were pale and lined. It had been a while since Father had grabbed my cheeks between his thumb and forefinger, but there was nothing there to squeeze any more.

I glanced down at my hollowed stomach. It groaned right on cue.

A heaviness snaked along my shoulders and burrowed in my chest. Maybe I was being too harsh on myself. Of course I was going to have lost some weight. I hadn't eaten nearly as much as I usually would, and I'd been moving a hell of a lot more.

The girl that left the village was now a woman of the kingdom.

Under the mirror, a shabby wooden shelving unit supported a wash basin and jug. I dipped my finger into the warm water. It must have been refilled recently. I draped a towel and wash cloth over my arm and carried the jug and basin back to my room.

"Take your clothes off," I requested.

Nathaniel shuffled awkwardly. "We should probably catch up with the others first."

I ignored him and began to unbutton his tunic.

Firm hands grabbed my wrists to stop me, and his eyes conveyed the same.

"What's wrong?" I asked, although I was scared to know the answer.

"Nothing."

His mouth said but his expression told me something else.

"Let me take care of you," I pleaded.

"You don't need to do that," he smiled as he tucked my hair behind my ear.

His expression soft but somewhat guarded.

"I want to…please?"

He let go, allowing my hands to continue.

My fingers trembled as nerves crept in. The silence between us roared loudly in my ears while my heart and mind warred with one another over why Nathaniel seemed so uneasy.

I took my time, one by one.

The black fabric slipped from his shoulders to pool at the floor like an unveiling of an art piece.

I knew he was exquisite clothed, but no amount of preparation could have readied me to see him this way.

He stood there in front of me, vulnerable and powerful in equal measure and it sparked a fire in me. There was a shyness to him being exposed while I stood back and took him in. He was almost submitting to me, and it pleased me.

My eyes made plans for the path I wanted my hands to trail. Palms either side of his thick neck gliding over the swell of muscles and sloping down to his broad shoulders.

My hands fidgeted at my sides, fighting the urge to grab him greedily.

My gaze following the dip in the centre of his muscular chest leading down to stacked ab muscles. His skin like caramel. And like caramel I was melting at the heat this man had provoked in me.

I traded places with him, bringing him out of my shadow and into the spotlight cast by the small window into the dull bedroom. I wanted to get a better look.

I spotted his mark, just like mine.

A smile crept into the corners of my mouth at the reminder of what it meant.

This man belonged to me.

Then, something else caught my attention. I noticed a half-moon scar beneath his right pectoral. It was dark and thick. I hadn't noticed at first as it followed the curve of his chest muscle. Brown and blue bruising mottled his ribs, which I'm sure were new injuries, but the thin lashes along his abs were not. They were barely visible in the dull light of the room, but there were many of them, and I wanted to hurt whoever caused them.

I was curious if there were more odes to injury incised on his skin, and I circled him around until his back faced me. There was shame in the way he swivelled slowly.

A horrified gasp escaped me, and his head drooped low.

I rushed him, throwing my arms around his body and pressing myself into him. My face rested against the most shocking of the many scars, and I knew what had caused it.

The sigil on that evil son-of-a-bitch's possessions: the armour his soldiers wore, the tapestries on the walls, the flags and banners, and apparently, his men. His men. He branded them as though they were his property.

Nathaniel attempted to remove my arms from his middle, but I held fast, so he twisted himself in my grip to face me. He huffed a small laugh before enveloping me in those strong arms of his. He brought a hand up and held my head to his chest and allowed me to linger there.

"Don't feel sad for me. We all have stories."

His words rumbled under my ear.

"I want to kill them all," I pouted.

"Got a thirst for blood now, have we?" he chortled.

I knew he was trying to lighten the mood.

"Not funny," I mumbled, doing my best to stay serious.

He tilted my head back so he could look at me.

"All of my scars are a part of the journey that led me to you."

Tears flooded my lower lids. I blinked and swallowed them back. I wasn't worth his years of torture.

"I'm grateful for each one. If you are my prize for enduring it all, then the pain was just."

He offered me a sympathetic smile and the calming strokes he caressed my hair with humbled me. This was his pain, not mine.

"You smell," I chuckled, using humour to divert my overwhelmingly heavy emotions.

His laughter shook me.

He stepped back and I unfastened his trousers.

As I lowered them, I couldn't help but steal a glance as my face aligned with his midsection. I looked up at him awkwardly, like I'd been caught in the act, my cheeks flushing with heat.

My appearance amused him as he flashed a coy smile.

I promptly stood.

"Sit down," I told him.

The bed groaned under the pressure as he did as I ordered. I unlaced his boots under his prying eyes and laid them to the side along with his socks, then took his trousers off the rest of the way.

The water trickled from the washcloth as I wrung it over the bowl. "May I…?"

A nod of approval.

His legs parted and made way for me to stand closer and my body tingled at the closeness.

I held back his hair with one hand, which surprisingly still looked well kept, and began with soft strokes on his forehead and over his perfect features to remove the crusted blood. He closed his eyes and revelled in the soft warmth of the washcloth and my tender touch. The silky skin of his eyelids glistened and were garnished with thick, luscious lashes. I remembered him during battle with his hood up in fierce combat. His cloak billowed about him as he swirled from one opponent to the next. An all-powerful warrior. He was a far cry from the man in front of me. This man looked like he had been through the wars. Well, what else did I expect. He had gone through the trials of battle in Brigsbane and Oakenvale and then again at my bedside not knowing my fate.

I knew the others hadn't seen him this way. He wouldn't have allowed it. He was always strong when it came to them, not that he was being weak now. In fact, allowing himself to be this vulnerable around me was nothing but strong. I admired him for it. Appreciated him for letting down his walls with me.

The dark rings under his eyes that I assumed were from exhaustion were actually bruises. The bridge of his nose was slightly swollen, wider and bruised, and the dry blood streaked from his nostrils across his cheek, I realised, was his. The bump and slight crookedness of his nose was gone, and I wondered if whatever had caused this injury had righted the previous break.

It took everything in my power not to climb into his lap and let him cradle me like a baby while I wept for the fact that he was hurt and had been hurt so many times over the years.

I was overly conscious of the possessive grip he had on my thighs, holding me in place between his legs.

I rinsed the cloth, pinkish tendrils tingeing the water. I wiped the soot from behind his ears and down his neck. The water glistened on his skin like a sheen of sweat. I didn't miss his throat bob, and it pleased me that he was struggling with composure just as much as I was.

I pried his grip from the back of my left leg with difficulty. He huffed a laugh, and I could tell he was deliberately resisting. I washed his hand, taking care to get around the sides of his remarkably well-manicured nails, despite circumstances, and in all the creases of his knuckles and calloused palms. With the blood and dirt wiped away, his knuckles were still red and grazed.

I ran the cloth up his strong, corded forearm before repeating the process with the other one. I imagined those hands all over my body and in my hair. I released a shuddering breath as his hands fell back into their default position just below the crease where my thighs met my backside. The skin there felt more receptive now.

I rinsed the cloth once more. The water turning murkier. I wiped along his collarbones and the hollow of his throat and down the centre of his rib cage. His muscled chest rose and fell. I caught sight of his mark, and I dared myself to touch it. My fingers slowly moved toward his chest, grazing the small brown teardrop mark.

I gave in to the weight of his stare as he studied me. I had never intended for this to feel so erotic. I'd just wanted to wash him, to care for him the same way he had done for me, but all I could think of was mounting his lap and pressing my body so close to his that you couldn't tell where I began, and he ended. I craved the closeness. I ached to touch him.

"You're hurt?"

It was a question but also a reminder, as if to deter him, if his thoughts were just like mine.

He shook his head in denial. "Not anymore."

I smiled at his insinuation that I had somehow healed him, and he grinned, pleased that I sussed his implication.

"I've missed you," he admitted.

"I'm sorry I took so long," I replied, before I placed a tender kiss on his lips.

His tongue swiped the place where it hit as he dragged his bottom lip into to taste it and the moment turned from tender to primal. He lifted the backs of my thighs and seated me on his lap. Every inch of me was thrumming for him as he groaned whilst he dragged me into position.

"I'm never letting you go again." His voice low and possessive, like his arms, which enveloped my back like prison bars. His eyes were filled with sincerity.

"I'm not going anywhere," I insisted.

-39-

I paused in the doorway, tenting my hand across my eyebrows while my eyes grew accustomed to the low spring time sun.

I heard a sigh to my left and found Colm and Sylvie on a bench on the porch. His arm was draped along her shoulders, her head leaning into his neck. They weren't saying anything. Sylvie watched her fingers interweave with his, I'm sure, relishing the fact that this was almost lost.

I was overcome with gratitude—a mere fraction compared to the sheer solace she must be experiencing.

I didn't want to interrupt, so I lingered in the doorframe surreptitiously.

The sound of a throat clearing behind me startled me.

"There she is!"

Colm jumped to his feet so quickly you would never have known he was impaled on a spike only a few days prior.

I marched to him, thumping the ground with my feet to be certain it was not an illusion, to be sure I wasn't asleep and this would all become another nightmare.

I threw my arms around his neck, which caught him completely off guard. We had grown close, but we hadn't yet been this affectionate.

I felt him stiffen as he straightened himself, and my arms unlatched to his conspicuous but pleased expression.

"I missed you too, Red."

I watched the light dance in his eyes, before my barrage of stinging, 'How dare you kill yourself for me,' slaps began. He hopped back and wrapped his arms around himself, making wincing noises while hiding a sly smile.

Sylvie stepped between us.

"I'm sorry. As much as he deserves a beating, I'm feeling rather protective."

"Sorry, Sylvie." I apologised to her, glancing around her side to scorn him with a glower, while he remained hidden behind her, playing a big baby.

"Where are the others?" I asked when I noticed there were a few less of us than I'd expected.

"They'll be back."

Colm crept out from behind the safety of Sylvie's back with a rather smug grin. I presented my open palm in threat. He cowered and giggled. I don't care how smug he thinks he is; I'll take all of it.

"They're in the capital to help with the unrest. The people have a lot of questions, and they're looking to authority to answer them," he continued. "Except there isn't one," he sighed. "It'll take time for us all to adjust, and they just want to know what to expect."

"Most of them are happy that Bellinus is…gone." Sylvie chose her words considerately. "But they're lost and looking for direction."

"So, give it to them," I replied. The answer was obvious to me.

"Give them what?" Colm asked, perplexed.

"Direction. You're the heir to throne, Colm," I pointed out.

"I…I don't want…no." He stuttered like he hadn't even realised that without his father and mother, with his siblings gone, he was the next in line.

"Sylvie would make a magnificent queen," I suggested with a tempting grin, trying my best to sell it.

I wasn't wrong. She would make a magnificent queen, and I would be honoured to follow them as rulers of our kingdom.

Our kingdom.

"I would, wouldn't I?" She laughed, as she straightened her back and carried herself like royalty would and waved graciously.

"Think about it," I insisted.

"If it's what the people want, then perhaps I would consider it. Sylvie, you would have to want it too," Colm replied while searching his wife's face for a hint of what to do. "But I have no idea how to govern a kingdom," he addressed the group.

"If I may," Nathaniel interjected with a level of authority to his tone that spurred an attraction in me. I could feel the energy between us heightening as he moved out of the door frame and brought himself closer. "You could be the King and Queen and rule with equal partnership. You could hire a counsel, maybe a representative from each district, and the people would vote for certain outcomes."

"I'll consider it," Colm repeated, with a tone that begged for us to change the subject.

Being the youngest royal, he probably never thought he would ever become head of state.

"Ah, you're awake." Meg emerged from behind the house with the bucket she used for chicken feed, which was usually vegetable scraps, potato skins, corn, and seeds. "Hate to break up the reunion. Can I have a word?" she asked.

"Yes!" Colm replied a little too enthusiastically. He really did seem desperate to get away from the discussion of kings and queens.

"I'd like to talk to Rose alone, if that's okay?"

It wasn't me she looked to for permission. Nathaniel nodded curtly. I know he said he would never let me go again, but surely, I would be allowed to go to some places without him.

Inside the house, Megarra filled a kettle with water and popped it on the stove. She tore nettles from their stems and placed them in a teapot. A whistle alerted us that the water had boiled, and she poured it into the teapot before bringing it over on a tray with two mismatched mugs.

"So, you can ride Sable too?"

It was all I could think of to fill the silence. Much better than sitting here counting the speckles in the finish of the pottery mug.

I hoped she hadn't sensed the undertone of jealousy. I had thought that Sable and I had a special bond that only her and I shared. Silly, I know, to feel this way about a wyvern, as if our relationship was exclusive.

"She let me ride her, yes."

Her tone was gentle as she tried to coax me from my spiral of envy. "But," she continued, "only because you needed her."

I stopped fiddling with the rough skin that now edged my nails and met her gaze.

"She heard your screams," she responded to my quizzical look.

I placed a hand across my throat as I remembered the noise ripping from it.

"But you showed up immediately?"

It couldn't have been more than five minutes before they arrived.

"Hmm," Megarra laughed whilst pouring us a cup of hot nettle tea. "The moment the wyverns landed after dropping you all off in Brigsbane, she began to get restless. They say animals can sense things that humans can't. She lowered her back to me and bleated a noise, and I knew what she was suggesting."

I didn't know what to say.

I knew how hard it must have been for Meg to leave this place for the first time in so many years, and not only that, to return to the place that had caused her so much trauma.

She did that for us.

"That can't have been easy," I spoke gently.

I wanted her to know that she could talk to me if she needed to. "I'm truly grateful to you."

"Well, I had a debt to repay."

My brows lowered at her admission. What debt? She didn't owe me a thing. I owed her, if anything.

"She saved me, so I had to help her daughter."

Tears had crept into her eyes as she stared at the mini whirlpool she was creating in the tea with her spoon.

I blinked in contemplation.

What could she possibly mean?

"I'm sorry. Who saved you?" I pressed.

She watched the whirlpool simmer out and smiled at a seemingly fond memory she'd found there, before looking me dead in the eyes.

"Millie," she said. "She's the reason I survived."

I lowered the cup I had brought to my lips before I was able to take a sip. It was like a ghost had walked in the room. I was frozen in thought, as the hair on my arms immediately stood up.

Her eyes flicked to the wispy erect hairs and back to me.

"I told you how I almost met my end," she went on. "My final words, the prophecy. I muttered them with magic. If I were to die, I wanted someone else to know the will of destiny."

"The whisper on the wind," I mumbled.

Her face lit up at my words.

"You know it?"

"He…Bellinus, told me." I explained.

"Your mother was a witch, child, just like me. It had been years since I'd met another. Our kind was already low in numbers when Bellinus began slaughtering those he had no use for or us witches, who could challenge his power. When I whispered those words, I released them on the wind to find the ears of those with magic in their veins."

This was the second time I'd heard that my mother was a witch, and I still can't quite accept it as truth.

They must be mistaken.

"She always knew that you were special, and the whisper she heard was enough proof. She sensed you'd be in danger. She said she had to kill the king before he could come for you. You were just a child…"

I stood up abruptly, the scuffing of the chair legs on the floor cutting her off and began to pace the room. I ran my hands through my hair, unable to comprehend that this woman they spoke of, and my mother were the same person. I had so many questions I wanted to ask. My mother had been born and raised in that village. Had she known she was a witch? Was she the only one? Deep sadness weighed on me at the realisation that I would never have the chance to ask her.

I looked to the ceiling and counted the exposed beams and drew calming breaths in and out before reclaiming my chair.

Meg assessed me before deciding it was safe to continue.

"…When she reached the Deadlands, she was greeted by my wyvern friends. They could sense her magic. They led her to me. She spent weeks healing me and helping me. She helped me with this place." She gestured to our surroundings. "She taught me to forage, and which herbs I could use for healing various ailments. We were only together for a short time, but she made such an impact on me. I will never forget her. Your mother was just as important a part of the prophecy as you are, my dear."

I hadn't noticed the tears until one dripped from my chin and burst on the back of my hand. I filled my lungs like it was the first breath I'd taken in minutes. I stood from the table and approached her side solemnly. She rose from her chair timidly, and as she did so, I pulled her into a tight hug. I hugged her, just like I wanted to hug my mother. I felt her tension melt away like it was the first time she had been held this way. She needed this just as much as I did.

"Thank you." That was all I could muster.

To think that Mother had been here made me feel closer to her than I had in years. To think that she was a part of the same battle that I was fighting spurred me on and motivated me to make sure that we triumphed. Her death would not be in vain. I would do my utmost to honour her, to show courage such as she had, to be selfless, and put those I loved before myself. I would make sure to achieve great things, just like the destiny she always spoke of.

I knew exactly where to start.

-40-

Lis, Tuck, and Thoran returned that evening on the backs of wyverns.

I had looked for Sable earlier and had thought they may be hunting or sleeping in their dens.

It seemed we were all able to fly with them, although I felt smug at the fact that Sable arrived riderless.

"We gave them a date next week to reconvene regarding moving forward." Thoran was discussing their visit to the capital with Colm and Sylvie. "On the topic of recovering bodies, geomancers have already begun lifting the collapsed parts of the castle to retrieve loved ones. We have advised them to leave the throne room for now until we'd had a chance to consult with you about what you want to do with, well, you know."

The atmosphere changed like the difference in pressure before a big storm. It just emphasised the fact that Colm had lost so much overnight. His parents, his last living sibling, his home.

"Part of me wants to say that I don't give a shit what you do with them, but I'd be lying, and that confuses me more than anything."

Sylvie rubbed the span between Colm's shoulders.

"It hasn't sunk in yet, darling. You haven't had a chance to grieve. You've lost so much; you've lost your home..."

"No, I haven't," he interrupted. "My home is wherever you are."

"Okay, well we are more than happy to take care of it for you," Tuck offered.

Colm nodded once.

"We salvaged these from the parts of the castle we could access." Lis had gone over to fetch two large bags and unzipped them, revealing books and scrolls. She took one from the top of the bag. "We found a prophecy that matches something that the king...Bellinus, said." She corrected herself as she sat next to me on the porch and drew my attention to the scrolled handwriting on the stained page.

"Bellinus stated something about possession of all the powers, meaning he would be immortal," Lis stated. "Well, we found this passage between the pages of a diary in his nightstand..."

TIME HATH NO END
LIFE HATH NO DEATH
BORN NEW FROM OLD
ONE VESSEL HOLDS ALL

"...You can see why he might have interpreted it to mean that he would gain immortality if he were to be the 'vessel' that holds all powers. But..."

She rummaged to find a diary bound in animal hide; you could feel its presence like a living thing. A shudder rippled down my spine.

"Sylvie, I remember you saying that you found something in the Book of Man that mentioned something like 'prophecies form as twin souls born,' and then Meg told Rose another part of her prophecy…"

She was so energetic in divulging her findings

"…When Megarra told you your prophecy, it came with an extra verse. Bellinus only knew this verse…"

She held up the paper from his nightstand.

"…Which then leads us back to what Sylvie read in the Book of Man, that prophecies are in two halves just like Twin Souls."

There were some mumblings around the group, and I wondered if they were agreeing with her or, like me, had struggled to keep up with her excited rambling.

"Which brings us…" Thoran encouraged her.

"Sorry, yes, we found this passage, which we think is the rest of Bellinus' immortality prophecy. Look at the way it's written, the sentences are formed the same; there are four lines in each…."

> RARE BECOMES COMMON
> CAULDRON BREWS A STORM
> THE FLOWER BUD BLOOMS
> DAWN WILL UNITE ALL

"So, you see, with the full verse, it doesn't seem like the recipe to immortality at all," she finished.

The faces around me wore lost expressions.

"So, what do you think it means then?" I pressed, equally lost.

"Well, we don't know," Thoran chimed in. "The way they are conveyed, it's like riddles. They could be interpreted in many ways."

"Time continues, life goes on, someone will be or has been born that will hold all the power; they will bring us all together?"

Megarra had joined us. We had been so deep in discussion we hadn't even noticed her arrival. She had startled me with her input.

"I'm just spit balling." She laughed at our expressions, a mixture of 'When did you get here?' and 'She could be on to something.'

She continued chuckling as she entered the house with her basket of laundry she had just taken down from the line.

All heads turned to me.

"What?" I questioned suspiciously.

"I don't suppose you hold all the power?" Lis asked.

All eyes were on me now, considering if Lis' theory could have some substance to it.

"Erm…no." I replied quite certain.

I think it's something that I'd be aware of.

"But on the battlements," she started.

I had wondered when someone might address that. I'd only been awake for a couple of hours and already the subject had been broached twice.

"That wasn't me," I cut in. "So many attacks were being thrown around, so many elements against each other. I think it just became one angry concoction."

No one looked convinced.

"And how do you explain the fact that no one on our side was hurt?" she pressed.

"We had a shielder with us, didn't we? Maybe they managed to protect us," Nathaniel offered in defence.

"That's a pretty precise shield," Tuck countered.

"Well, sometimes when people are pushed to the brink of survival, they can do extraordinary things," Nathaniel responded.

He flashed a look at me that told me he agreed with what they were insinuating, but his job right now was to protect me above all else, and protected I felt.

"Indeed."

Colm ended the conversation with one word.

I felt his eyes on me, but I couldn't look at him. It was as if I was see-through, and he could see the memory of what happened after he'd plummeted from the battlement wall.

I was sure someone had filled him and Sylvie in by now.

It had felt like it had come from me. Driven by my grief and rage, but that was just elemental power, and anyhow, the more it crossed my mind, the less I believed it was a product of me. I could not read and control minds or heal others or rejuvenate. I didn't hold all the power. In fact, I didn't feel very powerful at all.

"Well, perhaps I can concern you with something else?" Nathaniel began to cut the tension.

Their conspicuous eyes left me for him, but their faces still wore evidence of difficult conversations that needed to be had. He raised his eyebrows in acknowledgement of the atmosphere and decided to continue.

"I accompanied Megarra on a forage earlier. I was appointed basket carrier."

"Well, yes," Colm laughed at what I can only assume was a mental image of Nathaniel traipsing reluctantly behind Meg carrying her wicker basket like that's all he was good for.

"We gathered lots of wild garlic and dandelions and such, then we paid a visit to the wyverns hide."

Stone faces awaited the rest of his story unsure what the point of it was.

"It turns out the delicious bone broth and meats we have consumed have been the discarded parts of wyvern supper."

I swore he went green.

Colm jumped up but stood still as the information rooted him to the spot.

"I'm going to be sick," Lis announced.

"Wait." Nathaniel halted the commotion. "When I confronted dear Megarra, she replied..." He brought a finger to his lips preparing himself. "Waste not, want not my dear..."

An amalgamation of sounds swarmed the group. Some retching, some cursing the gods, and then there was the laughter. Tuck clutched his stomach while he howled at all the reactions. I supposed it was a little gross but most of our meals contained something dead.

"To be fair to her, she did only pick up the freshest looking bits," Nathaniel added.

This accelerated Tucks laughter like fuel on a fire. He drew a finger below his eye, catching tears before they fell. He held a handful of thick fingers to his chest and sighed the deep breaths that laughter had robbed him of.

"Where are you going?" Colm skipped, kicking up dust clouds as he reached my side.

"Just thought I'd find Sable," I replied.

There was a tension between us since earlier, but it could have been my imagination.

"May I walk you to your wyvern, milady?" He crooked his elbow and flashed me an encouraging grin.

Definitely my imagination.

I was over the moon to be in his joyous company. So many things had changed, but it pleased me to find that he had not. I obliged and linked my arm with his.

"I haven't thanked her yet for helping us, for saving you," I told him.

Nathaniel had shared with me the aftermath of the war in the days that I was recovering. As soon as I'd heard Colm lived, I had sprung from my bed and thrown on the first clothes I could find and fixed my hair. It wasn't until I looked at Nathaniel and saw how much he'd neglected himself that my excitement to find Colm was overtaken by my desire to take care of Nathaniel.

"I haven't thanked you yet either."

He stared at me with kind eyes. I looked away, almost ashamed that he had been so hurt because of me and ultimately for the fact that I had murdered his father.

"You don't need to thank me," my words caught in my throat.

How do I say, 'Sorry I killed your dad, but he was an evil bastard?'

"I'm sorry," I kind of blurted out. It was the best I could do without choking on tears of guilt.

"Hey," he calmed me.

He stopped me in my tracks, bracing me with his hands on my shoulders and lowered his face to capture my gaze. His eyes glittered with benevolence and altruism.

"What you did was already written. Besides, it was just a scratch," he offered in an attempt to make light of the situation.

He placed my palm back in the crook of his elbow, and we continued our stroll.

"It was not!" I argued.

"Well, no. I was definitely impaled," he laughed.

How was he so cool about it?

"But luckily it missed all the important bits and left me with a puncture wound, which your wonderful wyvern cauterised for me to stop me from bleeding out on the flight back. Thankfully, I was unconscious for that bit."

"Wow," I breathed.

I hadn't even considered the journey back or how they'd healed him. All I could think about was the fact that he was dead, and now he's not, and I was just simply elated. I hadn't thought about the how.

"Plus, girls love scars," he chuckled.

Rather a sweeping statement, but I did think of Nathaniel and the jagged lines on his perfect skin. Each bump and imperfection telling a story. A story of strength and survival. A story of his fight to live and love and protect. I thought of the trauma behind each one and how they shaped the man I loved.

"I'd do it again, you know," he said, snapping me out of my daydream.

I raised my eyebrows at his claim. He's mad if he would be happy to do that more than once.

"I'd maybe try to tackle a little lower next time rather than over the bleeding wall, but what I'm trying to say is, I didn't hesitate. I was honoured to give my life to save yours."

Sable wasn't far from the house. She had curled up atop a flat rock, breathing heavily. I clambered up to meet her and perched myself beside her, leaning back against her curves.

She opened an ochre eye to acknowledge me before closing it again nonplussed. Her scales had soaked up the sun's rays, transferring warmth into my still aching back, soothing me like a heated cloak.

"Thank you," I started. "Not just for saving Colm, but being there when I needed you."

She huffed at my show of gratitude.

Not one for sentimentality.

Got it.

I closed my eyes, calmed my senses, and allowed myself to exist in the moment. I had held so much tension in my body as of late. I was on constant high alert, scared for myself, scared for my friends, scared for my people.

I shut the door.

I shooed it away like a cat and shut the door on it.

Now it was just me.

Alone.

I was sprawled on a cosy rug with my back to the fire, the warmth penetrating my bones and driving out any lingering cold and fear.

Footsteps crept down the wooden staircase. A velvet baritone hummed a lullaby, and as he entered my line of sight, in the flickering orange glow radiating from the hearth, he smiled the most breathtaking smile and continued his soothing song.

In his arms was a bundle of blankets.

He stopped in front of me, carefully crouched, and laid the bundle into the curve of my torso.

I instinctively pulled it towards me. He leaned down and kissed my forehead, and I felt the love seep beneath my skin. He then leaned to the bundle and did the same to it.

When my eyes followed his movements, I saw that the bundle had a beautiful peach face, blush-kissed cheeks, and a perfect button nose. Delicate black lashes lined the baby's eyelids. A blotch of purplish-red stained one eyelid and part of her cheek.

I stroked the birthmark with my fingertips, and the baby huffed a delicate little noise.

A sweet smell like milk and honey wafted up my nostrils. It was so divine. I imagined it was what heaven smelt like.

Just then, the front door burst open. The wind howled and the rain came down in sheets, and in the frame of the dark night sky stood a shadowy figure. I stared at him, adjusting my focus, searching for details of who our visitor was.

As I stared, I noticed his shape begin to morph, as shadows unfurled from his sides like wings. Lightning cracked and thunder rumbled, and with the flash of light, he was gone.

I looked back down at the bundle I was curled around, and they too were gone.

"Nathaniel," I called as panic began to rise.

"I'm here," he replied.

I felt his grip on my arm, and as I looked to my side, everything went black.

"Nathaniel!"

Louder now.

My heart was pumping fast, stealing my breath.

"Rose, I'm here."

I blinked a few times, and Nathaniel materialised before my eyes. I threw my arms around his neck and gasped with relief.

"Hey," he soothed. "You were having a bad dream."

A bad dream? I was dreaming...?

I glanced around and noticed the sky was velvety black and dotted with stars, shimmering like silver sequins. I was still on the rock with Sable, who was camouflaged in the dark of night.

"You want to tell me about it?" Nathaniel offered.

What would I say? 'It wasn't a bad dream. The most part was actually wonderful. You placed a beautiful baby into my arms while I warmed myself by the fire.

Our baby.

Heaven.

It felt like heaven.

"I'm okay," I assured him as I pulled on that heavenly feeling.

He sat beside me, leaning against Sable.

I felt her fidget at the addition. A short gust left her nostrils as she settled down once more.

"It's peaceful up here," he pondered as he laced his fingers between mine, rubbing small strokes with his thumb.

"I'll say," I sighed. "I didn't even know I'd drifted off."

"You were out for a couple of hours. You must still be healing," he reasoned.

"What about you? Have you had a chance to rest?" I asked, assessing the bags under his eyes, wondering if he would lie.

"I will," he insisted. "I wanted to talk to you first…about us."

"Okay."

Uncertainty wobbled my words.

My palms begin to sweat.

Nathaniel looked down at our joined hands in silence, and dread seeped into me.

I was certain of my love for this man, and I was sure that he felt the same. He told me so only a few hours ago.

He was my Twin Soul.

Something flashed across my memory. Something that Sylvie had said about Twin Souls not always being compatible. What if he felt that we weren't a good match? What if it was Greer all over again? Did he pretend to care about me so that I would kill the king? Did he plan to let go of me now that it was done? Maybe he really was a seer, and he could see that there was no future for us. We had gotten so caught up in everything and held onto the only thing that felt good in all the bad. Did he mean to revoke his proposal?

Oh gods, I was spiralling.

Surely not.

He wouldn't have sat beside my bed until I woke otherwise. He wouldn't have taken my hand. I realised that my relationship with Greer, uncovering the truth about Sandy and confronting Pastor David, had really messed with my mind. I was suffering with the inability to separate truth from lie. I felt so insecure and uncertain about myself and couldn't trust myself to recognise when someone was being genuine or not. I had a lot of work to do. I knew I needed to be kinder to myself. None of it was my fault.

He inhaled deeply.

I held my breath.

"In such a short time," he began. "We…"

He huffed in frustration.

"The last few weeks."

He stopped again.

He seemed flustered, like he was trying to choose his words carefully but was struggling to find the right ones. This was doing nothing for my confidence. Letting someone down gently is difficult, and he's clearly finding it hard. We let ourselves get so swept up in things. Used one another for comfort in moments of despair.

"Rose, I," he attempted before stopping himself again.

"It's okay," I said, removing my hand from his. "You don't have to say it. I get it. We had no choice but to spend so much time together recently, but the job's done now. Mission complete."

I did my best to sound nonchalant.

"No, it's just," he started.

"No, it's fine," I cut in. "I understand. Sylvie told me that not all Twin Souls are compatible. All of this was so intense, so I could understand if emotions got the better of you. It's cool."

My voice wavered on those last words, and tears welled in my eyes.

He swiftly moved to crouch in front of me, grabbing my face with both hands capturing my eyes with a desperate expression.

"You've got it wrong. I'm sorry," he said. "It's my fault. I'm not doing this properly."

"Doing what?" I asked, impatience creeping in.

I was on a tightrope and losing balance.

"Rose Harlow, I love you more than I've ever loved anyone or anything."

My body trembled with relief.

"I want us to be together always. Where you go, I go."

Tears made tracks down my face as I nestled into his hand and closed my eyes.

A moment ago, I'd managed to convince myself that he didn't really want me, and these tears were pure relief that I was wrong. Never have I ever wanted to be more wrong.

"I want you," he assured me.

Had he heard my thoughts? "I want you to be the one that shares my soul. I want you to be the one that I lay down with at night. I want you to be the mother of my child. I want you to be my wife."

He now had tracks on his cheeks to match my own.

I placed my forehead to his and felt his love radiate like the sun's rays. It soaked into my bones, like the heat from the hearth in my dream. I remembered him there, and his velvety voice, and the beautiful bundle that he placed against my body, and the bliss, the absolute bliss that I felt.

Nathaniel pulled back and looked at me with awe. "I saw it."

"What?" I asked.

"What you just saw. Your dream," he replied, wonder struck. "I felt what you felt."

"Should I give you two privacy?"

I'd forgotten Sable was there, and she did not sound best pleased.

"No," the word left both our mouths.

We looked at one another, confused.

"You heard her?" I quizzed.

"Yes," he uttered slowly with uncertainty. "That is new."

"If you don't mind, I was rather enjoying my sleep."

Sassy wasn't a word I thought I would use to describe a wyvern, yet she was.

"What did you want to talk about?" I asked as we resumed our positions laying back against the comfort of Sable.

"Nothing," he replied. "I just wanted to make sure that you knew that I meant what I'd said before. I want us to have millennia."

"We will," I promised.

"Now, tell me more about that dream."

-41-

Nathaniel

I'll never forget her face this morning when I presented her with her mother's dress.

Just when I'd thought I'd seen every expression her beautiful face could make, she showed me one that almost brought me to my knees. It was love and solace, immense unadulterated gratitude.

There was woe in the moisture that collected along her lower lid that didn't fall with sorrow, but from joy.

Her dusky-pink tinted lips curved as laughter parted them.

She clutched the ivory lace to her chest and exhaled a breath that she had seemed to be holding for some time, like she had reunited with an old friend after many years. Not too different from the way I sighed when I'd finally found her.

She locked eyes with me and shook her head. I could see her lips attempting words.

"How?"

A while ago I'd accompanied Megarra on a forage for food and medicinal herbs. We had brought men from the capital and a couple of wyverns to assist us in not just finding food and herbs for Megarra's clinic, which we had built at the edge of the Deadlands, where it met Thane, but also to lift some trunks of felled trees that we would use for more buildings.

Rose's father had helped build safe routes through the forests to connect Sandy and the Deadlands to the rest of the kingdom and beyond.

Those that were loyal to Bellinus had fled, including the tosspots from the Upperlands and the plants in Sandy. Disappointing for me, as I couldn't wait to get my hands on that bastard, Greer. We knew we would have to deal with them again at some point, but for now, we were concentrating on getting the building blocks in place for a vast peaceful community, and to do that, we had to tear down all borders and make pathways for people to move freely.

The land was resourceful and abundant. And along with stone, clay, and wood, aranimmanis silk was harvested from abandoned webs and used for constructing sturdy nets and strong fabrics.

Dana, an elderly spindle lady from Fermyn, had discovered a way to spin the spider silk to make fine threads to use in the creation of hard-wearing materials that could last many years.

Thus, lead me to the answer as to how.

"Thank you," she sighed as she discarded the dress and threw her arms around my mid.

I clutched her close and breathed her in. Her earthy, sweet, nutty scent was intoxicating. It reminded me of marzipan and pastries, and I just wanted to eat her up."

You know, I'd have married you wearing a vegetable sack," she stated.

"Yeah, but that won't do," I replied. "Plus, I got myself something special to wear too."

Her eyes filled with exuberance.

"Really?" she exclaimed.

I laughed at her infectious joy.

"Really," I confirmed.

"Can I see it?" She wore a cheeky mien, and she already knew the answer.

"I want you to get to the top of that mountain and see me like you've just set eyes on me for the first time," I told her.

She rolled her eyes at me playfully. "You're so romantic."

She pecked my lips.

"I still don't know why we must climb the mountain, though. Can't we just fly up?" She quipped.

I knew she was winding me up. That part of the ceremony was equally as important to us both.

"Or we could just have a small ceremony in the chapel?"

She squealed as I threw her over my shoulder and spanked her behind.

It took nearly three hours to reach the summit. I had hiked as fast as I could without breaking into a sweat. I didn't want to smell overripe when she met me at the top. Not that she would judge me. Her skin was probably glistening itself from the strenuous climb.

I arrived before her. It was intentional. I wanted to see her rise over the top and walk towards me like a bride walking down the aisle to meet her groom, except there was no aisle on the top of the Sacred Volcano, just a huge pit of bubbling heat, and she would appear on the opposite side.

I straightened the lapel of my black suit jacket, which Dana had adorned with the same embroidered rose pattern as my cloak. It was an important detail to include as tribute to her and the journey we had travelled to get here. A red velvet pocket square and delicate rose buttonhole added a pop of colour, again a testament to her, the colour of her incredible hair and her namesake. I had combed my hair back and parted it to the side, but my defiant waves had managed to spring free during the ascent and danced around my forehead. I gave up trying to push them back.

I clasped my hands in front of me to stop the nervous quivering.

Colm rested a hand on my shoulder to brace me.

"She's almost here," he said. "I can sense Sylvie."

The butterflies in my stomach were rampantly beating their wings. It wouldn't surprise me if they weren't butterflies at all, but miniature wyverns, setting fires in my belly, burning me from the inside out. I could feel the heat on my cheeks and the back of my neck.

I took out my pocket square and dabbed away the sheen of sweat beginning to build.

Colm chuckled beside me.

"What's so funny?" I mumbled, without taking my eyes away from the edge.

"She's complaining."

Colm was laughing harder now.

"Sylvie?" I asked.

"No, your betrothed," he chuckled. "She said that she would like to see you do this in a dress."

A smile pushed through my nervous disposition, and I sent a message down our bond, letting her know exactly what I would do with that dress later. We had agreed to keep out of each other's minds on the climb for fear of hearing doubts or comments driven by the enervation from the trek, but I thought she could do with an incentive to give her an extra boost.

I felt her annoyance fade, and I imagined her smile matched mine in wideness. I could feel her skin prickle in reaction to the image I sent her and the tingle that built at the base of her spine.

"Dude..."

Colm's laughter ceased.

Time slowed down as she emerged over the edge of the Sacred Volcano, like the sun rising from the horizon. Her glow was the same, although she put the sun to shame. She had an aura of yellows and pinks emanating from her. Dusk had started to settle, and she was a beacon in the dull light.

Megarra and Sylvie had accompanied her up the mountain, but I did not see them.

It was only she.

I could not see her father or the wyverns. I couldn't see Tuck, Lis, or Thoran, or any of the few others that had joined the procession. Only her. If she were to be the only one I could see for the rest of my life, then I would die a happy man.

I swallowed thickly as I took her in. She was angelic. It was as if she was floating toward me, and it took my breath away. I could feel the emotion creeping to the backs of my eyes.

Her hair was parted in twin braids that draped over her shoulders. She had something dotted through them, but it was too far for me to see clearly.

Suddenly, I was all too aware of the distance that separated us, and I had to force myself not to take the shortcut by leaping into the bubbling lava and attempting to swim across. I would if she asked me to, I thought. I would do anything for her.

"Unwise, I'd say." Sable, saving me from peril.

My quick paces turned into a light jog into a desperate sprint. She dropped the bouquet of red roses she had grasped at her front and sped toward me gathering bunches of her skirt in her fists.

Our bodies slammed together like waves crashing on the shore. My mouth devoured hers like I'd been starved from her for years, not just for the night. A stupid Sandy superstition that said it was bad luck to spend the night together before the wedding. My hands roamed over the laced fabric on her bodice, and I yearned to tear it from her.

"Hey," she giggled.

Our foreheads pressed together, panting to catch our breaths.

"You look sensational."

She stepped back and rotated on the spot so I could view her fully. The lace clung to her waist. I was jealous of the way it held her. I imagined running my hands along the lines of her curves. The way the fabric was taut across her thighs. I could see how hard it must have been for her to manoeuvre up the mountain when it hugged her so tightly.

Those thighs.

Gods, she was killing me.

I could see now that the flecks of colour in her braids were daisies. It reminded me of the first occasion that we got to spend time together after the battle. We had taken a picnic to the river, and she had made me a crown of daisies. She called me her king, and it took everything in my power to resist taking her right there and then. I wish I could say that was the last time I had to resist her, but I'd been resisting her every day since we met, saving ourselves for the night of our bonding.

She ended her twirl with an awkward expression and an adorable chuckle.

"That was cute," I told her, and we both giggled then.

I mimicked her rotation to join her in her bashfulness, which encouraged another giggle from her. Gods, I loved that sound, and I loved it more that I was the cause of it.

"You look...incredible actually." Her voice was filled with wonder.

"You sound surprised," I mocked offense by clutching my chest.

"I mean, you always look incredible, but I've never seen you like this." I noticed her eyes widen and blink rapidly, and her throat bobbed. "You're stunning."

It was as though she'd reached into my chest and clutched my heart in her hand.

I brought my hand up to cup her face and hoped the look in my eyes told her how valuable she was to me. No amount of money, gold, or jewels could compare to her worth. I placed a tender kiss upon her lips, still swollen from how forcefully I had kissed her before, and we swayed to the tune of our own melody.

Her skin was slightly more weathered than when I'd first met her those many moons ago. I felt guilty and held myself personally responsible for all the trauma she had endured. Each ordeal, each injury, whether physically or mentally, had etched lines into her skin and left a mark on her heart. I made an oath that I would make it up to her for the rest of my life.

Her baby hairs clung to her forehead, and I smiled at the way they curved and swirled, adorning her face with pretty patterns like fine finishing details. I noticed a golden shimmer along her cheekbones, catching what little light remained from the day, complementing the mossy green fractals glistening between the darker and lighter shades of hazel in her eyes. The wide bridge of her nose had been kissed by the sun so often that it left evidence in the form of freckles. Her lips were plump and full, and I just wanted to take them into my mouth and bite them. The dimple on her chin was one of my favourites of her features.

I tousled her floral braids between my fingers.

"Shall we get married then?" My voice low and so relaxed from our gentle swaying.

She nodded intently while gazing into my eyes. That look was enough to disarm me completely.

"Today is the day that I become whole," I announced to our friends and family gathered atop the mountain. "She is the other half of me."

I looked to my love as we grasped hands, facing one another.

"What I lack, she makes up for. And in all my downfalls, she lifts me up. For every doubt I harbour, she is the optimism that drives that doubt away. She is the light to my dark, the good to my bad, the twin to my soul."

A tear slid down her cheek, and I kissed it away.

"Nathaniel Blackmore, you are me, and I am you. We will never be apart again, until death takes us from this life."

"Rose Elodie Harlow, you are me, and I am you. I will honour and cherish you until the day we both shall perish."

-42-

Rose

If I was told that today would be the day that I died, I would slay Death itself. I would barter and bargain for my existence because now I had something in this life to live for. I had fought so hard for it, and I would continue to fight for whatever the future had in store for me. Whatever that might be, I would do it all with him by my side.

Bound in blood and vow, we stitched our souls together in a moment of raw tenderness.

Eternity is what we promised to each other.

He is love and the ground beneath my feet and the sky above my head.

He is love and the air in my lungs and the blood in my veins.

He is love and all that I see.

He is the other half of me.

I let him in.

I let him hear it and feel it.

The words I had wanted to say aloud but kept just for him.

Nathaniel's eyes bore into mine. His lashes shuttered in slow strokes with lazy smiles. I studied the glow of the setting sun caressing his face. He was so perfect. The connection between us more intense than before.

The energy tingled like static electricity where he held me against himself, his arms enveloping me. I had reached around his waist and laid my face to his chest, and I started to sway to the melody of his heartbeat; the only music was the whistle of the wind as it rippled over the peak of the Sacred Volcano.

He tucked a tendril of hair behind my ear, and I stole the opportunity to press my cheek to his palm as I placed a kiss there.

"I adore you," I told him.

His dimples deepened as his smile widened.

"I adore you."

So, this is what it felt like to be loved.

To be cherished.

It was euphoric.

"So, what do we do now?"

I knew what we did now. I just wanted him to tell me. To finally give us the green light. It's what we had been dancing around the past few months. My want and need for him only increased the more time I spent with him, and I was beyond relieved that today I didn't have to hold back any longer.

"Well, we consummate…" he said awkwardly.

Was he nervous?

We had had several intimate moments, and he knew exactly how to make my body sing.

I wrinkled my nose. "Sounds so…clinical."

Nathaniel's deep, throaty, velvety laughter gave me flutters in my core. I loved that sound, and I made an oath to myself that I would try my best to always fill our home with laughter.

"Okay."

He laced his fingers with mine and leaned in until his breath was a whisper in my ear.

"You want to know what happens now?"

"Yes."

I wondered if he could hear my breathlessness through our bond.

"Now, I make love to you so painfully slow, until I push you over the edge again and again. I'm going to drown in your arousal while you kiss me back to life. I want you to feel me everywhere. *In here."* He put a finger to my temple. "Here." He put his hand on my heart and ran it slowly down my torso and cupped me between my legs. "And here."

Air was coming and going in ragged breaths, and a buzzing sensation vibrated below his hand. Tingles ran down my spine and pooled in my lower back.

"You will feel me deeper than you've ever felt before, and when my name is the only name you remember, I will allow myself to come undone with you. *Inside you."*

A throbbing heat at the apex of my thighs as my heartbeat seemed to pulse there. My lungs suddenly forgot how to work.

He pushed himself against me to show me that he meant every word.

"Breathe, my love."

I shakily exhaled as he captured my mouth in a hard and passionate kiss.

I glanced around at our loved ones that had gathered atop the Sacred Volcano to witness our bonding, and as politely as possible, wished they would all fuck off now.

How could I converse when all I could think about was racing back home and giving myself to him in whatever way he pleased? How could I let them congratulate me with hugs and kisses when his touch was the only touch I craved to feel?

We could have had the ceremony in a number of different places, but we wanted to do it this way. The same way Jacobi and Adama, the first of man, had done.

We started on either side of the mountain and dragged ourselves up it so we could feel even just a fraction of what they went through to find each other. We cut our palms and interlocked our fingers, squeezing droplets of our blood into the mouth of the volcano. We uttered the same vows that had been recorded in the Book of Man, and we went through the gruelling task of resisting one another for months so that we could 'consummate' after the ceremony.

We wanted to honour Jacobi and Adama, but we also wanted to honour us. We too were born under the Crimson Moon and had gone through our own arduous journey to get here. We hoped to last the years that they did and hoped that we could create a flourishing haven, just as they had.

I looked to my right and saw Nathaniel being embraced by our friends. Congratulations and boisterous back patting. It made me smile as I thought of the first time I saw him embraced in such a fashion with Colm, back on the night I had first met him and Sylvie. We had come a long way since then.

To my left, Megarra was saddling up. She had somewhat bonded with a wyvern over the weeks, and they had become quite the team. It seemed she had taken Colm's words in esteem and had started to treat the wyverns a little better. They had responded quite well to this and rewarded her so. I caught Sable's eyes, and she bowed her head to me.

I turned to make my way toward Nathaniel and the others and stumbled into an obstacle at my feet.

Nathaniel was on his knees, his face contorted with agonising grief. I tried to say something, but my words were drowned out by his wails of despair. He grasped his head with both hands, grabbing chunks of his hair at the edge of the hellfire. I desperately turned to my friends for help but found no one there. He was shaking with anguish. I could not break him out of it, and I was aware of how dangerously close we were to the edge.

Finally, I heard the steady beating of wings over the frantic thumping of my own heart, loud in my ears. Sable would help me. She could pick him up in her claws if I were unable to break him free of his torment.

A great black shadow came over the edge of the mountain, the sky behind a tinge of light blue. The wyvern landed with less of a thud and a lot less dust than usual, and I realised that it was not a wyvern at all. This creature had fanned membrane wings but the feet of a man, and it was pacing towards me in powerful strides while folding its wings away. My feet glued to the ground, partly from terror but mainly because I didn't want to leave Nathaniel's side.

"Magnificent, aren't I?" The creature spoke. His words sounded as though two voices were speaking at once.

I couldn't put my finger on it, but there was something familiar about it. What he said and the way he said it.

He was right in front of me now, and I could see his features as clear as could be in the dull light.

"What's the matter? King got your throat?"

His hand shot out as quick as a dart and grasped my neck, violently shaking me. I teetered on the lip of the lava pit, the heat causing sweat to run down my back. I couldn't say anything, not for lack of wanting to, but I didn't know the words to choose, and if I did, his hand was a vice, and no sound would come out.

It was Bellinus, but not as I remember him. He was not the aged and tired man slumped in the throne. His hair was jet black, not peppered with shades of grey. His eyes like blue skies, just like Colm's. But where Colm's eyes crinkled in the corners because he was always joyously laughing, this man's lines were between his brows. Even when his face was wearing a neutral expression, a deep crevice creased the skin there. His once wrinkled face was plump and filled with youth...rejuvenated.

"If only you could see your face."

His laugh was sinister.

"You're alive, but how?" He mocked my surprise in a shrill feminine tone.

"I was never dead. It was simply...metamorphosis. I absorbed some rejuvenation from Sylvie, and finally I had the strength to complete our experiment.

"Years ago, we extracted DNA from a young wyvern still contained in its egg. We injected it into my bloodstream, but your bitch of a mother's curse weakened me. I wasn't strong enough to complete the transformation. What you saw at the castle was the next stage of metamorphosis. Think of it like a caterpillar turning into a butterfly."

He spread his wings like a peacock spreading its feathers, and I tried to break free, but I was paralysed by his hold on me.

"The thing about prophecies, Rose Harlow, is that they can be rewritten, and I have rewritten ours," he snarled. "The kingdom may have fallen, but its king has not. It is the Rose that will wither and die," he spat, before he released his grip and evaporated before my eyes.

I threw my arms out and grabbed the air, desperate for purchase. I was falling into the scorching heat ablaze at my back. Wind whipped past my ears and on it carried Nathaniel's screams. I caught sight of him stretching his arms out towards my plummeting body, but he wasn't quick enough. I saw the moment that the realisation hit. Pain struck his face, contorting it in a way I hadn't seen before. A cry escaped my throat, not because I was about to die, but because of the sheer sorrow I knew I would leave him with.

We had just found each other, just bonded, just made whole.

The last thing I saw before my world went black were Colm, Tuck, and Thoran anchoring Nathaniel on the edge as his body jerked forward, longing to dive in after me.

And the last thing I heard was my pounding heart coursing terror through my veins and the screeching of my wyvern as she leapt from the edge, before Death finally claimed me.

Printed in Dunstable, United Kingdom